THE THIRD ORDER

A NOVEL

Wendy Sura Thomson

Author of
Summon the Tiger

DEDICATION

This book is dedicated to two of my strongest musical influences: Eveyln Micheletti, whose family comes from Umbria, Italy; and Dr. Frederick DeHaven, who gave me the opportunity to sing a concert in – and fall in love with - Assisi.

ACKNOWLEDGMENTS

I cannot say enough about the extraordinary assistance I received from Dana Layman, Carol Hunter, Diana Wolfe Plopa, Donald Levin, Tom Sura and Andrew Lark., for which I will be eternally grateful. I also wish to thank my stalwart editor Jefferson, who kept me honest.

CHAPTER ONE

Maggie pushed open the apartment door, kicked her Ferragamos unceremoniously under the hall table, and dropped her briefcase and purse on the table. She took off her coffee-stained coat and threw it on the chair as she closed and locked the door.

Stupid fucking jerk. Who brings an open coffee on the subway, anyway? Stupid fucking people in general.

She stopped to rub the back of her neck with a little groan. It had been one hell of a long day.

Ben came up behind her, gave her a little hug, and moved her long, mahogany hair to the side so he could rub her shoulders. Maggie's first reaction was to pull away; at this particular moment, she wanted nothing to do with the human race. She stiffened at his initial touch but then relaxed. Ben – sweet, gentle Ben. He was not the problem. He was stalwart and patient with her. None of this was his fault. She sighed and stretched her neck appreciatively. After a minute, she turned to him, placed her arms around his waist, and smiled as she looked into his warm brown eyes. "Thanks, hun. You always have a knack for calming me down."

He kissed the tip of her nose, smiled, and said, "I take it we are ordering in tonight?"

"Not until we break open a bottle of wine and my blood pressure drops a hundred points or so," she replied, heading for the kitchen. "Red or white?"

She returned with a nice bottle of Cabernet and two wine glasses. She tucked her leg under her as she descended into the sofa in one fluid movement, glasses in her left hand, bottle in her right. Ben watched in fascination; he still had a hard time taking his eyes off of her. Maggie's slightly wavy hair framed her perfectly oval, porcelain face. Her arresting storm-gray eyes, fringed in thick, dark lashes, immediately commanded attention, if only for their alternating piercing and laughing personalities. Maggie was of average height, but she was sinewy and strong, a remnant of years spent in ballet, and had a catlike grace that was entrancing just to watch. And that was what had caught Ben's eyes in the first place – how she moved.

~

One wintry Saturday in February, over a year earlier, and quite new to the city, Maggie decided to visit the Museum of Modern

Art (MOMA.) She had been so wrapped up in her new position and had been working such long hours that she had developed absolutely no social life.

I have got to get out and see where I now live. She had checked the *New York Times* for events and settled on the MOMA. It was somewhere she could go by herself, and she could go during the day. New York was still a bit intimidating.

As Maggie approached the museum, she was struck by the modern architecture.

This is certainly not old, solid stone and arches. The building itself was just as interesting as the art and was so very unlike those found in Fife, Scotland, where Maggie had grown up. She was struck by the openness, the glass, the relative sparseness of the place. She spent the first several minutes simply staring at the building.

As she went up a flight of stairs, she saw a banner at the entrance of a gallery: "Lilly Reich: Designer and Architect." She paused and made a note of the location of the gallery, and after a quick walk through the rest of the museum, she started down a staircase to return to the Reich exhibit. She was forced to move to the left side to get around an arguing couple who had simply stopped on the stairs. Just as Maggie was abreast of the two of them, the woman turned to leave and tumbled into her. Maggie managed to keep her balance, deflecting the falling force while recovering in time to catch the woman and right her.

"Are you okay?"

Flustered, the woman brushed Maggie off with a curt, "Yes, thank you. Damn boots." Her face flushed a bit as she turned to her companion. "George, why is it that this woman had the presence of mind to help me, while you just stood there?" George stammered something and moved past Maggie as if she didn't even exist. Maggie watched as the two continued down the stairs, totally unaware of anyone but themselves.

So rude. This is the New York I heard about.

Her thoughts were interrupted when a man came up beside her and touched her elbow. "Are you all right? You were kind to make sure that woman didn't hurt herself."

"Oh, I'm fine," she replied. "Growing up with three brothers teaches a little sister to always be ready for mischief."

He grinned. "Do I detect a brogue? You wouldn't be Irish, now, would you?" Maggie flashed a quick grin back and then, appearing as indignant as she could manage, retorted in her broadest brogue, "Nae, laddie! I'm as Scottish as the dee is lang!" She laughed.

"I-I am so s-sorry!" he stammered. "I hope I didn't just deliver the worst insult imaginable."

"Och, nae. Happens all the time. I dinna mind. Dinna fash yersel." The man's brow furrowed, so Maggie said, "And now I will revert back to the King's English. Thank you for your concern."

"I was just worried there was going to be a jumble of people at the bottom of the staircase," replied the stranger. "I'm glad you didn't get hurt."

"You *cannot* be from New York," she said, her lingering irritation with the rude couple filtering into her tone. "From what I have seen, manners and New York have been separated for a very long time." She looked down and, with both hands, smoothed out her clothing.

The man grinned. "I was behind the three of you and saw the entire incident. No, I am not originally from New York, and no, not everyone in this city is as self-absorbed and rude as that couple was. Please don't be too hard on the rest of us."

Maggie turned and settled her gaze on this man, studying him a bit. He had a gentle and open face. He was a good six feet tall, of slender build, with straight brown hair, neatly trimmed, and brown eyes the color of hot chocolate. There seemed to be a layer of amusement behind those eyes and just a hint of a grin in his lips. He was casually dressed in a leather jacket over a button-down shirt, a pair of jeans, and a pair of brown leather laced-up short boots. His entire aura spoke comfortable: comfortable with people, comfortable with himself…just comfortable. Maggie could feel her irritation start to melt away.

"So, where did you grow up?" she asked and then abruptly caught herself. "I am so sorry. I shouldn't be so direct."

"I'm not offended," replied the man. "Ann Arbor, Michigan. And you?"

"I grew up near St. Andrew's in Fife," she replied, extending her hand. "I'm Maggie."

The man took her hand and shook it somewhat ceremoniously. "And I am Ben, fair lady. Very pleased to make your acquaintance." His flirty affectation made Maggie grin. "How did you end up in New York?"

He's just as direct as I am.

"Half from spite, I think," she answered with a quirky grin. "It was either New York or London. My parents expected London, so here I am."

Ben laughed. "Should I infer you might be just a tad bit headstrong?" he ventured.

"I don't think I'd call it headstrong, exactly. Well, maybe," she conceded. "I was shuttled to dance lessons and dressed in pink frills and lace. What I really wanted to do was go exploring Loch Leven with my brothers. I wanted to go with them, but that's not what proper young ladies did. Boring."

Ben could picture a little red-headed girl, arms crossed over her chest, making a stand. He grinned at the vision.

"What brought you to this exhibit, Ben?"

"I am working on my dissertation," Ben replied. "I hopefully will earn my PhD in architecture from Columbia in a few months."

"Impressive! What led you to architecture?"

"I have always been interested in amazing structural designs, especially of ancient buildings. The arches with keystones. Flying buttresses and the strength seen in old, old structures that have allowed them to remain for hundreds, even thousands of years. I find it fascinating. I must come by it honestly: my father teaches at the University of Michigan's engineering school."

"So, why this Lilly Reich exhibit?" Maggie was genuinely interested.

"My dissertation is on comparative design of Renaissance and modern architecture. And what about you? Why did you come?"

"Frankly, I didn't have much to do, and I thought I might take a tour of the MOMA. That's what people call it, right? I have never been here before; this exhibit just happened to be showing."

"So, you are not here for the architecture? Not for Lilly Reich?"

Maggie laughed. "I didn't even know who Lilly Reich was. I'm actually in finance – a far cry from architecture. I work at Lehman Brothers, in derivatives."

It was Ben's turn to laugh. "You have now officially switched over to a foreign language. I confess I have nothing insightful or pithy to contribute. Give me bricks and mortar. Have you seen the entire exhibit?"

"No. I was actually just starting."

"Would you like a guided tour?"

Maggie paused. "You know, in all honesty, I probably will get a lot more out of the exhibit with someone who actually knows something about what I am seeing. Sure! Lead the way."

Ben and Maggie spent the next two hours walking the exhibit. Ben was in his element and offered insight and background that Maggie found interesting, both on subject and personal levels.

This is a very bright laddie – who is certainly passionate about architecture.

As they came to the end of the exhibit, Ben said, "The museum is closing soon. Would you like to catch a bite to eat? La Grenouille is right around the corner."

Maggie glanced at her watch, looked rather sharply at Ben, and made a snap decision. "Sure! But I think that calls for a full and proper introduction. I am Maggie Fraser. Margaret MacAlpin Stuart Fraser."

Ben turned in front of her and did a silly, slight little bow. He intoned in a most serious voice, "Frederick Benjamin Tyler at your service, ma'am. And may I say, that's quite some moniker you have."

"I told you my parents were traditional. While my name doesn't exactly follow the old Scottish naming tradition, my parents were intent that a couple of the family names got carried forward. MacAlpin comes from my mother's side – Stuart from my father's. They were grandmothers' maiden names somewhere along the line." The two began moving toward the exit.

As Ben held the door for her, he said, "Well, I like it! And you can tell me all about that during dinner."

"Aren't you the charming one."

Soon, they were enjoying their meal at La Grenouille. As they conversed, Maggie found herself drawn to Ben's intelligence and quick sense of humor. But what was most appealing to her was his apparent calm, his "I've got this" demeanor. He just exuded emotional strength and confidence. And she just loved that it seemed there was always a grin hiding just under the surface, which could be seen in the upturned corner of his mouth and a certain twinkle in his eyes.

"When did you come to New York?"

"Oh, about three months ago. I graduated last year from St. Andrew's. I had several offers, the two most appealing from RBS and Lehman, and decided it would be Lehman."

"RBS?"

"Oh – sorry. Royal Bank of Scotland. In London. My parents were none too happy with my decision, I must say. Oh well…"

Ben laughed at that and then toned it down quickly, seeing he was getting looks from other patrons. "I am sorry. It's just that I can picture the conversation. Did they just shake their heads sadly or get a bit indignant?"

"I could tell they were sorely disappointed. But you know, they are Scots; not a lot of words need to be said. They both have very expressive body language. Very evident disapproval."

"Are they over it?"

"Not entirely. It will take a bit more time, I think." Maggie bent over to pick up the purse she had slipped beneath her chair. "This has been delightful, but I should be going. I have to get up very early tomorrow morning."

"Fair enough. I have the luxury of being able to sleep in a little."

"Please do not remind me. I'm jealous."

After their meal, as they headed out the door of the restaurant, Ben asked, "Maggie, do you suppose we can see each other again?"

"I think I would like that very much." She pulled out her business card and gave it to him. "Here's how to contact me. I really hope you'll call."

Ben hailed a cab for Maggie, opened the door for her, and grinned. "I think you can take that to the bank."

"Take that to the bank?"

"A colloquialism. It means 'you can count on it.'" She broke into a wide smile, squeezed his hand, got into the cab, and left.

~

Ben called the next day. And the day after that. They started meeting for coffee Saturday mornings before running in Central Park. They made a pact to try restaurants featuring different ethnic cuisines a couple of times a month, which turned into every week, which then was supplemented by nightly calls, which then was supplemented by spending every moment between Friday night and Monday morning together. They were finding more and more to like about each other as, together, they discovered New York. And come late October, Ben asked Maggie an important question.

"Maggie, do you suppose I could ask you to come to Michigan and meet my parents?"

She hesitated only a moment before answering, "Yes. Sure! I would love to see Ann Arbor. And meet your parents, of course."

Ben and Maggie were in Central Park, having just finished their usual Saturday run. It was an absolutely beautiful day – mid-sixties and sunny. The trees were not quite at peak color, but they were nevertheless breathtaking.

"Well, then! That's great! So, now that has been settled, there is just one more thing." Ben got down on one knee, pulled out a ring case, opened it, and said, "Maggie, may I introduce you as my fiancée?"

The other morning runners, seeing a man on bent knee, stopped and formed a loose circle around the two. "Come on," one started calling. "Go ahead!" said another. The ring of runners started clapping while continuing their enthusiastic encouragement. Maggie looked around and started laughing.

"Did you set this up?"

"Absolutely not!"

"Well, that's a shame, because this is rather delightful." She looked at him very tenderly. "Stand up, Dr. Tyler. Please do not bend before me. Stand beside me, and I will say yes." She grabbed his hand and guided him up, to the roar of approval from the onlookers. Ben grabbed her by the waist and pulled her towards him.

"You have just made me the happiest man to have ever walked the face of the earth."

"That's quite a tall statement, sir," teased Maggie. "But I am happy you feel that way. I love you, Frederick Benjamin Tyler. I would be proud and happy to be your wife."

"And you will forever more be my Maggie May," replied Ben, kissing her gently.

~

Ben and Maggie flew to Michigan for Thanksgiving. As they pulled up to Ben's parent's house, Ben said, "I am sure you will love my parents. They are great."

"I hope you feel the same way about mine," Maggie said with a bit of a catch. She was sure Ben would be in for quite the culture shock.

Ben walked in the door with a big greeting.

"Happy Thanksgiving!"

The Doctors Tyler, both PhDs, rushed to the door: she from the kitchen, he from the den. "Oh, so good to see you!" cried Ben's mother as she hugged her son. She turned to Maggie, and with an outstretched hand grabbed Maggie's.

"We have heard such lovely things about you! Very glad to meet you!" She leaned over to give Maggie a kiss on the cheek.

Ben's mother was taller than Maggie. She was of slender build, like Ben, but she had startlingly blue eyes, very fair skin, and hair that was thick and absolutely snow white, cut stylishly: shorter in the back, raking down to chin length in front. She was quite strikingly attractive.

Ben shook his father's hand and then turned to introduce Maggie. "And here's my soon-to-be bride, the lovely Maggie MacAlpin Stuart Fraser."

Maggie shook Dr. Tyler's hand.

Ben gets his coloring from his dad. Dr. Tyler was tall like Ben but a bit stockier, and he had the same warm brown eyes. His brown hair was graying at the temples. He was dressed very appropriately for a college professor: khaki slacks and a crewneck sweater over a collared shirt. He had the same easy manner as Ben, and Maggie instantly felt comfortable.

"Very nice to meet you, sir."

"Sir?" Will replied, smiling broadly. "That's a bit formal, my dear. Please, call me Will."

Ben turned to Maggie, teasing, "Maggie MacAlpin Stuart Fraser. Are you intending to keep all of those names and just add Tyler to the string?"

Maggie laughed. "Oh, we Scots keep all of our names. Even death certificates are filed under maiden names. And married names – however many of them there might be."

"Now, don't you be thinking you are going to go for the Guinness record for most names," teased Ben. "Adding Tyler will be enough."

Ben's mom interrupted. "Hello. My name is Barbara. We have been very eager to meet you. Let me show you to your room." She turned to go up the stairs and paused on the bottom step.

"Your room is at the top of the stairs, on the right. I am not sure what will make you more comfortable – a room with Ben or a separate one. Please know that Will and I are not sticklers about sleeping arrangements. If you and Ben want to share a room, that's fine with us. We don't stand on much ceremony."

Maggie found that incredibly refreshing, and so very different from the reception Ben would be getting from her parents. The thought made her grin.

Barbara continued up the stairs, turned at the top, and, with outstretched arm, said, "Here is your room, Maggie. If you need anything, please let me know. The bath is the second door to the left." She pointed down the hall. "Now I will let you get settled. I am very glad you are here." Barbara gave Maggie a big, warm smile and gave her arm a little squeeze before she headed back down the stairs.

Maggie opened her small suitcase and started unpacking. She put her toiletry case on the dresser and laid a nightgown across the foot of the bed. She then stood up and looked around. The room was comfortable, with large double-hung windows on two of the walls. It was not fussy: it was wallpapered in a large but subtle taupe and cream plaid. Plain cream-colored drapes hung at the windows, and there was a small patterned rug by the double bed, atop dark-stained oak flooring. The dark oak sleigh bed was covered in a simple cream-colored coverlet and adorned with a matching pair of pillow shams. To the left was a smallish rustic dresser – *probably a family antique*, she thought – and at the foot of the bed was a taupe upholstered bench. The bed was framed by a matching pair of nightstands, also probably family antiques, and they each sported non-identical lamps that appeared to have been oil lamps at some point. In all, Maggie thought it represented the personalities of a couple of professors perfectly.

Ben appeared at the door. "Is this all right?"

14

"It's delightful." She walked over to the door and gave him a hug, a smile, and a kiss. "This is perfect. Your mother offered us a room together, you know. I can tell you right now you will *definitely* not get the same offer from my parents."

"I would never expect it. But to tell you the truth, I think I would feel a bit funny sleeping together under my parent's roof at this point. Awkward."

"That doesn't surprise me a bit. We will have the rest of our lives for that. I really think that I can bear sleeping alone for a long weekend."

Ben grinned. "Darn!" He turned to point down the hall. "My room is across from the bathroom." Changing the subject, he added, "Mom says dinner is almost ready. My sister Sarah and her husband will be here tomorrow about noon, so we can watch the Lions play football before dinner."

"Football on Thanksgiving? Is that a thing here? Not that we share the same celebration across the pond. The closest thing we have to this is St. Andrew's Day. But football?"

"Oh, yes. It's a sacred tradition: Detroit Lions football on Thanksgiving Day. Since 1934. Every year. It's nearly a religious event for some."

"Well, that's a bit odd," muttered Maggie. She paused. "I think I'll go down and see if there's anything I can do to help in the kitchen." She turned to head down the stairs.

Barbara was already putting food on the dining room table when Maggie walked in.

"Anything I can do?"

"Not much, dear. Maybe grab the rolls and butter dish. Everything else is already here." Turning to the den, Barbara called, "Will, dinner's ready." She then turned to the staircase. "Ben!" she said in a louder voice. "Dinner's up!"

Maggie waited for Ben to come down the stairs as Will came in from the den. Barbara was standing at the table.

"Maggie, if you would sit here," Barbara said, pointing to a chair that faced the kitchen. "Will sits here, and this is Ben's seat." Maggie smiled and sat down. She looked around the room briefly: it was warm and unpretentious. Quiet. The walls were claret over white beadboard wainscoting, with wide white baseboards and crown molding under the coved ceiling. The entrances from the front hall and kitchen were gracefully arched, and there was a claret oriental rug under the table. There were those same large, double-hung windows on two walls, framed by plain claret shantung drapes. The table itself sat six and was centered under a rustic wrought iron chandelier. There was a long table pushed up against one wall that could be used as a serving table, above which hung a large contemporary painting, evocative of perhaps a sunset through a fall forest. The walls picked up the colors in the foliage in a most attractive way. All in all, it was a very comfortable room.

Conversation flowed easily over a meal of grilled salmon, spinach salad, steamed carrots, rolls, and a lovely Viognier. Maggie found Barbara and Will as warm and welcoming as Ben, and she felt immediately at home.

"So, Maggie, have you and Ben thought at all about wedding plans?" Barbara asked.

"Oh my, not much. I am sure my parents expect the ceremony to be held in Scotland. But I am not convinced that is an absolute: it's quite a burden to ask people to travel internationally for a wedding. Truthfully, Ben and I haven't set aside a chunk of time to start planning. Ben should meet my family first – he might end up changing his mind." At that, Maggie grinned broadly and winked at Ben.

Ben winked back. "Not a chance. We are planning on spending Christmas in Scotland," he continued. "We'll focus on wedding plans between Christmas and New Year's. I am exploring an invitation I received from the Polytechnic University in Milan. They have provisionally extended an offer for a fellowship in their architectural heritage preservation program, starting in September next year. I rather like the idea of a Scottish wedding, if you two, Sarah, and Jake would be willing to make the trip. We could then continue on to Italy. Great place for a honeymoon."

"That sounds delightful!" said Will. "I love Scotland, actually. We went there several years ago. Lovely country, lovely people."

"I would love it, too," added Barbara. "Tell me about your family, Maggie."

"Well, my parents are recently retired and live near Dunfermline, in Fife. I have three older brothers: Callum, Dougal, and Duncan. Callum is single, Dougal is married with three children, and Duncan is married with two. Callum lives in London, but both Dougal and Duncan live in Edinburgh."

"Well, that settles it, then," pronounced Will. "It certainly is easier to get four people to Scotland than it is to get twelve people here."

"You know you didn't need that excuse," teased Barbara. "You love your travel."

"Ah, hun, you know me too well," said Will as he reached over to squeeze Barbara's hand. It was easy for Maggie to see where Ben got his manner – this entire family had an easy affection for each other that Maggie found quite endearing.

"So, it sounds as if late summer, early fall next year?" asked Barbara.

"We think that might work well," replied Ben. "Besides, Scotland is lovely in the fall."

"Well, please let us know when you pick a date," said Barbara. "I will block out the entire months of August and September in anticipation."

Maggie stood up and started to clear the table. "Oh no, Maggie," protested Barbara. "You are our guest!"

"I insist! It's the least I can do for the room and board you are providing."

Ben got up and joined her. "Mom, Dad, you go relax. Maggie and I will take care of this. You need to rest up for the big day in the kitchen tomorrow."

Ben and Maggie set to cleaning the kitchen: Ben rinsing dishes, Maggie loading the dishwasher; Ben scrubbing the pots and pans, Maggie drying. They fell into a comfortable, stress-free interlude that kept their hands busy while their minds unwound from their respective days. "Your parents are wonderful, Ben," said Maggie as she hung up the dish towel.

"I knew you would fit right in. I just knew it. So, would you like to go into town? We could take a walk around central campus and then grab a quick cup of coffee on State Street. I think you will like Ann Arbor."

"Sure! Let me grab my coat." Maggie ran up the stairs as Ben went into the den to tell his parents. In no time, the two were walking around central campus. "This is called the 'Diag,' Ben said as they were in the middle of that plaza. Maggie looked around at the surrounding buildings.

"Which one holds your dad's office?"

"Oh, the School of Engineering is across the river, over on Beal Street. The medical campus isn't here either. It's over by Fuller, northeast of here. And the stadium and athletic areas are over there." He pointed to the southwest.

"This place is absolutely massive! Not exactly walkable."

Ben started laughing. "That's why it has its own bus service. This is the US of A, where everything is big."

The night was clear, crisp, and calm – perfect for an evening stroll. Ben and Maggie headed over to State Street and ducked into an espresso shop that was nearly deserted – students had already left for the holiday. They grabbed a couple of lattes and headed towards a couple of overstuffed leather barrel chairs by the fireplace.

"I've been meaning to raise the subject of your potential fellowship," said Maggie. "We haven't spoken about how exactly that might fit with my career."

Ben fidgeted with his coffee cup. "I know, Maggie. Can you give me some time to learn more about it? I am not sure even how long it might last."

"I have no problem saving this year's vacation to add to next; that gives me a good month off. But Ben, I am not sure if Lehman would consider a leave of absence to tack on to my vacation. I think I could maybe wrangle another month. But more than that? I am just not sure."

Ben sighed. "That's what I get for falling in love with a brilliant financier. Sweetheart, I totally respect your career. Let me find out more. Then we can figure out what we will do."

"That's fair." Maggie finished her latte. "Think we should head back?"

"I was just going to suggest that." Ben stood up from his chair. He took Maggie's cup with his and returned them to the counter. "Let's blow this pop stand."

Ben and Maggie walked slowly back to the Tyler's, arm in arm. The realization that she always seemed warm when she was next to Ben flashed through Maggie's mind, and she smiled to herself. She tilted her head to look up at him as they stopped at a crosswalk.

"What?"

"Oh, nothing." She turned and looked up at him. She loved his eyes: there always seemed to be a shared secret right behind them; they always seemed to hint at a wink, a nod, and a knowing grin. "I was just thinking how happy I am."

Ben smiled and squeezed her arm, squiring her across the street with the changed light. *All is right with the world tonight*, he thought. *It's all good.*

~

By the time Maggie awoke the next morning, she could already hear a blender working away in the kitchen and could smell fresh-brewed coffee. She quickly dressed and headed downstairs. Barbara was whipping up something –Maggie couldn't tell what – and there was a freshly baked pumpkin pie on the counter. The sink was full of bowls and pans, and the faintest scent of turkey was starting to drift from the oven.

"Are you hungry, dear?" asked Barbara. "If so, there are croissants over in the breadbox and some ginger jam in the fridge. Milk or cream in the door, and sugar in the cupboard to the right of the coffee pot."

"I'll take you up on the coffee, but first, I'll tackle those pots and pans. You have your hands full."

Maggie poured herself a cup of coffee and started washing the pots and pans. It didn't take long – there was only a handful of large prep cookware.

"Is there anything else I can help you with?"

"Oh, not right now. There's a bit of a rush stuffing the turkey and getting it into the oven, but after that, I get a break until a couple of hours before dinner. Thanks for doing the dishes!"

"Well, just let me know." Maggie grabbed half a croissant and headed into the den, where she heard Ben and his dad in conversation. She walked in and headed over to Ben, leaning down to kiss his head.

"Good morning!"

Ben pulled her head down by the back of her neck to give her a kiss. He smiled up at her. "Good morning, lovely lady."

Will smiled at this exchange; it was so familiar to him. He saw himself and Barbara in it. He felt confident that the affection would not wane over time, that it would be constant. As constant as the affection he shared with his wife. Will was sure Ben and Maggie had a very solid relationship, and it gave him a very warm, satisfied feeling. His son had chosen well.

"Can I get either of you anything from the kitchen?" asked Maggie. "There's more coffee."

"Oh no, hun – I'm fine," answered Ben. "I've already had a couple of cups."

Will simply shook his head.

"So, Maggie, is this your first Thanksgiving?" he asked.

"Yes. I am looking forward to it. I've seen pictures of the spread, but never actually sat down to partake. It looks amazing in pictures."

"I think you will like it. It's quite the tradition. Kind of kicks off the holiday season."

"Well, I certainly am looking forward to the experience. One for the record books. I hope I didn't interrupt your conversation."

"Not at all," said Ben. "Dad and I were actually discussing my dissertation. We were discussing the tradeoffs between durable architecture, which takes a long time to build, and current building codes and practices that, while quite a bit faster to construct, give us comparatively throwaway structures. Population growth and job market movements make quick and easy very practical…but there's something about a tear-down mentality that seems somehow a bit sad. I guess I like solid and more permanent."

"I think you just described us," smiled Maggie as she bent down to give him another kiss. "I think I'll go upstairs for a bit and tidy things up. I will leave you two to your musings."

After Maggie had made the bed and straightened up, she called her work voicemail to see whether there were any urgent messages.

Of course not. The entire nation is off today. She made a note to herself to try and not be so tied to her work.

She looked around the room and wondered what to do next. Barbara had everything under control in the kitchen, and Ben and Will were deep in discussion. She glanced at her watch: it was only 10 AM. She had not brought a book to read, and she didn't know the area well enough to take a long walk. She wondered when Sarah and her husband were due to arrive, and then she decided to go back downstairs to try and find a newspaper or some other reading material.

Success! She found a copy of the *Ann Arbor News* on the console near the front door. She picked it up and carried it into the living room. She settled down in a wingback chair by the window and started to read.

She had gotten all the way to the sports section when the doorbell rang. Will headed towards the door, swung it wide open, and extended his arms for a big bear hug as Sarah entered.

"Hey there, my little girl! How are you? Happy Thanksgiving!"

Will reached over to shake Jake's hand. Hey, Jake! Happy Thanksgiving to you! So good to see you!"

Ben was right behind his dad, and Barbara behind him. The foyer was getting crowded, so Maggie stayed in the living room doorway. Ben gave his sister a warm hug and shook Jake's hand, and then he stepped back a bit so Barbara could make her way over to Sarah and Jake.

This is just like in the movies! All the hugs, smiles, and affection…just like in the movies. Maggie was very drawn to this family; she could so see becoming a part of it.

Ben walked around Barbara and, taking Maggie by the arm, brought her over to Sarah and Jake. "I would like to introduce you to your future sister-in-law. This is my Maggie."

Maggie started to extend her hand but immediately withdrew it as it became very apparent that Sarah intended to give her a hug. A big, warm, sisterly hug. Maggie noticed that Sarah smelled like warm vanilla.

That fits.

Jake reached over and shook Maggie's hand, flashing a rather brilliant smile at her. "Very nice to meet you."

"Likewise!"

Two more. Two more warm, affectionate people. What a great family… I am going to really enjoy being a part of this.

While Ben was busy taking coats, Will checked his watch. "Game's on in half an hour," he mentioned as he turned towards the den. "Pre-game has started. I'm going to turn the TV on."

"They are playing Kansas City today," said Jake. "Should be a pretty good game. Think Detroit will win?"

"Doubt it," replied Ben, following his dad into the den. "The Lions are five and seven – another so-so season." The three men disappeared into the den.

~

Ben and Maggie headed back to New York on Sunday. It had been a wonderful getaway, and Ben's family had been so welcoming – the long weekend had made Maggie feel relaxed and wonderful. However, it only took one day of the subway and Wall Street to make it feel like a distant dream…and Ben's dissertation defense was scheduled for mid-December. Life got back to normal in one short day, and it lasted until the pair headed off to Scotland for Christmas.

Ben and Maggie landed in Edinburgh on December 23. Maggie's brother Dougal was waiting for them after they cleared customs.

"Dougal! I'm so happy to see you! I've missed you!" she exclaimed, giving him a big hug. His hug lifted her off her feet. He set her back down and put his hands on her shoulders to push her back a bit so he could study her. "Well, New York hasn'a done you puirly." He was grinning broadly.

Maggie grinned back, and grabbing Ben's hand, she pulled him over. "Dougal, meet my Ben." She looked up at Ben, smiling excitedly. "Ben, my middle brother, Dougal."

Ben and Dougal shook hands. And although Dougal was smiling, Ben could tell that he was being closely evaluated.

"Nice to meet you, Dougal. I've been looking forward to Christmas and meeting Maggie's family."

"Well then, we should be on our way," commented Dougal rather abruptly as he started to shepherd Maggie and Ben out. He led them to his car and popped the trunk. "Put your bags in the boot, and we'll be off."

Ben took the back seat so Maggie and Dougal could talk. Maggie was very excited to be back in Scotland; Ben could tell. She was almost electric, displaying a level of animation that he rarely saw. Maggie was chatting a mile a minute, and Dougal seemed to be kindly indulging her.

Ben studied Dougal from the back seat. He was fair, like Maggie, but his hair was a much lighter red – strawberry blond. His eyes were blue, but not blue like Ben's mom; they were a paler blue. Dougal was fairly heavily freckled, although the freckles had faded some with age. He was only slightly shorter than Ben, with a stockier build. He was not heavy, but he had a build that probably would be prone to weight gain in the future if he didn't watch it. He was already developing a small pot belly.

While Maggie and Dougal were catching up, Ben quietly surveyed the landscape. He couldn't help but notice the stone: low stone fences, old low-slung stone cottages; lots of stone. The occasional modern home stood in stark contrast.

It wasn't long before they were on the Forth Road Bridge.

This reminds me of the Mackinac Bridge. Same design: bridge suspended from a pair of towers.

"Excuse me, Dougal. How long is this bridge?"

"Two and a half kilometers. This is the longest suspension bridge outside of the United States."

"There's a bridge that is very similar to this in Michigan, where I grew up. There's a bit of a scale difference, though our bridge is five miles long. I wonder if the architects shared design principles. They use the same principles of physics."

Maggie laughed. "Ben, you do live and breathe architecture."

Ben laughed with her. "I suppose I do, Mag. I suppose I do."

A lull settled over the car after they crossed the bridge into Fife. Within a few minutes, Dougal pulled off the motorway onto Wood Mill Road. A few minutes after that, he turned left and stopped in front of a startlingly bright-green garage with a brown two-car door that abutted a substantial stone wall, perhaps five or six feet tall.

"And here we are!" exclaimed Dougal quite jovially as he popped the boot to fetch the luggage. He and Ben grabbed the luggage and walked the few feet to the corner and then right to an opening in the wall that was flanked by a pair of square stone pillars and protected by a dark wood and wrought iron gate. Dougal swung open the gate and stepped aside, motioning for Ben and Maggie to proceed up the eight stone steps, walled on both sides, towards a stately, all-stone Victorian home. The metal plaque set into the right entrance pillar quietly announced: "Ayton Lodge."

The proportions of Ayton Lodge were tall, narrow, and consistent across all design elements. The home had a steep-pitched roof, and atop the center peak was mounted a cross. To the left of the centered entrance was a curved set of windows, intricately framed in mahogany shaped like a quarter of a pie, topped by a quarter-of-a-dome oxidized copper roof. Ben stopped on the top step and simply gazed in admiration.

This! This is right up my alley. What a marvelous structure!

"Are you coming, Ben? Or are you just going to stand and stare?" teased Maggie, amused.

"Maggie, are you kidding? Look at this place! This stone…this…this permanence. Hard to find many like this back home." Ben dropped his bags, tilted his head back, closed his eyes, and took in a deep breath. "Ahhh, I belong in a place like this."

"Come along now. I am sure my family is eager to meet you."

With that, Ben picked up the two bags and headed towards the front door.

Dougal had already entered, placed the bags he was carrying to the side of the staircase, and turned around. "Mum and Da must be out back. I'll go and fetch them."

It was awkward waiting in the foyer for the hosts. Ben put the two bags near those Dougal had carried in and looked around. He was drawn to the sunroom. "Maggie, do you suppose we could wait in the sunroom?"

"Of course." She headed towards one of the two chairs near the window. "Come on in! This is my favorite room in the entire house."

The sunroom was small and cozy, with a petite circular table perched between two high-back chairs. Maggie and Ben took off their coats, sat down, and waited for her parents.

"I feel like I am waiting for an interview," commented Ben.

Maggie laughed. "Probably not far off. Both my parents and brothers have always been quite protective of me. Once you get to know all of them, though, I know you will come to like them, even though they are far more reserved than what you are used to. They are all very, very good people. Very straightforward, honest, and proud. It will just take a while."

The two fell into silence. It wasn't long before Dougal returned with Alexander and Ailsa Fraser. Ben quickly rose to his feet, but Maggie beat him to it, running over to give her mother a warm hug and kiss on the cheek before turning to her dad to give him a hug, too.

"I am so glad to be home! And see what I brought!" she said excitedly as she turned to Ben, grabbed his arm, and dragged him over to her side. "This is Ben!"

Ben could feel a stiffness that settled into both Alexander and Ailsa, even though it was nearly imperceptible. He extended his hand to Alexander and said, "Very nice to meet you, Mr. Fraser."

Alexander's handshake was businesslike: strong and assertive. He took his pipe out of his mouth with his left hand, and the sound that he made while shaking hands was the closest thing to a "harrumph" Ben had ever heard.

Ben then turned to Ailsa. "Mrs. Fraser, very pleased to meet you." Ailsa's handshake was warmer that Alexander's; for that, Ben was grateful.

She smiled at him. "How was your trip, Dr. Tyler?"

"Pleasingly uneventful, ma'am. Dougal was quite the chauffeur, for which I am thankful. After being in the air for so long, I am not sure driving on the left side of the road would have been a very good idea."

"We are pleased that you have come," said Ailsa. "Are you hungry?"

Maggie answered, "Very, Mum. You wouldn't, by chance, have made any scones now, would you?"

"There are some in the kitchen," said Ailsa as she turned towards the back. "I made them, knowing you would ask. Come – sit, and I will put on a kettle for tea."

Maggie clearly favored her mother. She had the same oval face and mahogany hair. However, Ailsa's hair was fading and streaked with white. She had the same build and natural grace as Maggie; the largest difference between them was that Ailsa's eyes were blue. Very blue – blue like Ben's mother.

Mr. Fraser was impressive looking. He had thick, pure-white hair, although, given his age, the white must have been quite premature. His eyes were a piercing blue-green, and he had chiseled features and a square jaw, firmly set. He was reasonably tall, with a physique that bespoke a very athletic youth. He even walked very firmly and purposefully. It was difficult to imagine him ever ambling.

Dougal and Alexander sat at the dining room table while Maggie and Ailsa went to the kitchen. Ben, remembering Maggie had told him how traditional her family was, sat down with Alexander and Dougal.

"I understand you recently received your PhD in architecture," said Alexander. "What do you intend to do with that degree?"

"Well, sir, I intend to teach."

"Have you been offered a position?"

"The Polytechnic Institute in Milan has offered me a fellowship, sir. Maggie and I are planning on visiting there on our honeymoon."

"A fellowship is not a permanent position, correct?"

"No, it is not. However, both of my parents are professors at the University of Michigan, which has a highly regarded school of architecture. My goal is to get a position there after the fellowship."

Just then, Maggie and her mother came in with a steaming teapot, a tray of fresh-baked scones, some clotted cream, and some ginger jam.

Ben rose to pull out a chair for Ailsa. Maggie gave him a wink as she set down the tray.

Ailsa turned to Maggie. "Maggie, have you settled on wedding plans?"

"Well, we thought it would be nice to be married in the abbey."

"Oh Maggie, here in Scotland! How lovely!" Ailsa's face lit up.

Ben thought he heard another "harrumph" from Alexander, but this time, it was much quieter and significantly softer in tone.

"We are going to need to stop off at the abbey to make arrangements," said Maggie. "We will wait, though, until after Christmas. I am sure they will be very busy before then."

"Do you know when?" asked Dougal.

"Fall," replied Ben. "Maybe early September. I hope that the abbey can accommodate us."

"If not, you might consider Craigmillar Castle. It's lovely and convenient," said Dougal. "That's where Kate and I were married."

Maggie nodded at that. "Your wedding was lovely, Dougal." She turned to Ben. "Ben, it would be a lovely venue."

Changing the subject, Maggie turned to her mother. "Mum, when are Callum and Duncan getting in?"

"Duncan, Jessie, and the bairns are driving up on Christmas day. Callum is flying in on the Eve. He has sair missed ye, lass."

"And me him, Mum," said Maggie, a bit wistfully. "It will be so good to see them all. And Dougal," she continued, turning to her brother, "How are Kate and your bairns? They must be getting so grown."

Dougal grinned. "Aye, that they are. Sometimes, I wonder how Mum and Da did it, and we only have the three."

The conversation continued, polite and trivial, for quite some time. Ailsa finally got up, saying, "We should get you settled. Why don't you both come with me?"

At that, Dougal said, "I should be getting back to Edinburgh. Nice to meet you, Ben." He reached over to shake Ben's hand. "And you, Mag…glad you made it back home." Placing his hand on her shoulder, he gave her a wink. "Da, we should be here late morning, Christmas."

"Thanks for fetching us, Dougal," said Maggie.

"Couldn'a leave you to your own defenses, now, could I?" he teased as he walked out of the room.

Ailsa had prepared two rooms as far apart as the home allowed. She placed Ben closest to the stairs and Maggie down the hall. Ben grinned at Maggie as he placed his bags in his room. She winked back, picked up her luggage, and followed her mother down the hall.

The next day, at breakfast, Maggie offered to pick Callum up from the airport. Her parents quickly agreed. Ben and Maggie borrowed the car and headed back to Edinburgh. They had a few hours to kill, so they parked the car and headed over to Princes Street. Maggie, not wanting to carry presents from the States, needed to buy for her family. As they entered store after store, Ben was amazed at just how decisive she was. "Perfect for Duncan," she said as she found a lovely cashmere scarf – in less than five minutes. "Kate will love this," she said as she found a gold necklace in as much time. And it continued until, in ninety minutes flat, Maggie had presents for her parents, her three brothers, her two sisters-in-law, and her five nieces and nephews.

Ben loaded the packages into the trunk. "That was amazing. Have you always shopped so efficiently?"

Maggie laughed. "When pressed, yes. Not one to dawdle."

They left for the airport, parked the car, and waited at the gate. Callum rarely checked baggage. Maggie and Ben stood as the passengers walked into the terminal. Callum was one of the first to deplane, walking very decisively, overnight in hand. Upon seeing Maggie, he broke into a wide grin and strode right to her. He dropped his bag and picked her up right off the floor in a big bear hug.

"There you are!!! You are well, Mag?" he asked, putting her down.

"Good to see you, too, Callum! Life's not done you puir."

Ben stood to the side, watching. To his eyes, Callum was as fit a man as could be. Not muscle-bound, not a football player, not a wrestler. Fit like a runner – sinewy like Maggie. Ben just sensed that Callum's reflexes were amazing, that he simply exuded a store of energy waiting for release. His hair was reddish brown, trimmed short. He had his father's square jaw and Maggie's gray eyes. He was of average height, and except for the aura of energy bursting to be set free, had no remarkable physical characteristics that would make him easy to identify.

Maggie pulled Callum over to Ben, turned, and flashed a brilliant smile.

"Ben, this is my oldest brother, Callum. And I think he's wonderful."

Callum grabbed Ben's hand and gave him a very firm handshake. "Very glad to meet you, Ben." Unlike with Dougal, Ben felt a sense of warm sincerity from Callum.

"Very happy to meet you, too. I am quite glad to be here."

"Thank you for picking me up, Mag," said Callum. "I don't have any other luggage – we can head to the car straight away."

The three headed to the car park. "So, how is London?" asked Maggie.

"As always. It's good to be home for the holiday. I am quite looking forward to some good single malt and some cranachan – with family."

Maggie smiled. "Dougal and Duncan and their clans are driving up tomorrow. We have you all to ourselves tonight. We can catch up without a gaggle of bairns."

Callum turned to Ben. "Not to ignore you, Ben. How has your visit been so far?"

"Lovely. We've not been here long, but I love Scotland. And I really love your parents' house."

Maggie interrupted, saying, "Callum, Ben lives and breathes architecture. You'll have to excuse him." She gave Ben a wink.

"It's good for a man to have a passion, Mag. Nothing wrong with it being architecture."

The trip back to Dunfermline was uneventful, and it seemed to take no time at all. Ailsa was just putting dinner on the table when the three arrived. Perfect timing. The five engaged in small talk over roast, neeps, and tatties, and then Alexander brought out the MacAllan's.

"An 18! Wonderful!" exclaimed Callum.

"I have a 25 for tomorrow," replied Alexander.

"Impressive!" said Callum. "Must be a high holiday, that's for certain."

"We have a lot to celebrate," interjected Ailsa. "Everybody home? Maggie and her man? I could not ask for more."

The group retired to the parlor, single malts in hand.

"So, Callum," began Ben, "what is it you do in London?"

There was an uncomfortable silence for a moment, and then Maggie said, "Ben, Callum can't talk about his work. I'm sorry I didn't tell you earlier. He works for the government."

Callum interrupted Maggie, saying, "Ben, I work for MI6. That's about all I can say. I'm sorry." He paused. "I understand you recently received your PhD in architecture? That's very impressive."

"Yes and thank you. Freshly minted, as they say."

"Have you secured a position? I understand you wish to teach."

"I am investigating a fellowship in Italy. That is, if we can get it to work around Maggie's career requirements."

Alexander's body tensed up, and a slight disapproving shadow of a frown danced across his brow.

"Maggie, I am sure that once you are married, you will see that your husband's career should be your focus, too."

There was another uncomfortable silence. Maggie, not wishing to cause an argument, demurred. "We have a lot of planning between now and then, Da. Ben and I will cross that bridge when we come to it."

Believing that a change of subject was immediately called for, Ailsa interjected. "Callum, Ben, and Maggie are planning on marrying here! They are considering the abbey. Or maybe Craigmillar. Any suggestions, one way or the other?"

"Personally, I would choose Craigmillar, but the abbey is lovely, too."

Maggie jumped in. "Callum, if I could, I would have you as my man of honor." She grinned, and Ailsa gasped just a bit.

"I have an idea!" said Ben, wanting to defuse Maggie's cheeky suggestion, which he was sure was meant to shock her parents. "Maggie, you have no sisters, and I have no brothers. What say I ask Callum to be my best man, and Sarah can be your matron of honor?"

Ailsa let out a small sigh of relief. "Maggie, that seems like a perfectly reasonable suggestion."

Maggie looked seriously at Ben, pondering, and then at Callum. She paused.

"Actually, I think that's a brilliant suggestion. Callum?"

Callum grinned and reached over to shake Ben's hand. "I would be highly honored to be your best man."

And Alexander simply harrumphed. Just a bit.

~

Christmas day broke cloudy and gray, but that didn't dampen the high spirits at Ayton Lodge. Dougal and his family arrived slightly before Duncan and his clan, and soon, the Fraser grandchildren were running up and down the stairs and all around the house playing hide and seek. It was happy mayhem.

"Weans!" cried Ailsa from the kitchen as she was assembling hors d'oeuvres. "Noo jist haud on! I'll skelp your bahooky if I ketch ye!"

Ben looked quizzically at Maggie, who laughed and then translated. "She told the children to slow down or she'll slap their behinds."

Ben laughed. "Weans?"

Maggie grinned. "It's short for "wee ones.""

"Is there a class I can take for Scottish? No – wait. I have a better idea. Why worry about taking class when I have my very own translator."

Maggie smiled tenderly. "That, you do. That, you do."

She headed towards the kitchen, saying, "Mum, let me give you a hand."

"Anything I can do?" asked Ben.

Maggie called over her shoulder, "Well, maybe you can tame the weans." She laughed.

Ben thought a bit and then headed over to the staircase. He caught the next child running down, grabbing her by the waist. "Would you like to hear a story about cowboys and Indians?" She stopped wiggling at hearing that and then shouted to her siblings and cousins. "Cowboys and Indians!!" The other four came running, and Ben took them into the sunroom.

"Let me tell you about the Lone Ranger and Tonto," Ben started. The five quickly sat cross-legged on the floor in front of him, and peace came to Ayton Lodge as Ben enchanted the children with a tale of the Wild West.

Supper was soon served, and the family chatted easily: Duncan, the physician, told of humorous patients; Dougal, the history professor, relayed hapless students' pleas for favorable grade treatment. Callum was spared demands for interesting stories – everyone knew his work was off limits. Kate and Jessie, wives to

Dougal and Duncan respectively, were strategically seated within arm's reach of the children at the far end of the table. Ailsa and Maggie were seated between the women with children. The men, who were seated together, were as far away from the bairns as physically possible. This arrangement allowed for the conversation.

After supper, gifts were exchanged, and Duncan and Dougal, with their respective families, drove back to Edinburgh. Callum spent the night, and the next morning, Ben and Maggie drove him to the airport.

As they pulled up to departures, Callum turned to Maggie. "Will we see you at Dougal's for Hogmanay?"

"Wouldn't miss it! See you then!" She gave him a big hug. "So good to see you, Callum. I've missed you."

He grinned widely and rubbed his knuckles good-naturedly on her head. "Me too, Mag. Good to have you home for a bit." He then shook Ben's hand warmly.

"See you next week, then!" He grabbed his overnight and quickly headed through the door.

Ben turned to Maggie. "And what is Hogmanay?"

"It's New Year's Eve. Bigger than Christmas here. Huge in Edinburgh. Maybe they will let you be the First Footer. Supposed to be someone with dark hair – and you saw my brothers. Not a dark hair betwixt 'em."

Ben sighed. "Something else for you to explain. But we do have a week for me to get up to speed. I probably will need every minute of that."

~

Hogmanay came quickly – the week between seemed to fly by. This time, the Frasers gathered in Edinburgh, where they all went to the street party on Princes Street for the fireworks, and afterward went to Dougal and Kate's. The clan stopped at the front door and waited even after Dougal unlocked it. Dougal turned to Ben as he flung open the door, sweeping his arm expansively as he invited Ben to enter first.

"Legend has it that if the First Footer is a tall, dark, and handsome man, the year will be a good one. After you, Dr. Tyler – bring us all good luck!"

Ben straightened up, hesitated just a bit, and then took an exaggerated step across the threshold. The rest clapped and laughed as they followed him in. He turned and grinned widely. He waved his arms wide, with great grandiosity.

"Happy 1997!"

"Well done, love," said Maggie as she went to his side and gave him a quick hug. "Well done."

Ben grinned. "Thanks for prepping me for this," he whispered into her ear. Maggie just grinned.

Kate and Jessie busied themselves putting the children to bed upstairs as Dougal brought out the single malt.

"Anyone prefer Drambuie instead?" he asked as he started pouring the whiskey.

"I'll take a Drambuie," said Ailsa, and Maggie piped up, saying, "MacAllan neat."

Drinks poured, the clan settled in the parlor and chatted as they finished their drinks. It was after 1:30 when Alexander, Ailsa, Ben, and Maggie left for Dunfermline – when they got to Ayton House, they all promptly went to bed. Maggie and Ben left for New York the next afternoon.

~

Maggie and Ben settled on Craigmillar for their wedding, on September 15, 1997. Callum was best man, and Sarah was Matron of Honor. All five "littles" were in the wedding party, which thrilled them. Ben insisted on wearing a tuxedo, but the Fraser men, all four of them, were in their dress tartan kilts and Prince Charlie jackets. The little girls were dressed in white frocks with Fraser tartan sashes, and the little boys were also in Fraser kilts. Maggie carried red roses to complement the red in the Fraser tartan, and Sarah wore a red gown. The entire wedding party looked splendid. It was a perfectly beautiful day; the castle was magnificent… the day was absolutely perfect. Ben and Maggie spent the night in Edinburgh, flying out to Italy the next day for their two-week honeymoon.

~

CHAPTER TWO

Maggie rolled over and looked at Ben, who was still sleeping. She smiled to herself.

I feel so content. My life is perfect.

She quietly slipped out of bed, not wanting to wake him, and went over to the window. She opened both the inside and outside shutters and looked out. The sun cast a very golden morning glow over the countryside. They were in a hotel on the edge of Milan, and between the very distant hills and the edge of town were a couple of fallow sunflower fields. Maggie thought it must have been a remarkable sight when the sunflowers were in bloom. Nevertheless, it was a glorious September morning. She looked down and twirled her wedding ring just a bit. Wearing it was still a novelty to her.

They had been in Italy for ten days already, first arriving in Venice and then traveling to Rome and Florence before landing in Milan, where Ben had interviews and appointments with staff at the Politechnico di Milano. Maggie was so in love: in love with Ben, in love with Italy…in love with marriage and this honeymoon. She twirled her ring once more, smiling to herself. She had never felt happier.

She went back and sat on the edge of the bed.

Ben rolled over, opened his eyes, and smiled at her. "Good morning, Mrs. Tyler."

She leaned down and gave him a kiss. "Good morning, Dr. Tyler." She looked at the alarm clock. "I hate to rush you, but if we are to get some breakfast, we have to get to the cafe soon."

Ben groaned, but he rolled over and sat up. "I am starved," he admitted. "Food trumps lazy, I guess." He glanced at the clock. "I need to meet Dr. Bondarelli at eleven… I'd best get my butt in gear." He stood up as he looked out the window. "Nothing like fresh air! Love it!" He came around the bed and leaned over to give Maggie a quick kiss.

"We need to roll."

The newlyweds quickly dressed and headed to the café, where they ordered a typically Italian breakfast: cappuccino and viennoiserie. Ben, truly hungry, ate two.

"What are you going to do today while I am at the university?"

"I am going to tour the Duomo di Milano. It's magnificent, I hear."

Ben grinned. "I must be rubbing off on you," he teased. "I'm sure it will be fantastic." He glanced at his watch. "I've got to head out. See you around six?"

"Can't wait. Love you."

"Love you, too." Ben slid back his chair, rose after leaving lira on the table for the bill, and headed out the door.

Maggie went back to the hotel room to grab her camera, and then she headed to the Metro station. She had purchased a two-hour self-guided audio tour, and after that, she returned to the rooftop to gaze at the Alps. She then headed back to the museum and then back to the archeological ruins underground. In all, she had a very pleasant and full day. She checked her watch and, realizing it was nearly five, headed back to the hotel.

Ben was already in the hotel room when Maggie arrived. The first thing Maggie noticed was a very worried look on his face.

"What's the matter?"

"Did you hear about the earthquake in Assisi?"

"No! Was anyone hurt?"

"No, but it was a fairly massive quake. Dr. Bondarelli asked if I would go with a group from the university tomorrow to assess the damage to the basilica. Would you mind terribly?"

"Oh no! Is there a lot of damage?"

"Significant – I hear half the town has been damaged. The team wants to check two things: the soundness of the basilica and the condition of those Giotto frescos."

"I will be fine here, Ben. I will get tickets to visit da Vinci's *The Last Supper*. You go. They invited you for good reason. I am sure you can help with the assessment."

They obviously know how knowledgeable he is. That's my Ben!

The next morning, Ben needed no encouragement to rise. Excited by the opportunity to finally use all of those years of study, he was motivated and energized.

"Let's grab a bite before I head out."

Maggie quickly put down the hairbrush she was using, ran her fingers through her hair, and the two left for the café.

Maggie spent another very pleasant day touring Milan and studying its incredible art and history. She was coming to appreciate Ben's admiration for gorgeous, old structures that had stood through the centuries. She started to respect the structural permanence that inspired Ben. After her tour of the Convent of Santa Maria della Gracie and da Vinci's magnificent *The Last Supper*, she took a table in the piazza and ordered a cappuccino. The warm September sun caressed everything it graced, and sipping a cappuccino, Maggie simply enjoyed the moment. Right then, Wall Street and its frenetic pace seemed almost alien.

I could really get used to this.

She finished her drink and, checking her watch, headed back to the hotel.

*I can't wait to hear about Ben's day. I actually hope he accepts the job.
Maybe I could teach finance here.*

There were several policemen in the hotel lobby when she
entered. They all turned to her. She was surprised and glanced at the
concierge behind the desk. He had a very distressed look on his face,
and she was immediately filled with a sense of dread and alarm.

"Signora Tyler?" said a very kind-looking man.

"Yes," answered Maggie hesitantly.

"Signora Tyler, I am Chief Inspector Bianchi," he said as he
took her hand in both of his. "Come over here, please, and sit." He
led her to a sofa in the lobby. She glanced at everyone else in the
room, wondering what was happening. To a one, they all had looks
of concern and sorrow. Maggie's sense of dread grew disturbingly
intense.

Bianchi bade Maggie sit and then took a seat next to her, and
still holding her hand in both of his, he lowered his head for a
moment. When he lifted it up, he looked searchingly into her eyes.
He was obviously distressed.

"Signora, your husband went to Assisi to assess the basilica?"

Maggie simply nodded.

"This morning, while he and the team were in the basilica, a
terrible accident happened."

Maggie froze, and then the tiniest groan escaped her lips. She
felt as if she couldn't breathe, and it seemed that the edges of her
vision were going black.

"Part of the Basilica collapsed while it was being inspected," continued Bianchi. "Most of the evaluators were injured. Unfortunately, four were killed in the collapse of the roof."

Maggie tried to find her voice but couldn't. She put her free hand over the inspector's and pressed down. Her eyes searched his face frantically.

"I am so sorry to inform you that Dr. Tyler was one of the casualties," said the inspector very softly.

Maggie sharply drew in air and tried to withdraw her hands. She looked at Bianchi again and then around the lobby at everyone standing there. She yanked her hands free and, crying uncontrollably, ran towards the stairs, towards her room. She was stopped by another policeman, who took her into his arms and hugged her strongly. Bianchi came over to her and also put his arm around her.

"Signora, do you have anyone here?"

Maggie sobbed. "No. We are on our honeymoon."

"Signora, I am going to assign a policewoman to stay with you and take you to Assisi. You should not be alone at this time. Her name is Agent Leone. She speaks English. She will stay with you."

At this point, a slender policewoman, perhaps in her late twenties, came forward. Her uniform was impeccable, and her black hair was pulled back in a perfect bun. Against this professional severity shone a pair of soft brown eyes that spoke nothing but compassion. She placed her hand on Maggie's shoulder.

Leone said quietly, "Signora, I will have dinner brought in. You should try and get some rest. We will leave for Assisi first thing in the morning."

~

Maggie didn't sleep – of course she couldn't sleep. Her Ben was dead. That kept playing over and over in her head. She half didn't believe it.

They must have made a mistake. He will walk in and tell me how he escaped.

Then she would be jarred back into reality.

It's odd what happens when a person is hit with such a deep and unexpected tragedy. It's as if someone pushes a reset button in your psyche. Your entire life seems reset to zero. Your worries and concerns of just moments ago vanish – you can't even remember them. Things on a to-do list vanish. You end up parking yourself in this unfeeling, activity-centered compartment of your brain, going through the motions and doing what you know needs to be done, all the while not even addressing the emotions sitting in another compartment – knowing that if you move over to that emotion compartment, you can't function at all. So, in the meantime, you don't go there. You ploddingly stay in the activity compartment, doing what needs to be done at the moment but feeling wooden. Wooden, or empty, or concrete, or hollow – almost as if you are working from an alternate universe, watching, from a distance, someone you know is "you" doing things. And this was Maggie. Maggie, in this state, didn't need food or sleep to function for the next twenty-four hours: not just didn't need; she couldn't tolerate. She could not sleep: she was possessed of intense, restless energy. She could not eat: her stomach seemed to go into spasms if she tried to eat anything, to the point it hurt to eat.

Agent Leone picked Maggie up early the next day, and the two headed to the airport. The two women drove in uncomfortable silence: Maggie sunk in deep grief, Agent Leone not sure what to say. When they landed in Perugia, they walked out to a waiting police car, which was surrounded by several policemen.

"Signora, le mie più sentite condoglianze," said the policeman nearest the passenger door, taking her hand in his. His eyes were welled up in sympathy. Even though Maggie did not speak Italian, she understood his meaning. A second policeman then walked up, saying, "Signora, mi dispiace tanto per la tua perdita." He also took her hand, squeezing it. The solace offered by these complete strangers comforted her.

These people are so warm. They really care. And that thought made her start to cry.

Agent Leone wrapped her arm around Maggie's shoulders and led her to the waiting car. The two again fell silent: Maggie vainly attempting to regain her composure, Agent Leone silently giving her needed space. It didn't take long to get to Assisi – being in a police car allowed the two to drive into the city. Residents and emergency personnel were allowed in, but not tourists. Half the town was damaged or gone. Agent Leone drove as close as she could get to the basilica, and then she and Maggie walked the rest of the way. The basilica was cordoned off and bustling with emergency personnel. Agent Leone turned to Maggie and said, "Stay here a moment." She walked over to the chief inspector, who was standing by the entry door. In a few minutes, she returned.

"Signora, they have taken your late husband to the hospital."

Maggie hung her head and then looked over to the basilica. She turned suddenly to Agent Leone and said, "Give me a minute. I want to go speak to that monk."

"I am sure he doesn't speak English. Let me translate for you."

The two walked over to a tall, lean cleric – clean-shaven, perhaps in his mid-forties.

"Mi scusi, Padre," said Agent Leone. "Questa è la vedova Americana. Lei ha alcune domande per voi." *Excuse me, Father – this is the American widow. She has some questions for you.*

The monk turned to Maggie, took her hand, and said, "Le mie più profonde simpatie, signora. Il mio nome è Fratello Ventimiglio. Come posso aiutarti?"

Leone turned to Maggie. "I told him who you are and that you have some questions for him. He gives you his deepest sympathy and asks how he may help. His name is Brother Ventimiglio."

"Thank you," said Maggie to Leone. "Can you ask him, was he there when the roof collapsed?"

"Eri lì quando il tetto crollò?" said Leone to the monk.

"Sì, ero dentro con la squadra. Ho accovacciato dal muro quando ha cominciato a cadere, ed è così che sono sopravvissuto."

Leone translated, not turning to Maggie this time, but merely repeating the words in English. "Yes, he was inside. He crouched by the wall to survive."

Maggie then asked, "Where was Ben?"

"He was over by the tomb of St. Francis."

"May I see it?"

"No, signora. The basilica is not safe for you to enter."

Brother Ventimiglio saw the look on Maggie's face. He took her hand again, speaking earnestly and rapidly.

Leone translated. "He says that you are very welcome to return when it is safe, signora. Ask for him if you return. He will take all the time you need and show you everything you want to see. When it is safe."

Maggie looked up into Brother Ventimiglio's eyes.

"Grazie, Padre." She looked down for a moment and then turned to Leone. "Let's go, Agent. Let's go see Ben." She choked a bit on Ben's name, turned, and headed towards the car.

Maggie and Agent Leone walked into the hospital. Agent Leone went up to the desk and introduced herself and Maggie, at which point an orderly behind the desk quickly walked down a hall. He promptly returned, accompanied by two others – a woman and a man.

The woman walked right up to Maggie, extending her hand. "Signora, I am Professore Bondarelli. I am truly sorry for your loss. Such a tragedy," she said, shaking her head. "I feel so guilty for asking him to come here." Her voice trailed off as she fought back tears. "Such a loss."

She turned to acknowledge the man to her left. "Signora, this is a man from the consulate in Milano. He offered to assist with the arrangements. I assume you will want services and burial back in the United States?"

The man stepped forward and introduced himself. "Mrs. Tyler, my name is Alex Caldwell. I am so sorry for your loss. We are here to help you any way we can."

Maggie shook Mr. Caldwell's hand. "Mr. Caldwell, thank you so much for your generous offer. But right now, I think what I want to do is see my husband." She raised her hand into a fist and raised it to bite her knuckle. She was having a very difficult time keeping her composure.

The orderly stepped forward and motioned the group to follow him down the hall and into a small, dark room. The orderly switched on the lights – there, on a table in the middle of the room, was a corpse draped in a sheet. Maggie gasped at the sight, and Mr. Caldwell quickly went to her side, thinking that she might faint. Maggie straightened up and headed towards the table. She stood there as the orderly went to the far side of the table, near the head. He looked at Maggie with a questioning glance. She looked at him and nearly imperceptibly nodded her head. The orderly took the sheet in both of his hands and gently pulled it back. There was Ben, lying so still, ashen and bruised. There was still dust in his hair. Maggie started to cry and turned away.

The orderly pulled the sheet back up. Agent Leone walked up to Maggie. "Signora, perhaps we should sit down." She turned to the orderly. "Can you please get the signora a glass of water?"

The orderly left as the four went into the small lobby to sit down.

"Mrs. Tyler, where would you care to take your late husband's remains?" asked Mr. Caldwell.

Maggie thought for a moment. "I think he would want to go back to Ann Arbor," Maggie said finally. "Mr. Caldwell, have you notified Ben's parents?"

"No, I haven't. But I certainly can arrange that. We can have you accompany your husband back as soon as tomorrow. Which airport?"

Maggie quickly responded, "Detroit Metro."

The orderly returned with a glass of water, gave it to Maggie, and turned to address Agent Leone. "Can you please inform signora that the body will be ready to go home tomorrow morning?" Agent Leone nodded in acknowledgment. She then turned to Maggie.

"We should head back to the airport." She turned to Mr. Caldwell.

"Will you call me with the arrangements? I think it would be best if the remains were sent to Milano, no? Then Mrs. Tyler can accompany them back to the United States."

"Of course." Caldwell then turned to Maggie and gave her a business card. "Mrs. Tyler, please feel free to call me anytime. If there is anything else we can do, please do not hesitate to call."

Professor Bondarelli, silent for most of the ordeal, stepped forward and gave Maggie a hug. "I know there is nothing anyone can say, signora. We are all so deeply sorry."

Maggie and Agent Leone walked back to the police car and left for the airport. Maggie spent the ride back to Perugia with her head leaning on the passenger door window. She was emotionally exhausted.

The next morning was a blur. The consulate had made flight arrangements for that evening, and the casket was arriving at the airport late afternoon. Maggie was met at the gate by Agent Leone. She was carrying a taped box, which she gave to Maggie.

"Signora, here are your late husband's personal effects. I thought you might want to carry them on with you to make sure they didn't get lost."

Maggie took the box, a bit hesitantly, and then looked at Agent Leone. "Ma'am, I can't imagine I would have been able to navigate this without you. I am deeply grateful to you for your kindness and assistance. Thank you so much."

A sorrowful smile flitted across Agent Leone's face.

"Mrs. Tyler, I lost my brother very suddenly in an accident a few years ago. I remember how difficult that was. I can only imagine losing a husband." She reached into her pocket and brought out a business card. "Please contact me if you need any help. I think, had we met under different circumstances, we might easily have become friends. Go with God, Mrs. Tyler." There was a trace of a tear in her eye. She shook Maggie's hand.

"Your plane is boarding. Perhaps you should get to your seat."

Agent Leone walked up to the boarding agent and spoke a few words to her. The boarding agent signaled for Maggie to step forward to the head of the line and cleared her boarding pass. Agent Leone watched until she could no longer see Maggie on the gangway, and then she turned and left.

CHAPTER THREE

It was a long flight back, with layovers in both Frankfort and Chicago. Maggie didn't arrive at Detroit Metro until late the following night. The terminal was empty except for the people waiting for arriving passengers – hers was the last inbound flight of the evening. As Maggie stepped off the gangway, she saw Sarah and then, behind her, Ben's parents. Sarah rushed up to Maggie and gave her a warm hug, tears streaming down her face. She just stood there hugging Maggie, as if the hug could wash away some of Maggie's pain. That made Maggie cry uncontrollably. She had spent so much emotional energy holding everything together… Sarah's outpouring of sympathy let open the gates to so much of what Maggie was feeling.

Ben's parents walked up, and Sarah broke the hug. It was clear that Ben's mom had been crying a lot – her eyes were red. She looked as if she would break into tears again at any moment. Ben's dad looked so much older. His face was ashen, every wrinkle and crease somehow exaggerated. The sorrow was so palpable that a gate agent walked up.

"Are you okay?"

Maggie was in no shape to answer.

"We are here to pick up my son's remains," said Will. "This is a very difficult time for us. I'm sure you can understand."

"Give me a moment," said the agent, and he walked over to the phone on the desk. He came back after a brief conversation. "Please stay here a moment. I have sent for an escort for you. I am so sorry for your loss." He guided the four over to the lounge area. A few moments later, a man drove up in an electric trolley and motioned them to board. He drove them through the terminal to a small, quiet room near baggage claim.

"Do any of you have any luggage?" he asked. Maggie nodded. "May I please have your claim ticket? I will fetch your luggage and bring it here." He left for the luggage carousel, and a very uncomfortable silence fell on the room. No one dared speak for fear of unleashing all of their emotions.

Maggie's luggage arrived at about the time the casket did.

"I have made arrangements for the funeral home to pick up the casket," Will informed the agent. "Eagle. They will ask for Dr. Ben Tyler." At that, he choked up. He composed himself quickly. "They can't get here until first thing in the morning. Will that be a problem?"

"No, sir. We will take care of it." The agent hesitated a brief moment. "On behalf of Delta, please accept our condolences for your loss."

It was a long and uncomfortably quiet ride back to Ann Arbor. They arrived well after 1 A.M., and everybody went right to sleep. It had been a very hard day.

~

Sarah did not leave Maggie's side for days. She drove Maggie to the funeral home to make arrangements. She was by Maggie's side at the cemetery. She wrote the first draft of the obituary and contacted the local newspapers to get it published. But most importantly, she stayed by Maggie's side. She took Maggie on a long walk in the arboretum. She took Maggie on another long walk, this time along the Huron River. There were times of conversation and times of long silence... Sarah became Maggie's quiet bulwark of strength.

"Sarah, you have been so kind. I am so very grateful – I am not sure I can ever even find the words to convey how much what you have done has meant to me."

"Maggie, I have felt close to you from the moment we met. You are like a sister to me. I hope we can still be sisters."

Maggie gave Sarah a hug. "I was hoping we could remain close, Sarah. You are my one and only sister, and I would like to keep it that way."

The funeral came and went in a flurry of activity, handshakes, flowers, hugs, and condolences. It was on the next day, when there were no plans to make or people to thank, when the finality started to set in. Maggie was sitting quietly on the edge of her bed, staring at the still-taped box of Ben's personal effects, when Sarah came in.

"Maggie, what's in that box?"

"Ben's things from the accident. I haven't had the nerve to open it."

"Would you like to open it with me here? Or do you need to wait?"

Maggie hung her head dejectedly. "I imagine I should go through it. I'm just not sure I'm up for it at the moment." She paused in silence before continuing. "But I would very much like you to be here when I do."

"You let me know. Just say the word, and I will come right over. But now I think I need to go home. Jake expects me this evening."

Maggie rose and walked over to Sarah. "You have been my salvation, Sarah. I am not sure what I would have done without you the last couple of days. Thank you."

Sarah grabbed Maggie by the shoulders. "Maggie, you are a strong and resilient woman. Even so, please know that I will always be here for you. I am your sister-in-law...forever."

Maggie gave Sarah a hug. "Thank you again, Sarah. I will be going back to New York day after tomorrow, so you and I will have to open the box within the next day or two." She stepped back. "Finally, after all of these years...it's good to have a sister. At last."

~

Maggie called Sarah the next night. "Sarah, I'm leaving tomorrow afternoon. Do you have any time tomorrow?"

"Sure! Before or after lunch?"

"Let's grab a bite to eat and come back and open the box."

"Deal. See you then."

Sarah and Maggie went into town and grabbed a bowl of soup, and then they went back to the Tylers' home. The two went up to Maggie's room, and Sarah sat on the bed as Maggie picked up the box and sat down beside her. Maggie took a deep breath and looked at Sarah.

"Let me remove the tape," suggested Sarah. She took the box and gingerly worked the tape off with her fingernails. When it was off, Sarah stopped, box on lap, and looked at Maggie. "Are you ready for this?"

Maggie nodded her head, and Sarah lifted the lid off, putting it next to her on the bed.

Maggie reached over and pulled out Ben's shirt. She grabbed it with both hands and lifted it up to her face, smelling the fabric. It still smelled like Ben. A tear started streaming down her face. She buried her face in the shirt.

"Are you okay?"

Maggie nodded silently and put the shirt to the side. Under Ben's watch and wedding ring were his wallet and passport. Maggie put all four items to the side, lifting them up by the passport so she wouldn't have to touch the wedding band. Next were Ben's sweater, undershorts, and slacks. His shoes were on the bottom, stuffed with his socks. As Maggie was pulling out the shoes, she noticed something else stuck inside one of them. She pulled it out.

"Sarah, have you ever seen this before?"

Sarah shook her head.

"Neither have I. I wonder what this is doing in this box? This looks very old."

Maggie and Sarah were looking at a rusted piece of iron. An amulet, perhaps. It was shaped like a crescent, like the sun rising over the horizon, and was bisected by a "V" that extended both below and above the crescent. The "V" had a spearheaded shape on the top right side and a rounded design resembling a curved trident on the left.

Maggie held the object up, turned it around, and examined it. "I have seen something like this before. Back in Scotland. When I was in school. Whatever was Ben doing with something like this?"

Sarah reached over. "May I take a look?" She waited for Maggie to give it to her and then peered at it. "I have never seen anything like this before. You say it reminds you of something you saw as a child?"

"Yes, but I can't for the life of me remember what. If I can't remember, I'll ask Dougal. I'm sure he'll be able to identify it for me."

Ben's belongings were spread over the bed. Maggie put everything back in the box slowly, arranged as they were packed – all except the amulet, which she put in her pocket – and closed it up.

"Sarah, would you mind storing this for me?" Maggie handed the box to Sarah. "I think this will be my precious memory box. I have a lot of loose ends to tie up in New York, and it makes no sense for me to bring this box with me. I am not sure what I will do now that my Ben is gone."

"Absolutely. I will take it back home with me and keep it in a safe place until you return. Please remember, you are always welcome to come and stay with Jake and me. Anytime."

Maggie just sat there for several minutes. She felt heavy. Heavy with the weight of grief. Heavy with the weight of unexpected loss. And heavy with the loss of direction she was feeling. She just felt heavy.

"Thank you so much, Sarah. I will take you up on your offer after things settle down. I am not sure what I am going to do. I think I might take a leave from work and go back to Scotland for a bit. At the moment, I feel that it will be incredibly difficult to focus on work. I am not even sure I can bear walking into our…my…apartment." Maggie started to cry.

Sarah stood up at that. "Maggie, let's go to the arboretum and take a long walk." She pulled Maggie up. "Fresh air and exercise is a great tonic."

Maggie rose and grabbed a sweater. "That's a great idea, Sarah. I need to try and shake this."

~

Maggie's flight was early the next morning. She landed at JFK and hailed a cab into the city. She piled out of the cab, paid the fare, and turned to the door. She stopped and just stood there for the longest time. Finally, she pulled her keys out of her pocket, walked up the stairs, inserted the key, and opened the door, bringing her suitcase in. She looked around at the familiar furnishings: the table in the vestibule, the leather sofa, the walnut end table. She started to shake and headed toward the sofa to sit down. She was totally overwhelmed by the absence of Ben while sitting in this environment that simply screamed his name. She simply couldn't stay – she had the strongest compulsion to leave. Immediately.

She nearly ran to the door, flung it open, and ran out, slamming it behind her. She headed down the street towards the nearest park. She grabbed a cup of coffee at the corner shop and headed into the park, taking in the crisp fall air. It was almost exactly a year since Ben had proposed, and the autumn leaves reminded her of that wonderful day in Central Park. She sat on a bench and hung her head, crying softly. After a while, she composed herself.

I really have to stop this. I am going to drive myself crazy.

She got up and walked slowly back to her apartment. She put her clothes away and pulled out a frozen entrée for supper. She pulled the amulet from her pocket, studied it again, and put it in her jewelry box.

I will go into the office tomorrow. I need to get back to work. I am sure it will give me a welcome diversion.

She suddenly felt exhausted. She went to bed early and awoke at five the next morning. She went through the familiar motions: getting ready for work, jumping on the subway, getting off at Wall

Street, and walking into her office. She hung up her coat and pulled out her chair, turning on her computer. She had hundreds of emails to sift through.

Maggie got through her first day reading emails. As she headed home on the subway, she started to dread heading back to the apartment. She startled herself: when had it become "the" apartment instead of "their" apartment? Instead of "her" apartment? She wasn't even sure why she had noticed the change in grammar. She pushed the thought aside.

She found herself going to work early and leaving late. She also found herself staring into space frequently. Her heart just wasn't in it anymore, and she was having a difficult time concentrating. After a couple of weeks, she asked for an extended leave. She was going back to Scotland, just for a while. She needed to re-ground herself. She wanted to feel connected again. She called her parents, then she called Callum, and then she called Dougal. She packed a small suitcase and tucked the amulet in the corner.

CHAPTER FOUR

Dougal met Maggie at the airport and drove her up to Dunfermline.

"Dougal, when we get to Da and Mum's, there is something I want to show you."

"What's that, Mag?"

"There was an amulet, or something like that, that was in the box that the Italians gave me with Ben's belongings. It looks very old. I don't recognize it, and neither does Sarah. It reminds me of something from my childhood, but I'm a little foggy. I thought you might recognize it."

"Sure, Mag. But I'm not sure I know much about all things Italian."

"That's the thing. I don't think it's Italian at all."

When Dougal and Maggie got to their parents' house, Dougal brought in Maggie's bag and took it upstairs. Maggie lifted it up on the bed and opened it. She reached into the corner of the suitcase and brought out the amulet, giving it to Dougal.

Dougal let out a low whistle. "Maggie, this looks Pictish! Where did you say you got this?"

"It was in the box they gave me with Ben's belongings from the basilica. I didn't open the box until I got to Michigan, or I would have asked earlier."

"This just might be quite remarkable. We should authenticate it. Would you be willing to have it carbon-dated at the university?"

"They won't damage it, will they?"

"No. They can date it by gently taking just a little rust. I will make the arrangements at the lab if you like."

"Please do, Dougal. I am very curious."

Maggie put the amulet back into the corner of the suitcase, and she and Dougal went down to supper.

~

Maggie got up the next morning and headed to the dance studio where she had studied.

"Maggie Fraser!" cried Fiona Wemyss as Maggie walked in the door. "It's been forever!" She ran up to Maggie and gave her a big hug. "What brings you back?"

"Oh, I'm here for a while to recharge. Maggie didn't want to overload Fiona with her situation. "I was wondering if you needed any help for a month or two. Just a month or two."

"That would be wonderful, Maggie. These wee ones can always use more encouragement and guidance. When can you start? Do you have any set schedule?"

"Well, I really don't want to work full time. Either pick a couple of days per week or maybe a few hours a day. Whatever you might need."

"Well, what about working with the beginners Tuesdays and Thursdays at three in the afternoon. Would that work?"

"Perfect! See you Thursday! Now I need to go get some dance clothes and slippers."

Maggie headed over to the Starbucks on Carnegie Drive and took her coffee into Pittencrief Park. She sat down and sipped her drink, watching people strolling by. She started to relax – she felt it. The familiarity of Scotland was dimming the pain of New York. It was a welcome relief. She then set about finding new dance clothes and shoes.

She fell into a new routine: taking it easy, teaching a few dance classes, wondering what she was going to do going forward. The longer she stayed in Scotland, the less she wanted to return to New York. She wasn't sure that was good for the long term, though. The only thing she really was sure of was that she should not make any drastic moves. Not until she felt stable and sure.

About three weeks into this new routine, Dougal called. "Can you come with me tomorrow?"

"Wednesday? Sure. Are we going to the lab?"

"Yes. We have an appointment with one Oliver McQuiddy, a carbon-dating technician. Bring the amulet."

"What time should I be at your house?"

"Make it two. We'll head over together."

Maggie and Dougal showed up at the university lab at three on the dot. They were met by an overweight, middle-aged man in a lab coat.

"Dr. Fraser?" asked the man, reaching out his hand. "I'm Oliver McQuiddy."

"Glad to meet you," said Dougal. "I hope you can help us. This is my sister, Maggie," he continued, turning to her. "She has the object we would like dated."

Maggie reached over to shake Oliver's hand. "Pleasure to meet you."

"Follow me," said Oliver as he pointed down the hall. The three walked down a long hall to a secured door. Oliver swiped his badge, and the door opened. He motioned for Maggie and Dougal to enter.

Oliver walked over to the lab table, went to the far side, and turned around. "What is it you would like dated?"

Maggie reached into her pocket and pulled out the amulet. Oliver's eyes narrowed.

"Where did you get this?"

"Italy. I have no idea how something like this ended up in Assisi."

"Assisi?" asked Oliver. He was obviously very interested. "This looks Pictish."

"That's what I thought," interjected Dougal. "That's why we are here: we want to know whether this is authentic."

Oliver picked up the amulet with gloved hands and studied it closely.

"Assisi, you said. Would you mind telling me how this came into your possession?"

Maggie hung her head. Dougal stepped in, saying, "Maggie's husband was, unfortunately, killed in the recent Assisi earthquake. He was investigating the damage in the basilica when the roof caved in."

"He was in the basilica? Do you know where in the basilica?"

Maggie spoke up. "I was not allowed in, but a priest told me that Ben was near the crypt of St. Francis."

Oliver peered at the amulet again. "I would like to hold on to this for testing."

"No, that will not be necessary," said Dougal as smoothly as he could. "I would like you to take a small sample of the rust. I know that is adequate for dating. So, if you would, please scrape a bit off, and we'll leave you to your testing. You can call me when the testing is done. Over in the history department."

"Certainly." Oliver took the amulet over to a microscope and placed it on the stage. He then took an instrument resembling a scalpel in one hand and a small pair of pliers in the other. Looking through the eyepiece, he carefully scraped off a small pile of rust. When he was finished, he gave the amulet back to Dougal.

"It should take a few weeks for the results to be available. Here's my card – you can call for status any time."

"Thank you," replied Dougal, shaking Oliver's hand. "We shall be in touch."

Maggie reached over and shook Oliver's hand. "Very nice to meet you, Mr. McQuiddy. And thank you in advance."

Maggie and Dougal left and headed towards the car. "Dougal, didn't you trust Mr. McQuiddy with the amulet?"

"Mag, if that piece is genuine, it's priceless. I certainly wouldn't want us to walk in with something so potentially historically significant and leave with a replica. You must be very careful with that. Do you have somewhere safe for it?"

Maggie hadn't thought that the amulet would be as valuable as Dougal mentioned it might be. She thought a bit and then said, "Yes, I know somewhere quite safe. But first, I would like to take some pictures of it before I stash it. This has become quite the mystery – one that I would really like to solve."

"Come back with me to my office, Maggie. I have a digital camera there that we can use. I would also like some pictures. I can think of several people I would like to contact after the dating comes back. A picture would be quite useful."

Maggie and Dougal headed to his office and took several pictures. Dougal uploaded them to his computer and then returned the amulet to Maggie.

"Let's be off, then," he said, and they headed back to Dunfermline.

~

Oliver McQuiddy went over to his window and watched Dougal and Maggie leave. He waited several minutes, making sure they were well out of sight, and then he made a phone call.

"Master," he said into the phone, keeping his voice low, "would it be possible to call his eminence and ask him to send someone into the Vatican vaults for some research?"

Oliver waited until the voice on the other end of the phone stopped, and then he continued. "An article was recovered from the basilica's earthquake. It appears to be Pictish in origin. I am carbon-dating it, but it was found in the ruins around the tomb of our most holy saint. I thought we could research the journals of St. Francis to see if it was mentioned."

Oliver again waited until the voice at the other end finished, and he ended the call with a simple, "Thank you. I will certainly let you know of the outcome."

THE THIRD ORDER

CHAPTER FIVE

"Francesco, allez à la piazza - c'est jour de marché, et nous avons besoin de l'huile d'olive." Pica had just come from the kitchen, and she absentmindedly summoned her son to go to market and buy a flask of olive oil on behalf of the cook. It was market day in Assisi, the sun was shining on that brilliant day in 1191, and the piazza was filled with farmers and merchants from the surrounding countryside.

The young boy did not look up as he responded, "Maman, please speak Italian. You live in Assisi now – you've lived here since before I was born. Nobody speaks French."

"Mon petit chou, tu as raison, comme d'habitude," Pica teased. Born Pica de Bourlemont, noblewoman of Provence, she had wed a dashing Italian silk merchant and had left her home and country for this Umbrian walled city more than a decade earlier. While fluent in Italian, when she was distracted, she easily slipped back into her native tongue. She never pined for her former home, though; she embraced Italy, even naming her son Giovanni – Giovanni di Pietro di Bernardone. It was her husband who was so enamored of all things French. He had been in France conducting business when Giovanni had been born. Upon his return to Assisi, a delighted papa Pietro had started calling his newborn son "little Frenchman" – Francesco. The name stuck, and Francesco it was.

The Bernardone family lived a very comfortable life in Assisi. Merchant traders were a strong and politically important cohort in medieval Assisi, and Bernardone was one. Dealing in silk was a very lucrative trade. Pietro's business was buying silk from the Byzantines in Thrace, Greece, and selling it in Italy and France. Pietro provided a good life for his family, but he was away from home a fair amount. Pica had started relying on her ten-year-old son more and more as he grew.

"Francesco, take this," Pica said, handing him a few ducats. "Go to the market and see whether the oil merchant is there today. If he is, buy a flask of oil from him." Francesco took the money and rushed towards the door. He loved going to market: there was so much activity and so many things to spy.

"Don't run! You might break the flask!" were the words that floated out the door with him.

Francesco paid no heed; he only needed to be careful coming home. He ran down the narrow, cobbled street towards the piazza, the sounds and aromas attracting him as naturally as a bee to flowers. As he approached the perimeter, he slowed; now he must find the oil merchant. He started weaving through the crowds, past the farmers with chickens and eggs, past the basil and oregano, past the lemons and tomatoes and fish and flour and milk. Usually, the oil merchants were between the farmers and the goods merchants who sold cloth, baskets, pottery, tools, and jewelry.

The oil merchant was indeed there, just as he usually was. Francesco bought a flask of oil from him for his mother, but instead of heading back through the food merchants, he continued forward, towards the tools and implements. That was his favorite section of the market. He stopped to look at a knife: it looked like a soldier's knife. It had a leather sheath and a no-nonsense, woven leather handle. Francesco always stopped for things that looked as if they could easily belong to a soldier.

I will be a soldier someday, and I will need things like this. I will be a soldier as soon as I am old enough. I will ride into Apulia on my big white horse and join the crusaders there. Little boys will run up to me to touch my boots and horse. People in the street will part for my passing and bless my mission.

Lost in his thoughts and daydreams, Francesco suddenly realized that some of the merchants were starting to pack up to leave. He quickly backed up – and backed right into someone standing behind him. He just as quickly turned around, eyes to the ground, and he saw before him white linen brushing sturdy boots. His gaze rose to a dark leather cincture that held a large broadsword on the man's left side and continued up, past the large red cross that was appliquéd to the linen covering the man's broad chest, to the chainmail cowl that surrounded his thick neck. Above that was a very red beard, and above that, very blue eyes. Francesco could barely see that man's head, as tall as he was. He stumbled back in awe and amazement. He had backed into a Knight Templar.

The knight reached out to steady the boy. "Are ye all right, laddie?"

Francesco didn't understand the strange language and quizzically looked up. The knight, realizing he had spoken English, repeated the question in French, hoping to find a language they could both understand.

Francesco eagerly replied, "Oui, monsieur." He was thrilled that this knight spoke French! Francesco's eager reply drifted into awkward silence as his eyes settled on the sword in awe. That sword! It was so very large! In its scabbard, it was taller than him. He timidly reached out to touch it, but the crusader caught his hand in midair. "It is a dangerous move to reach for a man's sword, laddie."

Francesco quickly pulled his hand back, hung his head, and remorsefully said, "Je vous en prie, excusez-moi."

The knight smiled and, cupping his hand under Francesco's chin, gently lifted the boy's head up. "Manners, laddie. Simple manners."

No longer dumbstruck, the awkward awe wore off and was replaced with a torrent of words.

"M'lord, why are you here in Assisi? Do you have lodging? Are you hungry? Are you heading for the Crusade? Where is your horse? And that sword! I have never seen one so large! What kind is it? Wh–"

The knight smiled as he placed his hand on Francesco's shoulder. "Slow down, mon petit chou! One question at a time! I am returning from the Holy Land, heading back to my home in Scotland. Have you heard of Scotland?"

"No, m'lord. Where is that?"

"It's past France, across the water, north."

"They speak that strange language there?"

"Aye, laddie, we do indeed," the knight said with a laugh as he switched for a moment back to his native tongue. Francesco scowled.

The knight laughed again, this time a bit more heartily. "I think the next question you asked was if I had lodging?"

Francesco nodded eagerly.

"I just arrived this afternoon, and I ate at the tavern over there." The knight half-turned to point over his left shoulder. "My next job is to find an inn for the night. I already boarded my horse in the stable – the one just inside the city gate."

"Maman is French. You must come with me! You can stay the night – I am sure Maman will say yes. The cook is making dinner, and it smells delicious! Will you come and tell me all about the Holy Land? Did you fight the Saracens? I am going to be a soldier when I grow up! I am going to go to Apulia and join the pope's forces there!" Francesco's words were tumbling out his mouth with remarkable speed as he puffed out his chest and tried very hard to look older and larger than he was.

At this, the knight's laughter turned into a hearty guffaw. "A soldier now! And what does your maman say about that?"

Francesco scowled again. "She wants me to join my father, selling silk. Selling silk!! No!" Francesco defiantly crossed his arms across his chest. "I want to fight the Germans and the Normans! And ride a horse and have a sword and shield, and maybe a mace. And a knife," he added wistfully, turning to watch the tools merchant pack up his wares to leave for the day.

"What is your name, lad?"

"Francesco. Francesco di Pietro di Bernardone."

The knight extended his right hand, and taking Francesco's, he solemnly introduced himself. "I am Alan Fitz Walter, second high steward of Scotland, Knight Templar, dapifer to William the Lion, king of Scotland."

This introduction caused Francesco's mouth to drop wide open. A look of consternation fell across his face, as he wasn't sure whether he should kiss the ring on Fitz Walter's hand, drop to one knee, or continue standing. Fitz Walter recognized the child's confusion and took his hand.

"I think I shall take you up on your kind offer of dinner, as long as your maman agrees." Francesco could not believe his good fortune! He grinned and turned to lead Fitz Walter back to his house. "I need to make sure I don't break this flask of oil."

"Well then, we must go carefully," responded Fitz Walter with a grin. Francesco was liking this tall man more and more.

The two wended their way back through the narrow streets to Francesco's house, chatting as they meandered.

"You asked about my sword," said Fitz Walter. "It is the latest improvement in Highland weaponry. I had it made right before I left for the Crusade."

"I have never seen one so long, m'lord. It must weigh a lot."

"Aye, laddie. Even as big and strong as I am, I need two hands to use it. But if a man is strong enough, it is an excellent weapon. No enemy can get close enough to harm me."

At that moment, Francesco turned to Fitz Walter. "This is where we live." He broke through the door and excitedly called out to his mother, "Maman! Can we have a guest for dinner? He's right outside the door. He's a crusader!! He's dapifer for William the Lion, king of Scotland! He is heading back home from the Crusade! Please, Maman? Please? He just arrived in Assisi and doesn't have lodging, and he's hungry, and we have room, and we have dinner, right? Oh, please, Maman? Please?"

Pica put down her needlework, stood up, and approached Francesco.

"What is this? There is a nobleman outside the door? You did not bring him in?" Pica turned and headed to the door. Fitz Walter was standing to the left of the door jamb, and when Pica saw him, she stopped in amazement. She had never seen such a large, impressive display of masculinity. She curtsied, stood back up, and extended her hand.

"Please forgive my son's poor manners, m'lord. May I introduce myself? I am Pica, born of Bourlemont, Provence, wife of Pietro di Bernardone."

She spoke in Italian, though, and saw the consternation on Fitz Walter's face. Francesco came up behind her. "Maman, m'lord does not speak Italian, but he does speak French." Pica, slightly flustered, repeated her introduction in French. Fitz Walter took her hand, brought it up as he bent down, and brushed it against his lips.

"It is my honor to make your acquaintance, m'lady. I am Alan Fitz Walter, second high steward of Scotland and dapifer of William the Lion, king of Scotland. I am late of the Crusade in the Holy Land, returning to my home in Scotland. I hate to bother you, but your son tells me I might find lodging and respite here for the night?"

Pica curtsied again. "It would so honor our house to have your presence, m'lord. Francesco, go tell the cook we have a guest for dinner. And tell the housekeep to bring in extra hay and a linen cover to make a bed for m'lord."

Francesco was ecstatic! He ran off to do his mother's bidding.

Dinner was almost ready, so Pica and Fitz Walter headed towards the table, where Francesco's brothers and sisters were gathered. There were three younger children at the table; the fourth, a babe, was off by the window, in the arms of the wet nurse. Francesco returned and sat down at the table. Pica was at its head. She lowered her head, announcing with just that movement that it was time to give thanks. All four children bowed solemnly, hands in laps. Fitz Walter followed in kind.

"Thank you, Heavenly Father, for this wonderful meal we are about to enjoy. Thank you for your Son's sacrifice for our souls. Thank you for allowing us to feed your noble and honorable Christian soldier joining us this evening. We honor him as he honors You, fighting for Your glory. May your blessings continue to guide us and him as we fulfill Your purpose for us. In the name of the Father, the Son, and the Holy Ghost. Amen."

Everyone crossed themselves and proceeded to eat. Francesco was trying very hard to not obviously gloat – his siblings were intimidated, curious, and awestruck at the presence of their unexpected dinner guest; they all recognized that it was Francesco who had brought this exotic guest to their home.

Pica turned to Fitz Walter. "Sir, can you tell us of news of the Holy Land? Has it been rescued from the Saracens?"

"Unfortunately, we have not regained Jerusalem, m'lady. I accompanied King Richard of England, who remains in the Holy Land. We did lay siege and capture Acre, which the king believes grants him some advantage in dealing with the Saracens. There seems to be great respect between him and the Saracen leader, Saladin. We shall see whether the king prevails in regaining Jerusalem for the Holy See."

The children had long known that dinner discussions were for the adults. Had Papa been home, the children would have not even been at the same table. However, Francesco's curiosity had by now totally gotten the best of him.

"Lord, tell me of the battle. For Acre. Is that a city? A state? Did you ride your horse through the Saracens, swinging your sword? Did you lead your soldiers into battle? Did your squire go with you?"

Fitz Walter looked to Pica for guidance. Her nearly imperceptible nod told Fitz Walter it was acceptable to answer.

"Laddie, Acre is a city. For most of the time in Acre, the Holy Army merely laid siege, making sure nothing got in or out of the city. No tearing through swarms of infidels on horseback, sorry to say. The fight for Acre had been underway long before King Richard and I arrived – armies made up of Germans and Flemish, Italians from Ravenna and Verona, Danish, French, Frisians, and Armenians. The fight for the city had been going on for two years, and many of the initial men died from disease. I came with King Richard and eight thousand men; I am not sure the Christian army would have been victorious without the additional reinforcements.

We were storming walls, not rushing through hordes of men. Laddie, please understand that wars, while noble and required, are hard, cruel, dirty, and painful. Noble causes drive noble men, but the work itself is not kind, honorable, or pleasant. I am glad to return home to my wife, family, and land."

These were not the words that Francesco had been expecting. Fitz Walter took note.

"Francesco, I need to go bed down my steed for the night. I think you should come with me. As long as your maman agrees," he added, nodding his head towards Pica in acknowledgment.

"Yes, I think that is a wise idea." Francesco asked for permission to stand, eager to be off with his newfound hero.

"With your leave, m'lady," said Fitz Walter. Pica again nodded, and Fitz Walter and Francesco were off to the stables.

It was nearly dark, and the two walked through the narrow, winding streets in the dusky pre-night, barely speaking at first. Francesco was processing the surprising words of this fearsome, brave knight.

After a while, Fitz Walter said, "I have a son back home, you know. His name is Walter. He will be the third high steward when I have passed. He is about your age, I think. Nine?"

Francesco quickly corrected the knight.

"I am ten!" he said a bit fiercely.

"Of course you are. I haven't seen Walter in years, so it is a bit hard to judge. Please excuse me."

Fitz Walter continued. "I was so sure leaving for the Holy Land was the proper action to take. I never took into account how long I would be gone – never realized how long it would seem. I haven't seen my boy since he was a wee, wee bairn. He probably won't even know who I am."

"But aren't you proud of being a big, strong knight and warrior?"

"I am, no doubt, but being gone so long… missing my wife and son. Leaving behind the work of shepherding Scotland on behalf of my Liege Lord. Seeing so many men die. That could easily have been me, laddie. Then what would have become of my wife and son?

"You know, Saladin gave King Richard a horse when Richard's horse died. That single act of humanity and respect changed me, I think. Changed the way I thought about the enemy. They are men, just like me. And then when King Richard massacred the 2,000 captured Saracens over ransom… well, then I knew I needed to leave and go back to my home. My heart wasn't in it anymore. 2,000 men!"

As they approached the stable, Francesco finally spoke. "I never thought a knight would think that way."

Fitz Walter paused a minute before replying. "Laddie, it never should be easy to take another man's life. Even if he means you harm. Every creature on this earth has a basic right to life, your enemies included. Yes, it is important to protect yourself, and that sometimes means battling for your life. It is important to fight for God and for things bigger than you and me together. It is important to protect the Holy Land and to protect those who wish to make the pilgrimage to honor God's Son, Jesus. That is all very important. But it is also important to understand that the man you may be fighting is also one of God's creatures, whether he understands that or not. We should never take a life callously."

Francesco became very quiet at those words. He had never thought of that before, but there was a kernel of peace that was planted in him, one that, although it remained dormant, never quite died.

The two approached a stall halfway down on the left side. "So, here's my steed. He's a patient, faithful horse. He deserves to be cared for. He has always done my bidding, even in dangerous situations."

Fitz Walter brought Francesco over to the dappled horse, which was maybe sixteen hands high. Fitz Walter needed a horse that matched his stature. This was no stallion; this was a sturdy horse that screamed endurance and fortitude.

"I need to make sure I care for this horse as he has cared for me throughout my travels and battles. We need to care for all living things if we are to honor God the Father, don't you think? We have been ordained by the Father to care for all living things created by the Father as He created us. Remember that, laddie. We are stewards of these creatures that have been placed upon this earth to serve and protect us."

Fitz Walter directed Francesco to bring in fresh hay and scatter it around. Fitz Walter took a bucket and went to the trough to fill it, bringing it back to the horse. He also took a pitchfork and removed the droppings scattered in the stall. After he was done, he motioned to Francesco that they were finished.

"Remember to take care of all living things, boy." The two turned, bolted the stable door, and headed back through the winding streets up the hill to Francesco's home.

Fitz Walter rose at daybreak and went once again to tend his steed. When he returned, the household was up and bustling. There was a chicken stewing in the pot, bubbling over the rekindled fire. The housekeep was turning the haybeds and straightening the linen. The baby was fussing because the wet nurse had not yet fed her. All in all, it was a typical, bustling household morning. Fitz Walter was offered a crust of bread and a bit of wine, which he gratefully accepted.

Francesco had been sent to fetch water from the city well, and he came in with a sloshing bucket. He gave it to the cook and then turned and went over to Fitz Walter.

"Are you leaving today?"

"I was planning to, yes. I have far to go, and I do not wish to overstay my welcome. I would like to spend tonight in Cortona."

Francesco looked down a bit despondently. He knew the knight must leave; he knew better than to plead for him to stay longer, but he wished it didn't have to be so. Fitz Walter reached under his surplice and pulled out his pouch. He untied the leather laces that both closed it and secured it to his cincture, and opened it. He fumbled within it and finally brought out an odd piece of metal – a piece of jewelry. An amulet, perhaps, made of iron. It wasn't perfectly symmetrical; it wasn't ornate. Its shape was not square, nor oval, nor diamond. It was odd-looking. Francesco had never seen anything like it before.

"Francesco, I know you are disappointed that my stay here was short. I would like you to have this to remember me by."

"What is this?"

Fitz Walter extended his hand towards Francesco. "It is an amulet from Bute. Bute is where I live. There's an ancient monastery there – Kingarth. This is from Kingarth. It is a very ancient amulet. It is Pictish."

"What is Pictish?"

"A long, long time ago, in my land, there were different kingdoms. One of them was the Pictish kingdom. It has been gone for a very long time – so long that no one remembers its language or customs. This was given to me by the monks at Kingarth Monastery. The monks helped convert many Picts to Christianity. This was given to me as a reminder of my homeland and of my land's ancient history. A reminder to me that I need to return home."

"Won't you need it for the rest of your journey?"

"No, laddie. Of that, I am sure. There are Templar lodges with many knights all the way from here to home. I have my brothers in arms to safeguard me now. So, this is yours if you will take it. But it comes with conditions."

"Conditions?" Francesco was apprehensive.

"Yes. You must promise me that when you look at this amulet, you will remember that all creatures, big and small, friend and enemy, are God's creatures."

"I can do that." Francesco's voice reflected the relief he felt.

"There's more. If you become a soldier, you must become a good soldier. If you become a silk merchant, you must be a good silk merchant. And when you become a man, you must be a good man."

"I can do that, too." There was true sincerity in Francesco's voice.

Fitz Walter laid his hand on Francesco's shoulder. "I enjoyed our time together, little man. Take care of your maman until your father returns. You are a fine lad, and I am honored to have met you." Francesco bowed his head sharply to hide the flush he felt developing. Fitz Walter then approached Pica and, taking her hand, once again brushed it against his lips.

"I thank you, good woman, for your generous and kind hospitality. May your husband return soon and safe, and may the sun long shine upon you and your family." Fitz Walter quietly left several ducats on the table and then, turning, took his leave.

Francesco took his amulet and placed it in his own pouch, safely tucked away with the few other small, personal belongings he cherished. A flat stone he and his father had found while walking one day. A bead that had fallen from a vendor's stall and been left lying, forgotten. The very first baby tooth he had lost. And now the Pictish Crescent.

~

The four young men poured out of the inn, laughing and stumbling into the street. The cobblestones were bathed in twilight, the remaining glimpse of the sun hidden by the stone walls that surrounded the city.

"Giaco," Francesco said with a laugh, placing his hand on his companion's shoulder. "That barmaid wanted nothing to do with you! That last carafe of wine did you in, my good man."

Giaco's face reddened as he gruffly pulled away and turned to hide his embarrassment. "Leave me alone, Franco."

Pietro joined in, teasing Giaco about his hapless flirtation. "Perhaps the older barmaid would have taken to you more kindly, Giaco. Want to go back in and try? At her age, she would probably welcome your advances." At that, Giaco's three companions let out peals of laughter and pranced around, crudely acting out a welcomed flirtation.

"Leave me alone!" Giaco shouted gruffly. He turned and headed away from his drinking companions.

"No, no, Giaco. Don't leave angry," pleaded Tommaso. "I'm sorry. Come with us, Giaco. Come play passe-dix with us. No hard feelings."

Giaco stopped, thought a minute, and decided to join his friends – he loved to gamble. As they headed to Tommaso's, the talk turned to war.

"There's another call to arms. Did you hear? We are to march against Perugia," commented Pietro. "We were too young to fight in the civil war, but now! Now we fight!"

"Do you have armor?" asked Francesco. "My armor is to be ready by next market day."

"Ah, Franco, so you convinced your father. How did you manage that?" asked Tommaso.

"I told him that with all of the nobles that left to get away from the war, Assisi has few knights. I said that we might use the occasion to improve the standing of the house of Bernardone."

"Always prepared with a shrewd point," Giaco said, laughing. "I will join you, though. I will use my brother's armor. Now that he is married and has a family, his zeal for battle has waned."

"When are we to march?" asked Pietro. "I heard we are to gather in the piazza in a fortnight."

"We four should appear together – on horseback, in full armor. We can make a splendid entrance!" Giaco said excitedly. "And when we return victorious, we will be cheered in the streets!"

At that moment, they reached Tommaso's and went in to spend the rest of the evening on gambling and wine.

~

Francesco carefully donned his shiny new armor, covering it with an intricate, embroidered silk surplice. He was certain he looked splendid, which was very evident by the swagger in his gait as he headed to leave. He walked downstairs and said goodbye to his younger brothers, who were eyeing him enviously. He then turned to his mother, who was standing quietly with her head down. Francesco knew Pica did not approve of him leaving. He awkwardly gave her a hug, which she only halfheartedly returned.

"Come back, Francesco. Come back healthy and well." With that, Francesco walked out into the bright sunshine. He walked down to the stable to fetch his steed and was joined by Giaco and Pietro.

"Where is Tommaso?" asked Francesco.

"Late, as always, I suppose," answered Pietro. I don't think we should wait for him. He can catch up later." The three young men were eager to head towards the piazza with great pomp and circumstance, certain that their splendid appearance would turn heads in awe.

Their grand entrance wasn't grand at all. In fact, hardly anyone noticed. They stopped at the edge, where the street and piazza met, and saw before them a small sea of common men, almost all on foot, armed, in general, with all manner of farm implements. A few had swords; a few, axes. Mostly, they had clubs and pitchforks, shovels and scythes. They were milling around while a few men on horseback were rather ineffectively trying to get them organized. One of those horsemen noticed the three young men and rode up to them.

"Good! You," he said, pointing to Giaco. "You take that group." He gestured to the northwest. "You," he said, pointing to Pietro. "You take that group." He waved to the southwest. "And you," he said, addressing Francesco. "You take the men over there." He pointed northeast. Then he abruptly turned and headed off.

The three young men hesitated. Never having led men, or been in battle, they were not quite sure what to do. They watched as the man who had addressed them circled around a band of men, shouting to them to form a line four men wide. They then split up, went to their assigned stations, and did the same.

By the time they had arranged their men, the first group had already headed towards the main gate. Each group headed out in turn, down the steep hill towards Perugia, twelve miles away. As the last group passed through the wall, the gate was shut after them.

It took the rest of the day for this ragtag army to get to Ponte San Giovanni, where it bedded down for the night. Francesco sought out his comrades, whom he found down by the river. They were all dusty, tired, and hungry. They sat on the bank of the river and ate crusts of bread they had brought with them. None of them dared to speak what they were feeling: this was not the glory of triumphant battle they had anticipated.

"Has anyone seen Tommaso?" asked Pietro finally.

"No," replied Francesco. "I am not sure he made it out of the city."

"Well then, when we get back, he should groom the horses and polish our armor," stated Giaco. "Just like him to back out."

"And pick up the tab in the tavern," added Pietro. The others nodded in agreement.

"I think we should reach Perugia tomorrow before noon," said Francesco, changing the subject. "Do either of you know the plan for tomorrow?"

Pietro and Giaco shook their heads.

Francesco stood up. "I am going to find that man who directed us this morning and find out what we should do tomorrow. Stay here; I'll be back to tell you what he says." With that, he left. He meandered through the men bedded down every which way with whatever they had brought with them until he saw a makeshift tent. Heading towards it, he saw the man he supposed was the leader.

"Sir?" said Francesco.

The man turned. "Yes?"

"We were wondering, sir, what the plan is for tomorrow."

"What's your name, son?"

"Francesco, sir. Francesco di Bernardone."

"I am Andreas." The man extended his hand. "What is your experience? You are well outfitted, but from the looks of your armor, you either are new to battle or your old armor needed replacing."

Francesco lowered his head a bit. "New to battle, sir. But I have trained with my sword."

"I see. And your friends?"

"The same, sir."

"In that case, here are your orders. I will put your and your friends' units in the third wave. You will need to watch: I do not know whether the Perugians will come out to fight or whether they will stay behind their gates. If they come out to meet us on the battlefield, I will lead my men in the first wave. The second wave is led by Angelo." He pointed to his right, to a redheaded soldier in battle-worn armor. "Hold back until after Angelo takes the field. Do not take the field unless either I or Angelo fall back." Andreas picked up a stick and started drawing in the dirt. "Position your men here." Andreas drew a circle in the dirt and then pointed to the right and back of the circle. "Have one of your friends with you. Have your other friend position his men over here." Andreas pointed to the opposite side of the circle. "When and if you charge, flank the battlefield and come in laterally." He drew a line up the side and then towards the circle. "Do you understand?"

Francesco was filled with excitement.

I am really a soldier! I am a captain, leading men! The glamor of battle, lost by the river, had quickly returned.

"Yes, sir! I will go and tell Pietro and Giaco. By your leave." Francesco bowed slightly. Andreas waved him away, and Francesco rushed back to the river to share the plans with his comrades in arms.

Dawn arrived with a whisper. The sky was clear, the wind calm. Francesco woke when he heard the rustling of men getting up and gathering their gear.

Today is the day!

He rolled up his blankets and fastened them across the back of his horse. He rousted Pietro and Giaco, and the three washed their faces in the river before heading over to Andreas's tent. The foot soldiers were being organized into groups, and it wasn't long before Pietro, Giaco, and Francesco were each assigned a few dozen men. In short order, the entire brigade set off.

The first hour went slowly, and the initial excitement of the impending battle was wearing off. Francesco was lost in thought, daydreaming in the tedium, as the first wave of the little army followed a curve in the road and was lost from sight. He was immediately brought back to the present by the battle cries and sounds of metal hitting metal. The Perugians had come to them and set upon them by surprise.

Chaos ensued. The second wave was straddling the curve in the road; some of the foot soldiers, if you could call them that, had no choice but to fight. Those near the back of the line stopped dead in their tracks. Their captain went behind them, trying to keep the column going forward by riding back and forth. Some men charged ahead with abandon, and some slipped off into the woods as the opportunity arose. The rest rather reluctantly followed the bend in the road, into the fight.

Francesco frantically rode over to Pietro. "What shall we do? We can't flank like we were told – the trees are in the way."

Pietro looked around. "Maybe we can, Francesco." He called loudly, "Giaco!!" Giaco came galloping over. "Giaco, can you ride into those woods, wide around, and see what's happening? Franco, can you do the same on that side?" Pietro gestured right and left. "I will stay and organize the men into two groups. If we can get through the woods, we might be able to flank."

Francesco and Giaco quickly agreed and headed off on either side of the road.

Francesco knew the road: after the wide curve, the road headed through fields, and the tree line receded from the road.

That's where the fight must be. The Perugians must have been waiting where the trees open up.

He carefully wove his way through the woods and approached what he thought was its edge. He dismounted and started leading his horse forward. The war cries and the clash of metal were now joined by moans and anguished cries of pain. He must have been very close. He stopped and looked around, assessing whether he could get several dozen men successfully through these woods and positioned to attack.

Yes, I can, he concluded, and he started to lead his horse around to head back.

"What do we have here?" The words fell heavily on Francesco's ears. He hadn't seen any men as he had approached.

He froze and then slowly turned full around to face three men.

"Found ourselves a nobleman!" The men started to split up as they approached Francesco. The man in the middle grinned. "This one should fetch a nice ransom!"

Francesco's hand went to his scabbard, but with that move, he quickly found a sword at his neck. "I wouldn't be doing that, m'lord," said the grinning man. "Wouldn't want to have to kill you."

Francesco moved his hand away from his sword just as one of the Perugians took the reins of his horse.

"We can get a pretty penny for this horse. And the armor. And the tunic! Quite a handsome tunic. In fact, take it off."

Francesco slowly removed the embroidered silk tunic.

"Give it to me," demanded the man. Francesco complied, and the man put it on. He then danced around a bit, swaying to and fro, to the great amusement of his buddies, who were now behind Francesco, between him and his horse.

"Captured us a nobleman," said one of the men behind Francesco in a sing-song. The others laughed.

"Let's be going," he said as he shoved Francesco forward.

The three marched Francesco past the raging battle to an area where several other captured captains were being held. The armor they had been wearing was piled up on a cart, and their right hands were being strung together in preparation for the hike back to Perugia. Francesco was ordered to remove his armor, which he did, and he was then tied to the line of men. The last to join the prisoners of war was Giaco.

~

The group of prisoners was the last to head back to the city in case there were stragglers caught. Francesco and the others stood by the side of the road as several carts full of the wounded were allowed to pass first. Francesco had never witnessed anything like this pile of mangled men, and it horrified him. Next came the dead, piled high in a few more carts. Francesco simply hung his head.

It was only a few miles to Perugia, although it seemed much further to Francesco. Once past the city gates, he and the other captured Assisiati were led to the town dungeon. The dungeon consisted of three communal cells, dark, damp, dug out beneath the city center, and lined with stone. They smelled of feces, urine, sickness, and unwashed men. There were no seats, blankets, or windows. One by one, the Assisiati were interviewed so that ransom demands could be sent to their families. All of them were then just left there in one of two cells and fed once a day until the money arrived.

~

"Francesco, how long have we been here?" asked Giaco.

"Very long," replied Francesco wearily. "Hard to say when you can't see daylight. Months, maybe."

"Francesco…" started Giaco. His words were interrupted by coughing so severe it made his body convulse. "Francesco," he finally continued. "What if the ransom isn't paid? What if my family can't raise it to release me?"

Francesco peered at his friend in the dim candlelight. Although he knew that Giaco's family wasn't as wealthy as his own, he also knew that Giaco needed reassurance. Privately, he wondered the same thing, and he worried that Giaco would not survive to see the day if the ransom took much longer to arrive.

"I am sure you will be home soon, Giaco."

You don't look well, friend.

"If I don't make it home, Francesco, will you do something for me?"

"Of course. But you will get home, Giaco."

Giaco took as deep a breath as he could. Francesco could hear a rattle in his chest. "You know that pretty barmaid in the tavern?"

"The fair one with the dimple?"

"Yes, that's the one. Will you make sure to tell her that I thought of her every day?"

Francesco looked at Giaco quizzically. "Giaco, you never let on you felt so deeply! We all thought it was merely a wine-driven flirtation!"

"I never had the nerve. If I could do it all over again…"

"Giaco, Giaco…you will make it home. You can tell her yourself."

"But if I don't…"

"Of course I will, friend. Of course."

~

It was a day like every other the day Giaco died. He had gotten thinner and thinner, weaker and weaker. His coughing brought up blood, and his breathing became labored. Francesco was helpless to do anything but stay by his side, holding his hand and saying soothing things to comfort him. When Giaco died, Francesco crossed his dead friend's arms over his chest and lowered his eyelids for him. A deep sense of sorrow filled his heart. Francesco hung his head, simply kneeling there on his haunches, holding onto Giaco's now-lifeless hand and hoping that it simply wasn't so. Hoping that, miraculously, Giaco's eyelids would flutter or that his chest would rise again. Or even cough again. Anything. When the realization finally sank in, Francesco quietly said a prayer for his friend. There was nothing else he could do, and his tears fell onto Giaco's body.

When the jailer came with meager rations, Francesco told him of Giaco's passing. Shortly, a couple of men came and took away the body.

The day Giaco died – after his body had been removed – Francesco suddenly thought of Alan Fitz Walter.

"And then, when King Richard massacred the two thousand captured Saracens over ransom…well, then I knew I needed to leave and go back to my home. My heart wasn't in it anymore. Two thousand men!"

Ransom! Why is money more important than life? For want of timely ransom, my friend is dead.

Francesco withdrew into his own thoughts from that moment on, considering the lot of men whose striving for wealth caused such pain and hardship from the time men first walked the earth.

~

Francesco was very thin and sickly when the jailers came and got him. The sun, unfamiliar for an entire year, seemed to burn his eyes as he stepped out into the piazza. The glare was such that he could barely see his father standing there waiting for him.

"Father? Father, is that you? Oh, Father, you have come for me!" Francesco fell to his knees. "I am so sorry, Father. I am so sorry." Francesco was sobbing. "Giaco died, Father. Right there in front of me. Giaco died."

Pietro looked down at his son. "I doubt you can ride a horse," he commented rather coldly. "You'll have to ride with me. Can you make it to Assisi?"

Francesco was shocked. His father was so angry! "Papa, it is so very good to see you! I thought I might never see you again. Please don't be so angry."

"Angry? *Angry*? Francesco, I am furious! You *know* I did not approve of this 'soldiering' business! You *know* I always wanted you to join the family business!! Heaven only knows why I let you convince me to buy you armor, a horse, and your sword. Those cost me a fortune! And they are gone! And then the ransom! Do you know how much they demanded? It took me an entire *year* to raise it!

I swear, if it wouldn't have broken your mother's heart, I would have let you rot in prison."

Pietro's words stung. Francesco slowly stood up, truly remorseful, and hung his head. "I am very sorry, Papa. Please forgive me. I just want to go home."

"Well then, we will make it by nightfall if we leave now. After all I have spent on your ransom, I don't want to spend another sou at an inn here."

Francesco struggled to get on the horse, but with his father's help, he did. The ride back to Assisi was uncomfortable. Francesco couldn't recall seeing his father so angry. The two rode in silence: Pietro in a slow burn, Francesco in chastened apprehension.

Pica was just sitting down to eat when Pietro and Francesco entered. Upon seeing her wan and skeletal son, she raced over to him and led him to the table. "Oh, Franco! You are so thin! You must eat."

"Just broth for now, Maman. Broth and some bread, maybe. A piece of meat."

Francesco ate slowly, barely managing to finish his meal. There was more in front of him for this one meal than he had eaten over the course of three days in the dungeon.

"Maman, may I bathe? And then, please… I am so tired. I need to rest."

"Of course!" Pica rushed off to the kitchen to get the maid to boil some water for a bath. Before she returned to the table, she went upstairs and collected a clean chemise for Francesco.

"Your bath should be ready soon," said Pica as she walked into the room. "Here is a chemise for you. I think I shall burn the one you are wearing."

Francesco slept for an entire day. When he awoke, the first thing he noticed was the sky out the window. The chirping birds seemed so loud; he didn't remember noticing them before. The setting sun was streaming a shaft of golden light through the window, casting a warm glow across the floor. He hadn't noticed that before either.

He rolled over in his bed and felt the wool stuffing of the mattress cushion his thinly covered bones. He was acutely aware of the weight of his blanket. After a year of significant sensory deprivation, everything was astonishingly loud, and bright, and soft, and heavy. He lifted his blanket up, put his feet on the floor, and sat up. That made him dizzy – he sat on the edge of the bed until his head cleared.

Still not well.

He gingerly stood up. Someone had laid out stockings and a doublet, and there were a pair of shoes by the door. He slowly dressed and headed downstairs.

Pica was sitting in her chair with her needlework, just as Francesco had always remembered. She stood up as he entered the room.

"How are you feeling, son?"

"I think I should eat something, Maman, and then go back to bed. I feel very weak, and I'm still tired."

Pica sat with him as he ate. She sighed and placed her hand on his arm.

"Francesco, are you ready to settle down and take up being a silk merchant? Your father has been waiting."

Francesco hesitated. "Maman, my mind is so muddled right now. I need some time to think about what I have been through before I think of the future."

"Don't wait too long, Francesco. Don't dwell in the past; think of the future. Your father expects you to join him. He believes that you owe that to him." Pica turned away with that and went back to her needlework.

Francesco went back to his room and went over to the armoire to put the doublet away. As he opened the door, he saw his pouch of treasures – the pouch from when he was a child. He opened it… He smiled as he picked up the bead. He set the bead back in the pouch and then took out the skipping stone, looking at it wistfully. Those had been such happy, carefree days. He then picked up the amulet. He studied it as he remembered the brief encounter with the fearsome but gentle crusader. Fitz Walter's words had kept creeping into Francesco's thoughts:

Be a good man. Protect God's creatures. Even your enemies are men, just like you.

Francesco looked around and found a leather thong. He laced it through the amulet, tied it around his neck, and put it under his chemise, next to his skin. It hung nearly over his heart.

I will be noble and kind like Fitz Walter. I will be a good man. I will care for God's creatures. I will treat others like they are my brothers and sisters. And this amulet will be a constant reminder to be true to these vows.

CHAPTER SIX

Maggie wound bubble wrap around the amulet and placed it in the shipping box she had purchased. She stuffed crumpled paper all around it, closed the flaps, and shook the box to see whether anything moved. Satisfied that the amulet would survive shipment, she taped it up and took it to the postal service. In short order, the amulet was on its way to Ann Arbor, and Maggie headed to the dance studio.

She got up the next morning and headed to the railway station. She hopped on the train to Edinburgh and headed straight away to the university library. She had become quite curious about the Picts and decided to do some research. She soon came to realize Dougal's point: the vast majority of existing Pictish artifacts were stone carvings. If this iron amulet was genuine, it would be a monumental historical discovery.

Then why, and how, did this end up in Assisi?

Maggie mulled this over as she headed to Dougal's office.

First things first: find out if it is genuine.

Maggie knocked on Dougal's office door. "Anyone home?" She turned the knob. Dougal was at his desk, pouring over pages in a thick book. "Have a minute?" She didn't wait for an answer to walk in.

"Well, hello there, lass. To what do I owe this pleasure?"

"I've been over to the library reading up on the Picts. You were right: if this amulet is authentic it is a very rare and important find."

"I've been studying all things Pictish, too. And what situations might have arisen that would link Scotland and Assisi together. There is not much."

Maggie walked over to Dougal's desk as he sat back down, and she stood at his side as he pointed to the book he was studying. "The Picts were strong after the Romans left, not during. The only other connection I can make is through missionaries. St. Colomba and his followers were active in converting the Picts to Christianity. But that doesn't explain how something Pictish ended up in Assisi."

Maggie thought a bit. "It sounds very much like you believe the artifact is genuine."

"Maybe I am indulging in wishful thinking, but it would be simply brilliant if it were truly from the Kingdom of the Picts."

"What else have you found, Dougal?"

"Well, St. Blane was the bishop of the Picts. He established a monastery on the Isle of Bute. He is the closest link I can find, but I can find no record of him traveling to Italy. He died in 590... The Roman Empire left Britain in the four hundreds. If I were to guess, I would say that any link would be through missionaries, but I have no idea how at the moment." He spoke without lifting his head, still referencing the book before him.

"How long before we get word back from Oliver? We might be a little ahead of the curve here."

"You're right, Maggie, but it's just so intriguing. I can't help researching. It's fascinating." He closed the book and looked up. "I should be hearing from McQuiddy any day now. Are you headed back to Mum and Da's?"

"Yes, heading over to the train shortly. Please let me know when you hear from Oliver." She leaned over and gave Dougal a peck on the forehead. "Thanks for all of your help, Dougal."

He smiled. "Don't thank me yet, Mag. I'll ring you as soon as I hear back."

Maggie had fallen into a comfortable pattern: getting a coffee at Kingsgate and taking it over to Pittencrief Park, people-watching, taking long walks, teaching dance to the weans. It was a great environment to let herself heal. New York was becoming further and further away, and the more she thought of it, the more she knew she would not permanently return. What had been so important had been lost to the ether when Ben had died, and Maggie had no desire to go back and try to establish the life she'd so happily had with Ben. That left her wondering what she would do with herself. While she knew she wouldn't be happy teaching dance forever, she was unsure what path she would take. These musings filled her mind every day as she strolled through the park, coffee in hand.

Several days after her visit, Dougal called. "Maggie, can you meet me at my office? As soon as you can?" Dougal's voice was solemn and heavy, as if each letter of each word was filled with import.

"Of course. I take it you've heard back from Oliver?"

"We'll chat when you get here, Maggie. Make haste, will ye?"

"I'll head over to the rail station straight away, Dougal." She hung up the phone and picked up her purse. She was at the university in a little more than an hour.

When Maggie knocked at Dougal's office door, he opened it quickly, shepherded her in, and closed the door behind them.

"Maggie, McQuiddy's report came in." Just by the look on Dougal's face, Maggie knew what he was going to say. She caught her breath.

"It's authentic, isn't it?" Her eyes got round as she searched Dougal's face. His grin said it all. "Oh my! Now what, Dougal?"

"I am going to write a paper on it. We have the pictures, right?"

"Oh yes."

"And the artifact is safely secured?"

"Dougal, I am sure it is safe. I–"

Dougal interrupted her. "Don't tell me where, Maggie. It's actually best if I don't know where it is."

That startled her. "Are you worried, Dougal?"

"Not worried, Maggie, just cautious. This might just be a find of the century. I have no idea what might happen. I just need it safe. Safe until I get my paper published. We need to start investigating where we think it should end up. A museum, I would imagine. I don't want to alert the antiquary community before I get a chance to document what I know." He stopped for a moment and then continued. "Actually, you are a very big part of this. You need to fill in the circumstances about when and how it was found."

Maggie thought a moment, and then everything seemed very clear. Her musings about her next steps in life were suddenly in sharp focus.

"Dougal, I need to go back to Assisi and speak to that monk – Brother Ventimiglio. I will make arrangements immediately. And contact Agent Leone – she can translate for me." Maggie's mind was racing.

"Maggie, do you have a mobile phone?"

"I do."

"Make sure you take it with you. We need to keep in touch. And while you are doing that, I'll see whether I can figure out how your amulet got to Assisi from this end."

"It's a plan. Let me get on this."

As Maggie was walking out the door, Dougal added, "And Maggie, best if you keep this under your hat. We don't want to invite any trouble."

She turned and looked back quizzically. "If you say so, Dougal. But I think you are worrying just a little too much."

"Please, Maggie."

"Oh, all right, then." She left for the train.

The next morning, she got her morning coffee, but instead of heading to the park, she headed to a travel agency, where she made plane and hotel arrangements. Reservations made, she picked up a bite to eat at an old-fashioned fish and chips place, complete with lunch served in newspaper. She then went to the studio for her classes, heading back to Ayton Lodge in the late afternoon. She was alarmed to see a couple of police cars pulled up in front of her parents' home, and she ended up running the rest of the distance. She threw open the gate, jumped up the couple of stairs, and ran into the house. There was a policeman in the entrance, who turned as she entered.

"Ma'am?" he said, but she interrupted him.

"I'm Maggie Tyl… Maggie Fraser Tyler. This is my parents' house, and I am staying here at the moment."

"Mum! Mum!" Maggie frantically called for her mother.

"In here," called Ailsa. "In the study."

Maggie rushed into the study to find her mother standing amidst overturned furniture, drawers pulled out and thrown on the floor, and books and knick-knacks everywhere.

"Mum! Are you all right?" She rushed up to her mother. Ailsa was just standing there, frozen in the mess, not knowing even where to start.

"It appears that we've been burgled. The place was all turned upside down when your da and I returned from shopping today. Everything is just a fine mess." Ailsa's voice was flat and mechanical.

Maggie bent over and picked up a broken Dalton figurine. "Have you found anything missing?"

"That's the funny thing. What you would think would have been stolen is still here. The television. The silver. We haven't found anything yet, but just look at this place. Who knows at this point?"

Maggie gave her mother a reassuring hug. "I'll help you, Mum. No worries. Have you called Callum?"

"Yes, Mag. He's the first person we called. He said he'd come up on the next flight out of Heathrow."

"Do Duncan and Dougal know?"

"No, not yet."

Maggie thought a moment. "I think I'll try to call Dougal." She headed for the phone.

She rang Dougal's office, hoping he hadn't left for home yet. Just as she was about to hang up, he answered.

"Dougal, someone ransacked Mum and Da's house. Callum is on his way. I think we should tell him about our conversation this afternoon. I have a feeling this is no coincidence... Mum hasn't been able to find anything missing so far."

There was a fairly long silence on the line. "Maggie, is everybody okay?"

"Yes. No one was home."

"Maggie, I don't think this was a coincidence either. Please don't say a word to anyone but Callum. He'll know what to do." She heard unmistakable concern in his voice. "Do you think you will be safe in the house?"

"As long as Callum gets here, yes. Let me try and find out when he's getting in. I'll let you know what I find out. Are you heading home?"

"I was just walking out when the phone rang. Call me at the house. I should be there within the hour."

"Will do. Talk to you soon, Dougal."

Maggie hung up the phone and went back out into the hall. "Mum, I spoke to Dougal. He asked me to call him back when Callum gets here. Do you have any idea when that might be?"

The policeman, who had taken up guard in the hall, turned when he overheard the question.

"Ma'am, pardon me for eavesdropping, but Scotland Yard has requested that we stand guard here until one Callum Fraser arrives. When you find out when that might be, please let my captain know." It was obvious that the sergeant had no idea why a simple break-in merited such attention or why this unknown Callum Fraser had such influence.

"Thank you, Sergeant. Perhaps there has been a series of break-ins outside of your jurisdiction. I am very comforted that we will have such outstanding protection, though. Thank you."

At this, the sergeant smiled, obviously pleased with his important post.

Ailsa broke in, saying, "Callum said he'd catch the next flight. I don't know when that is, but flights from London to Edinburgh are quite frequent. He said he'd hop on the train from the airport, though. No need to fetch him."

Maggie looked around quietly for a moment and then looked at her mother. "It seems that we have to wait, then. Were you fixing supper? I hope so, Mum. Let me help. I'm suddenly quite hungry." She gently took her mother's arm and headed towards the kitchen. "Where's Da?"

"He's in the garage. I stuck a pot pie in the oven an hour ago. It should be ready soon. Would you go tell him it's nearly ready?"

Maggie headed out the side door, and she entered the garage to see her father, back to the door, picking up some tools. "Are you all right, Da?"

He turned around, tools in both hands. "Yes, Maggie. I don't know why anyone would make such a mess." He looked around at his tools and workbench. "Everything just dumped on the ground. All of the drawers pulled out."

"Anything taken, Da?"

"Not that I have yet discovered, lass. It's as if they were looking for something in particular, though. All of this mess and nothing apparently taken. I just don't understand."

"Mum sent me out to tell you supper is almost ready. Callum is on his way. Maybe he can make sense of this."

They closed up the garage and headed into the house. Maggie excused herself for a moment, saying, "Let me make a quick call to Dougal. He wanted to know when Callum was arriving." She went to the phone and called him.

"Dougal, can you call British Airways and find out flight schedules from Heathrow to Edinburgh? It would be great if you could pick Callum up and tell him what you know during your drive up here. You'll have to wait at the gate for him – he told Mum he was going to catch the rail."

"Great idea, Maggie! Will do. See you soon."

~

Dougal and Callum arrived a little after 10 PM. Callum went directly to the local police to get up to speed on what was known before he dismissed them. Dougal went right up to Maggie.

"I'm glad you are all right," he said openly…and quietly whispered in her ear as he gave her a quick hug, "I told Callum." He backed away and continued. "Let me go find Mum and Da."

"They are in the parlor waiting up for Callum. They will be surprised to see you, Dougal."

Dougal and Callum went to chat with their parents, but both Ailsa and Alexander were soon to bed, leaving the siblings to chat.

"What do you think of this, Callum?" asked Dougal as soon as he was sure that their parents were out of earshot.

"The timing is certainly suspect, especially given what you have told me. Who knew about the amulet?"

"The only people that know that the amulet is authentic would be the technicians at the lab at the university. Oliver McQuiddy was the one we spoke to directly. I have no idea who else may have worked on the testing. I also have no idea if any of those that might have seen the results told anyone else. Not very helpful, I know."

"There is a chance this was random. Possibly. I will follow up on that McQuiddy fellow, though. I take it the amulet was not here?"

"No," piped up Maggie. "Dougal asked me to put it somewhere safe, which I did. He doesn't even want to know where."

Callum thought a bit. "Not a terrible idea, Maggie. Are you sure it's secure?"

"I am, Callum. But I think that someone besides me needs to know where it is. Can I tell you?"

Callum smiled. "Like when we were wee bairns, Mag. Whisper in my ear."

She leaned over and whispered, "I sent it to Ben's sister in the States."

"Brilliant! Make sure that fact is not shared." He thought a minute and then added, "Do they know what it is?"

"No, I haven't had the chance."

"Best that you don't, I think. My current concern is for your safety. The two of you. If it's the amulet the thief is after, he may come after you."

"I have a ticket to Italy. I was intending to go to Assisi to speak to the priest who offered to talk to me about the earthquake. I should be safe there, don't you think?"

"I think that, for the moment, talking to anyone about the amulet might not be wise. Not until we figure out what's going on. The sergeant said they found no fingerprints. There were no broken windows: the lock was picked. This was not the work of an amateur. That is a bit troubling, and I have nothing to go on at the moment except to investigate the technicians at the lab. Dougal, has there been anything unusual that's happened around your office?"

"Nothing I can think of. But given this, I wouldn't be surprised if someone were to break in there, too."

"If that happens, at least we would know that both events are related to the amulet. Dougal, will you please vary your routines? Don't get coffee at the same place and at the same time every day. Drive to and from work using different routes. Don't park in isolated places. Try and be around other people as much as you can. At least for the next couple of weeks."

Callum was silent for several moments, thinking. "That Mum and Da's house was hit, and not your office or home, Dougal, tells me that Maggie is more likely the focus. Not you. Whoever did this might try rifling your office, but I doubt they'd try your house now that they've shown a few of their cards."

Maggie spoke up. "What should I do, Callum? Should I go to Italy?"

"I think that will be fine, Maggie, as long as you don't mention you have, or ask about, the amulet. Leaving here is probably one of the best things you could do at the moment. When is your flight?"

"Day after tomorrow. I called Agent Leone, and she is planning on meeting me in Perugia and coming with me to Assisi. I really wanted to ask about the amulet, though."

"Please don't. Not until we figure out what's going on here. Dougal said the only connection he could think of linking Scotland and the basilica would be the church. So, besides the fact that it is probably priceless to a collector, there just may be a religious angle. It's best to not say anything until I can figure out which motive it is."

"Callum, this entire incident might not be about the amulet at all. Aren't we presuming a lot?"

"Mag, please humor me. I just want you safe. You can wait a bit, can't you? I won't be able to hop a plane and be there in two hours if you need me."

"Oh, all right, then. I won't say anything. I'll just ask Brother Ventimiglio about what he remembers. And visit the place Ben died. I need to do that." Those last words trailed off, and Maggie hung her head.

There was an uncomfortable silence, and then Dougal spoke up. "Callum, I will do what you asked of me and let you know if anything out of the ordinary happens. I was going to research the amulet, but perhaps I need to do that a bit surreptitiously. Do you suppose it would raise any eyebrows if I used the students in my ancient Scottish history class to do the footwork in a roundabout way?"

Callum smiled. "Good idea, Dougal. Have you done anything similar in the past?"

"Aye, I have. Last year, I had a section on Dal Riata. Following that with the Pictish Kingdom actually makes a lot of sense."

"One last thing. Maggie, perhaps you should stay with Dougal for the next two nights?"

"Come on then, lass. Kate and the weans will love to have you."

"You'll have to give me time to pack for Italy, then. Go call Kate. Callum, you'll have to tell Mum and Da why I left without so much as a farewell. I'll be back in a week's time."

Maggie went upstairs to pack.

CHAPTER SEVEN

Maggie landed in Perugia and headed to the arrivals deck, pulling her carryon through the crowd. She spotted Agent Leone waiting at the curb.

"Thank you for meeting me." She gave the agent a hug.

Agent Leone smiled. "How are you doing, signora? You look well."

"Time with my family has been good for me. I think I am ready for this part – closure. I really appreciate you agreeing to translate for me."

"My pleasure." Leone put Maggie's carryon in the trunk. "I called Brother Ventimiglio. He is waiting for us."

It was a short drive to Assisi. As they entered, Maggie noticed that almost all of the damage had been repaired. Assisi was again a lovely stone city with enticing, narrow passages leading to homes with medieval-looking burnished wood doors, many arched, and window planters brimming with beautiful flowers. Agent Leone pulled into the Piazza Matteotti to park, and the two walked down to the basilica. As they approached, Brother Ventimiglio, who had been waiting for them, walked up.

"Buon pomeriggio, signora," he said, taking her hand. Maggie smiled.

"Signora, what would you like me to ask the father?" said Agent Leone.

"Would you please tell him that I would like to see where they found Ben? And then I would like him to tell me what he remembers about that day. Did he have a chance to talk to Ben? Where was he when the roof caved in? Pretty much anything he remembers. But first, I would like to visit where they found Ben."

Agent Leone spoke to Brother Ventimiglio, who nodded in eager agreement. He had been touched by the tragedy of this woman, widowed so early, and was eager to do anything to help her through her pain. He touched Maggie's elbow and motioned for her and Agent Leone to follow him.

The three entered the basilica. Repairs were still underway on the arched interior ceiling, and there was scaffolding that occupied much of the chapel space. The three walked along the wall to the lower level and then down the arched stone hallway leading up to a small altar that stood in front of an imposing stone edifice, ringed in a heavy iron grid, that held the remains of St. Francis.

Brother Ventimiglio walked to the left side of the altar, climbed the single stair, stopped, and turned. He pointed to the floor.

Maggie walked up and knelt down, touching the floor with her fingertips and bowing her head as a tear dropped to the floor. It was so quiet there, so quiet and peaceful. She leaned back on her haunches, head bowed, palms of her hands still on the stone floor, with her eyes closed. It was as if she were trying to entice the spirit of Ben from the floor and into her body. She stayed that way for several minutes as both Brother Ventimiglio and Agent Leone allowed her to grieve.

Maggie finally stood up, wiped her eyes, and looked at Agent Leone.

"Please tell him thank you and ask him to recount the day."

Maggie listened in somewhat of a fog of emotion as Brother Ventimiglio recounted the day the roof fell in. There had been art restorers, historians, and engineers with Ben, along with some clergy of the church, who had been in the main hall. One historian had been filming the damage when the roof had fallen in, and he had caught the collapse on video. Brother Ventimiglio had been grabbed by the arm by a fellow priest and pulled toward a side wall, where they'd both crouched against the wall, steeling themselves against the stone and dust. She learned that he had not seen Ben fall – he just knew where Ben's body had been found. Ben had fallen through the floor over the tomb of St. Francis.

Maggie turned to Agent Leone. "Can you ask the good father who gathered Ben's belongings? I would like to thank him or her."

After inquiring, Agent Leone said, "It was one of the emergency team, signora. He doesn't know whether it was a policeman or a fireman. Or maybe one of the paramedics."

"Thank you. If you ever find out, will you let me know? That box gives me something to hug when I miss Ben so." She stifled a little sob.

Maggie walked slowly around the main chapel of the basilica, watching the workers carefully restoring the Giotto frescoes. After a while, she motioned to Agent Leone that she was ready to leave. She somberly shook Brother Ventimiglio's hand, thanking him, turned, and left with Agent Leone.

Maggie returned to her hotel room, wondering how she could obliquely find out about the amulet that had ended up in Ben's possession.

I guess I will simply have to wait, at least until Callum gives me the okay.

She wondered what her next move would be.

Maybe I should go to the Vatican. I wonder if I can research the tomb of St. Francis there? Probably not a very good idea. Probably written in Latin or Italian, anyway. And my Latin is miserable."

She wondered what to do next. She could think of nothing more she could investigate without violating her promise to Callum. She didn't feel safe returning to Scotland either, not at the moment, at least. She certainly didn't want to be chaperoned everywhere.

Then she thought of Sarah. She decided she would go to Ann Arbor. She could do her research there, at the university library, without raising suspicion or being targeted. She called Dougal and told him of her plans, and then she promptly started to pack.

~

Sarah was waiting for Maggie at the airport. "So good to see you! I'm so glad you've come back!"

Maggie smiled warmly. "So good to see you again, Sarah. I've missed you!"

"How long will you be in town? Have you already made lodging arrangements? Would you like to say with us?"

"That's so kind. I would love to, actually. I don't want to bother your parents again."

"I am sure they would not be bothered, but I am glad you are coming home with me. We can pal around."

Maggie hesitated a bit. "Are you hungry? Can I buy dinner?"

"Take-out would be great. I know a great little place that has good service." Changing the subject, Sarah asked, "Is there a specific reason you've come back? I thought you were going to stay in Scotland for a longer time. Or go back to New York."

Maggie's voice was bathed in resignation. "I've decided my heart isn't in New York anymore. I don't think I'll go back there to live. At least not now. When I went back there, everything seemed so hollow. Just empty. My heart wasn't in my job anymore either, and it was so very depressing walking into the apartment. I just needed to leave."

"I'm so sorry, Maggie. It must be so hard for you," Sarah said quietly and gently.

Maggie took a deep breath. "I will be going back to Scotland from here, but I don't have a totally set date. Sometime within a week or so, I would imagine."

"Well, you are welcome for as long as you want."

"You are so very kind, Sarah. Changing the subject, do you know if I can get into the university library? I would like to do some research on the basilica in Assisi."

"The library is open to the public, but only students, faculty, and staff can borrow materials. The basilica?"

"Yes. I was just there. There's a part of me that wants to know what Ben was looking at. Silly, maybe. I just became curious."

Sarah quietly took Maggie's hand. "I understand.

"If you don't mind, I'll go to the library tomorrow and read. That way, I won't be in your hair. Or Jake's. I hope he will not be put out."

"Not in the least. Besides, he leaves for Chicago day after tomorrow on business. It will be good to have your company."

"So, what can I buy us for dinner?" The two piled into Sarah's car.

~

The next morning, Sarah took Maggie to the library.

"I need to do a bit of shopping, Maggie. I'll be back for you at two or thereabouts. Is that okay?"

"No need to come fetch me, Sarah. I'll get back before supper, I promise. Maybe we can catch a movie after dinner."

Sarah smiled. "That sounds great, Maggie! See you then!"

Maggie walked into the library and up to one of the catalog computers. Dougal was researching the Picts and connections with missionaries, so Maggie decided to research Scots who may have traveled to Italy in the Middle Ages.

She spent the next several hours researching timelines, Picts, and the various Crusades. It took little time, but she stumbled upon a thesis written by one Alan MacQuarrie in 1982 – *The Impact of the Crusading Movement in Scotland.* She found the copy and started reading. She soon realized she needed more than one afternoon to read it and take notes.

One for Dougal. His university – his department. He can get me a copy.

She pushed back her chair energetically, got up, pushed the chair back in, and turned to leave.

Maggie grabbed a taxi and headed to Sarah's and Jake's. Sarah's car was in the drive, so Maggie walked up and knocked on the door.

Sarah smiled as she opened the door. "No need to knock, Maggie. You're family. How was your day?"

Maggie smiled back but simultaneously shook her head. "I hit a brick wall. I've not yet figured out how…" – she hesitated – "…why I thought I could answer a very obscure historical question in one afternoon. Now I know why Dougal laughed at me." Maggie fibbed to cover nearly divulging her mission.

126

Sarah looked at Maggie quizzically. "A historical question?"

"Dougal and I have a bet. He bet I couldn't come up with a connection between Dal Riata and Italy in the early Middle Ages. After the Romans but before Dal Riata ceased to be. He was right. I came up blank. I owe him a nice bottle of MacAllan's. Darn."

Maggie wasn't used to lying, and she fiddled with her coat to hide her discomfort.

Sarah laughed. "Don't ask me. I have never even heard of Dal Riata."

"I don't think you will be at any disadvantage, Sarah." Maggie laughed. "I told you it was really obscure." Changing the subject, she asked, "Anything I can do in the kitchen to help?"

"I thought we could have salmon on arugula and then catch a movie. Very quick dinner. *Shakespeare in Love* is playing at the State. I hear it's a very good movie. Want to see it?"

"My treat. Dinner sounds marvelous."

When Maggie got up the next morning, she wondered how she was going to encourage Sarah to safeguard the amulet without saying too much. The last thing she wanted to do was put Sarah in any danger.

Callum is right, she thought. *The less anyone knows, the safer they will be.*

Over coffee, she looked up. "Sarah, I probably shouldn't, but do you think I could open Ben's box and reminisce? I don't know how healthy that is, but I miss him so."

Sarah looked sadly at Maggie. "We all do, Maggie. Just probably not as much as you do. Sure, we can open the box. It's upstairs."

Maggie and Sarah walked upstairs into Sarah's room. Sarah reached up to a shelf in her closet and brought down the box. She took it to the bed, where the two women sat down side by side. Sarah put the box on her lap and opened the lid.

Ben's shirt was still on top. Maggie pulled it out and buried her face in it. It didn't smell like Ben anymore. She had waves of ambivalent emotions: she was sad that she was losing the ability to feel Ben close; she was resigned that time was moving on; she was bothered that she was still feeling like a rudderless ship. She put the shirt aside and picked up Ben's wallet. She hadn't gone through it before. This time, she opened it and started examining its contents. There was his driver license – Ben smiling at the camera with that hallmark glint of amusement visible in his eyes. There were a couple of credit cards and Ben's Columbia ID, along with some U.S. dollars, some pound sterling, and some lira. He also carried pictures of his parents, a picture of him and Sarah from years ago, and a lovely picture from their wedding. Maggie's eyes welled up, and she slowly put everything back into the wallet. She placed the wallet on the bed and continued through the box. There, in the left shoe, was the amulet. She lifted it up and placed it on her palm as if she were weighing it. She turned it over and peered at it, looking for any markings she may have missed earlier.

"Sarah, there is something very special about this." She turned to face Sarah. "I think we need to put it somewhere safe. Somewhere it won't rust all over everything. I told Dougal about this. He is interested in this from an academic standpoint – he thinks it might be quite old. Maybe I should rent a safe deposit box."

"We have a safe, Maggie. It was in the house when we bought it. Come on and take a look." Sarah stood up and headed downstairs. She went into the living room, moved a chair, and lifted up the corner of the rug. There, sunken in the floor, was a small safe. Sarah punched in a series of numbers and lifted the top, swinging it on its hinge.

"This is perfect! Would you mind?"

"Not at all. As you can see, it's quite empty."

Maggie went back upstairs and grabbed one of Ben's socks. She put the amulet in the sock, wrapped the sock around the iron, and took it back downstairs. She placed it in the safe, and Sarah closed and locked it. She flipped the edge of the rug back down and pulled the chair back over the safe.

"Sarah, please promise me you will not mention this. Both Dougal and Callum have some concern about this amulet. If it truly is old, they are worried that some collector might try and make it their own. I am going to ask you to not tell anybody you have any knowledge of it."

"You are starting to frighten me a bit, Maggie."

"Sarah, I wouldn't worry," Maggie said as reassuringly as she could. "I think the two of them are being overly concerned. But they made me promise."

She stood up and took out her mobile phone. "I need to call Callum. And the dance studio – I have dance students that are missing me, I am sure." She fell silent for several moments. She stopped and turned towards Sarah.

"Sarah, I apologize. I am so lost. I have no idea what I want to do – I only have stumbled into things I don't want to do. I don't want to go back to New York. I don't want to spend the rest of my life teaching dance. I don't think I want to settle in Fife... I just don't know what to do."

Sarah took Maggie's hand. "Maggie, be kind to yourself. Give yourself time. I am positive that you will find your way. You have been through a lot. You just need some time."

Maggie squeezed Sarah's hand. "You are so kind, Sarah. I am so glad I know you." She stood up and walked to the door. "Service is better outside. I'll be right back... This shouldn't take long."

Maggie rang Callum, but he didn't answer. She put the phone away and sat on the step, wondering what she should do.

Do what Callum would do, she thought to herself. *Analyze.*

She went back inside and grabbed a pad of paper, writing down everything she could think of that might help her unravel her mystery. What did she know? The amulet had been made around 600 AD or so. The Pictish had disappeared around 900 AD or so. She'd picked that up at the library earlier that day. The First Crusade had started in 1095 AD. Maggie started jotting down facts and dates and connecting them with lines, but then she suddenly stopped.

St. Francis! I didn't research him! And that's where Ben was found…and the amulet!

She was both excited by this breakthrough and a bit irritated with herself that she hadn't thought of it before. She crumpled up the paper, threw it away, and went into the kitchen. She fixed herself a cup of tea and went to find Sarah, who was in the den watching TV.

"Sarah, I think I'll go back to the library tomorrow… Would that be okay with you?"

"Sure, Maggie. I'll be taking Jake to the airport anyway. You look excited."

"I had a thought I want to explore. Yes, it does excite me," she admitted sheepishly. "Think I'll head to bed. I want to get a fresh start tomorrow."

"Good night, Maggie." Sarah turned back to the TV. "I just want to finish watching the news."

Maggie got up early the next day, made a pot of coffee, quickly downed a cup, and caught a bus to the library. She headed right to the card catalog and looked up St. Francis. This time, she brought a pad of paper and started writing down the facts of his life. She didn't know what she was going to need, so she outlined everything. At the very least, she could take it back to Dougal and try to match it up with his work. The dates didn't yet make sense to her, but she wasn't concerned. What did catch her interest was the fact that St. Francis had been a soldier. That fact opened up an entire new line of opportunity. After several hours of research, she headed back to Sarah's.

"Sarah, let's go out for dinner. I think I will be heading back to Scotland soon. I found something I need to share with Dougal."

"You think you can win your bet?" Sarah was grinning.

"Not quite, but maybe close. We always have been competitive."

Sarah laughed. "I would have never guessed."

~

Dougal was waiting for Maggie in the Edinburgh airport concourse. "Good flight?" He gave her a peck on the cheek.

"It was fine. I was eager to get back, though. I need you to get me a copy of a thesis written by one of your doctoral candidates in 1982."

Dougal let out a hearty laugh. "Lass, you certainly get right to the point. Let's grab a bite to eat, and we can chat about our respective findings."

They headed to the Royal Mile Tavern for some fish and chips. While waiting for their pints, Maggie opened up the conversation.

"Dougal, besides that thesis I asked you to provide, I decided to research St. Francis. Guess what? As a young man, he was quite the man about town: he spent his days drinking and gambling with his buddies. And then he became a soldier. I'm thinking that it might not have been a religious connection, per se, that got him the amulet. It might have been a crusader, either going or returning from the

Holy Lands. Many of them took boats from Southern Italy across the Mediterranean instead of hiking all around the sea."

Dougal peered intently at Maggie, processing what he had just heard. "That's quite interesting, Maggie. I made no progress with the missionaries in Scotland. I think you might be on to something. Did St. Francis join a Crusade?"

"He wanted to. He actually started to go, but he became ill and had to turn back. After his religious conversion, he made a trip to Egypt and met with the sultan, not as a soldier, but as a missionary. He was allowed to preach in the court of the sultan, so he had many opportunities to run into foreign crusaders. Perhaps one of them was Scottish."

Just then, dinner came, and the conversation didn't continue until both had started eating. Maggie stopped, put down her fork, and quite abruptly asked, "Dougal! Pardon me... I was so taken up that I completely forgot to ask: have you had any incidents? Have Mum and Da had anymore?"

"Don't fash yersel, Mag. Everything's been quiet. And you?"

"No issues at all. Do you suppose we can carry on with our research?"

"I was thinking of heading over to the Isle of Bute. That's where Kingarth Abbey was. I was going to hunt down the local historian and ask about St. Blane and the Pict conversions. I can also ask about involvement in the Crusades. Maybe one of the early Stuarts was involved – Rothesay is their clan seat. Maybe a docent at Rothesay has records I can read."

"Can you get me into the library, Dougal? Besides that thesis, I'd like to read more on the Crusades. Maybe I can find a link."

"I like it, Maggie. Stay with us? You'll be quite a bit closer to the library."

"That will be grand." With that, they finished their dinners and headed out.

Maggie spent two days at the university library before catching the train to Dunfermline. There, she quickly fell into her prior routine: dance classes several times a week, coffee at the Kingsgate Starbucks, and walks in Pittencrief Park. She spent her evenings piecing together her notes on St. Francis and the Crusades. Maggie noticed another woman routinely getting coffee, just like she did. She was noticeable for her plainly styled hair, her lack of makeup, and her very simple clothing. After a few days, they started smiling at one another, and then they started to say hello. One morning, Maggie extended her hand and introduced herself.

"Hello. My name is Maggie, and I notice that you and I love our morning coffees."

The woman smiled and shook Maggie's hand. "Hello. My name is Martha. I have noticed you, too. Glad to make your acquaintance."

Martha freed her hand to grab her coffee, and Maggie noticed an odd scar on the back of her hand. It was an older scar – no redness left – so Maggie didn't inquire. She did notice that it was roughly square, maybe 3/8" across, located between the bones leading to the fourth and fifth fingers, perhaps an inch below her knuckles.

I wonder what happened. That looks like it would have really hurt.

Just then, Maggie's coffee was ready, so she smiled at Martha, grabbed her coffee, and headed over to the park.

Martha and Maggie ended up at the coffee shop at the same time the next day, but it was raining. They sat down together at a table.

"You must live near here," said Martha.

"Actually, my parents do. I'm just visiting at the moment."

"That's nice. How long do you plan on staying?"

"I will probably leave in a week or two. I'm thinking of taking a little trip." Maggie was uncomfortable telling this near stranger that she was rather rootless at the moment. Changing the subject, she asked, "I take it you work around here?"

"I do. I'm a sales clerk at one of the stores at Kingsgate."

"Well, then, this is very convenient for you."

Maggie glanced at her watch and said, "I think I'd best be going. Nice sharing a cuppa with you, Martha." She stood up, and as she walked out the door, she couldn't help but wonder what store had hired a woman who dressed so simply.

Dunfermline had its first snowstorm the following Wednesday. Maggie was sitting in Starbucks, reading the paper and sipping on her coffee, when Martha walked in. She had several shopping bags with her and had a difficult time opening the door. A man seated close to the door held it open for her – she smiled and thanked him. She walked up to Maggie's table.

"Mind if I leave these here while I order coffee?"

"Not at all."

Martha dropped her load and went to buy her coffee. She returned and sat down across from Maggie.

"This weather is nasty."

"It certainly came upon us quickly. I am not sure I am totally prepared for winter. You certainly have your hands full," Maggie added, nodding to the bags.

"Oh, those. Every year, my friends gather used clothing to give to charity. I agreed to drop these off."

"That's very kind of you. Would you like some help getting them to your car?"

"I don't have a car, but a friend of ours offered his. I told him I would bring these to his car. I'm supposed to meet him in…" Martha paused to look at her watch. "Meet him in fifteen minutes. It would be great if you would help. I wasn't expecting snow."

"Well, drink up, then, Martha. We have a mission."

Maggie followed Martha around to the back of the shopping center, where there was a dark-blue Peugeot waiting. Upon seeing the two women approach, a man got out of the car, walked around to the back, and opened the trunk. He stood by the side of the trunk while Martha held back, motioning for Maggie to put her bags in first. Maggie smiled at the man and leaned over to place her bags closest to the seat backs to give Martha's bags room. At that moment, the man and Martha pushed an unsuspecting Maggie into the trunk and slammed it shut.

CHAPTER EIGHT

"Now, now, young lady," said the strange man standing in front of her. "You really must not be frightened. You have been chosen…" He then abruptly stopped and giggled. It wasn't a giggle, actually, more of a chuckle. It was so extremely inappropriate to both the conversation and situation that it took Maggie aback.

Who chuckles after kidnapping a stranger? She had never experienced that behavior before.

I had better work on figuring this man out.

"You must become a follower of the Third Order. We know you have the iron crescent. You will give it to us." He stopped and looked her over carefully. "I never thought it would be someone like you." Again, he chortled. "Oh my." He chortled again, shaking his head.

Is this man daft? Maggie's eyes narrowed. *Eleven pence and three farthings short of a shilling.* She stood motionless, watching him intently.

The man composed himself and continued. "We will teach you the ways of the Third Order. The Third Order, the way it was meant to be." He shook his head in apparent disapproval of something… Maggie was unsure of what. He then muttered something to himself as if he were carrying on an internal conversation. He shook his head again.

"You will follow the Rule of Life for the Third Order. You will live a life of penitence, poverty, and prayer."

Oh, Lord. What have I gotten into?

"The first rule is simplicity of dress." He walked over to a table a few feet away and picked up a pile of cloth that Maggie had not noticed before. "Here, these are now your clothes." He handed the pile to Maggie. It consisted of a chemise, a long, plain skirt, and a tunic. The skirt and tunic were made of rough, handwoven linen – the chemise was made from a lighter fabric, possibly cotton. The skirt and tunic were unbleached and scratchy. There was no waistband in the skirt, no zipper, and no button. What passed for a waistband was a sewn pocket laced with a thin cord for tying. The tunic was made from fabric rectangles sewn together to form front, back, and sleeves. There was no collar, just an edge left open to slip over a head. There was a thicker cord, apparently meant to tie around the tunic. The chemise was fashioned in a similar, primitive fashion. Drawstring neckline, drawstring cuffs. And that was all there was.

"This is the dress for the penitent, as it was when St. Francis founded the order."

Maggie had remained silent, but now she found the nerve to finally speak. "Where am I?" she asked.

The man lowered his head and chuckled again. "That is of no concern of yours anymore. You are in a place without worldly distractions so you may follow the way."

"It will be quite impossible to 'follow the way' if I don't know what that is. Tell me what it is you think I should be doing, and why, exactly, was I kidnapped?"

Maggie noticed a very dark look flit across the man's face.

Not a good sign. I best be careful around this daftie."

The man composed himself. "Of course you don't know." He shook his head. "Lovely girl, you are. Such lovely hair. You must wear it back and tied. Such a shame."

At that, the man abruptly turned away and started muttering to himself. "Love the Lord, hate the body. Love the Lord, hate the body with its sins and vices. Chapter One." He seemed very troubled and started pacing to and fro. Maggie quietly watched, but every muscle in her body became tense. She looked around the room carefully, trying to figure out what to do if this man came at her. He was between her and the only door. Her eyes refocused sharply on him.

This man looked to be in his sixties, perhaps. He was mostly bald, wore glasses, and although he wasn't obese by any stretch of the imagination, he had a triple chin. He was wearing nondescript street clothes: plain oxfords, khaki slacks, belted high, and an oversized flannel shirt. If you passed him on the street, you would take him for an average pensioner. Maggie figured she was far faster and had much better reflexes. She had a good chance of getting to that door if she had to. What she didn't know was whether the door was locked.

After several minutes, the man's agitation abated. His muttering and pacing stopped. He just stood there, lost in his own thought.

Maggie sighed. "So, perhaps we should start at the beginning. Do you have a name? What shall I call you?"

"I am the master of formation," he intoned with deep resonance. "The master of formation of the true Third Order."

"The true Third Order? Is there more than one?"

That dark look flitted across the master's face once again. "The *true* Third Order. Not the defiled Rule of Life declared by the pope in 1978. I am the master of formation for the Third Order, with the Rule as written by St. Francis himself."

Maggie's eyes narrowed again.

So, we have a religious rebel daftie. A daftie that does not like change. That would explain the clothing out of the Middle Ages.

"Where can I read more about this Rule of Life?" Maggie asked.

"I will be your teacher," the master replied rather loftily. "You need not seek any other source."

I was afraid that would be your answer.

141

"So, what shall I call you?"

"You may call me Master. Follow me, now. I will show you your room."

Maggie had been so intent on her captor, and the location of the door, that she had not taken note of her surroundings. The two of them were in a cottage – an ancient cottage. It had thick walls; she could tell by the depth of the recess around the small, leaded windows. The room was small and dim, with no overhead lighting. The one door she noticed was made of sturdy oak and was in the far wall; Maggie assumed it led to outdoors. The floors were stone, covered with some old and worn rugs. The table from which the clothing had been fetched was of trestle design; it was heavy and coarse, flanked by two benches. Across from the door was an unscreened fireplace topped by a thick, rough-hewn mantle. Just above the mantle hung a very prominent cross.

The walls of the room appeared to have been plastered and painted once upon a time, but there were areas where the plaster had fallen off, exposing stone blocks. There were a couple of old chairs in front of the fireplace. Between the table, benches, and chairs, there wasn't much room for anything else.

The master headed towards a hallway to the left of the fireplace, motioning for Maggie to follow. They passed two shut doors, and then the master opened the door at the end. He pushed it open and stood to the side. "This is your room. Please change into your clothes. When you are finished, place your worldly clothes in the basket. Then you may come out. We will start prayers soon."

Maggie walked past him and into a very small, sparse room. It had one very small window, an iron cot, a small wooden table, and a kneeling bench. Above the cot was another, very prominent cross. The cot itself was covered in a heavy wool blanket that appeared to be handwoven. The basket of which the master had spoken was large, empty, and made of rattan. It sat in the corner. There was a small, worn rug over the stone floor by the side of the bed, upon which were a pair of neatly placed sandals. The room was chilly, and the clothes Maggie had been given would not keep her warm. Neither would the sandals. This room was meant for sleeping and nothing else.

Maggie changed into the clothes that had been given to her, during which her mind was racing. She racked her brain trying to figure out where she might be. She had started counting minutes from the moment the car had started to move. She'd gotten to 78 – that would make it about an hour and twenty minutes. They had only stopped for three lights the entire distance, so they must have gotten on the motorway. They hadn't gone south: she would have noticed the difference in sound had they taken the Firth Road Bridge. By process of elimination, they had to be somewhere within an arc going northeast to southwest from Dunfermline, approximately a hundred kilometers out. Less if they had headed east to the coast and then north and even less than that if they had headed west and then south to the Borders. So, maybe eighty to a hundred kilometers from Dunfermline. From what little she could see out the window, they were in a remote area. Beyond that, she hadn't a clue.

Maggie opened the door and walked out into the hall. The master was at the trestle table in the main room.

"You must always close the door behind you," he called down the hall. Maggie dutifully shut her bedroom door and walked towards him.

He stood up and walked over to the fireplace, motioning for her to join him. He knelt before the fireplace, again motioning her to join him. The thin rug offered little protection from the cold, hard stone floor beneath it.

This is going to be uncomfortable. I wonder how long this will take?

The man bent his head, crossed himself, and started to mutter to himself in nearly a whisper. Maggie couldn't make out what he was saying. She supposed he was praying. He intermittently would cross himself and then continue with his whispered chant. He was lost in his own world; Maggie wasn't even sure that he realized she was there with him. She kept her head bent and watched his hands – they were the only things she could see without moving her head. She noticed an unusual scar on his right hand – very similar to the one she noticed on the woman who had lured her out of the coffee shop.

I wonder if that's meaningful or coincidental.

Other than those musings, Maggie simply knelt there quietly, waiting for her next instruction. Her knees started to ache, but she knew better than to move. She was wary of this entire situation: she believed this "Master" was not rational, she had no idea what he might do, she had no idea where she might be, and she had no idea how she was going to extricate herself.

After some indeterminate time, the man crossed himself once more and then got up. She noticed he had a difficulty rising from the floor.

A weakness. If I need time, wait until he is kneeling.

"You will now prepare supper," said the master. He was strangely silent about the prayer session.

That's odd. She'd assumed she would be peppered with instructions or asked about how she prayed or something.

I wonder what he presumes.

The master headed through an archway into a small, primitive kitchen and motioned for Maggie to follow. There was a wood-burning stove, a farm sink, a prep table, a fireplace, and not much else in the way of kitchen appliances. Various pots, pans, and plates were stacked on some open shelves, and there were a couple of cast iron pans by the stove. There was a fire started in the stove, with a tin kettle of water steaming on top. Next to that was a cast iron pot, also steaming.

"Jack brings in food for us," said the master. "Until he returns, we only have broth and bread."

There is somebody else. I wonder if it's the man from the car.

The master continued. "Please set the table and serve the broth and bread." He turned and left to sit at the table.

Maggie pulled down some bowls and plates. She filled the bowls with broth and set them aside. There was a round loaf of bread on the prep table; she searched for a knife to cut the bread and found a dull one with a rounded tip mixed with eating utensils in a basket on one of the shelves.

No refrigerator.

She brought out a bowl and a plate of bread for the master and then headed back into the kitchen for hers. She suddenly realized just how hungry she had become. She sat down across from the master but waited. He was again deep in whispered chant, crossing himself several times. After a few minutes, the master crossed himself and started to eat. Maggie took that as permission and started to eat.

There was no conversation at the table as the two ate. Maggie was careful to time her eating so that she finished when the master did. When the last chunk of bread was gone and the soup bowls empty, the master swung his legs over the bench as he waved his hand dismissively towards her. She took that as her cue to clean the table and take the dishes to the kitchen. As she was washing the dishes, a car pulled up, and the master walked out the door.

The sun was setting, which gave Maggie some sense of direction. She was looking east, maybe southeast. She was in the Highlands, that was definite. Wherever they were, it was most definitely remote – there were no signs of humanity she could see.

If this is east, then the window in my room must face north. She wondered how she might be able to see what was to the west and to the south.

I think I must be in Perth. What's up here and looks like this? Spittal of Glenshee. Cairngorms National Park. The ski resort…

She stopped suddenly. She and her brothers had often gone skiing at Glenshee when they were younger. She peered out the window again. *I must be somewhere in the Glenbeg moors? The park?* She felt a growing excitement.

It fits the time in the car. It fits the topography.

She smiled to herself. She was reasonably sure she knew, at least in general, where she was. That was definitely a step in the right direction.

She was putting the bowls back on the shelf when the master came in, followed by the man who had taken her.

His name must be Jack.

"Margaret, you must go to your room," said the master. Maggie was startled: he had never called her by name before. She hadn't been aware that he even knew who she was.

My kidnapping was no accident. Maggie bowed her head and walked out of the kitchen. She noticed that Jack was casually leaning against the door jamb, watching her with what could be mistaken as amusement. She only had time for a quick glance at Jack, but he appeared to be in his mid-forties, maybe. Tall – perhaps six foot two or so. Tall and on the thin side, with broad shoulders. He had dark hair, which he had slicked back with some sort of hair preparation. That was all she could glean at the moment. She walked down the hall, went into her room, and closed the door behind her. She sat on the edge of her bed, wondering what to do – then she noticed that the basket was empty. Her street clothes – and shoes – had disappeared. She climbed under the blanket to keep warm. It was going to be a very long night.

A sudden thought made her sit up with a start – her door had no inside lock. She climbed out of bed and looked at the prayer bench. She lifted one side to see how heavy it was. Moderately…not heavy enough that it wouldn't budge, but heavy enough that she couldn't easily lift it up off the floor. She carefully lifted one side so it was resting on only one leg and pivoted the bench on that leg, moving the side she was lifting towards the door. She gently lowered the bench, walked to the other side, and repeated the maneuver. She thus very quietly walked the bench over to the door and placed it under the door latch. Not perfect by any stretch of the imagination, but better than nothing.

I will not get a decent night's sleep tonight. She climbed back into bed.

She could hear the drone of conversation coming from the common room but couldn't make out what the master and Jack were saying. From the tone, she knew that while it wasn't lighthearted banter, it wasn't emotion-fueled anger or frustration either. She finally drifted off into a fitful sleep.

It wasn't quite dawn when there came knocking on her door. "You must get up," said the master. Maggie rose and walked the prayer bench back to its prior place. Out from the covers, she became quite cold quite rapidly. As she exited her room, she closed the door against the cold.

The cottage apparently had as its only heat source the main fireplace. A stack of wood had been brought in and placed on the hearth. It seemed that a fire had been started the night before and had been banked overnight.

"Tend to the fire, Margaret," said the master.

"I don't know what to do," she answered.

The master seemed pleased for an opportunity to school Maggie. "Take one of the logs and disturb the fire embers. Then place several logs on the fire in a star pattern."

Maggie did as instructed, and soon, there was a welcome warmth coming from the fireplace.

"Now, Margaret, please fix breakfast."

Maggie went into the kitchen. Jack had apparently brought in eggs, which were sitting in a basket on the prep table. There was also a canister of oatmeal, a quart of milk or cream, a fresh loaf of bread, a small slab of bacon, some carrots, an onion, some fresh peas, and a few potatoes. Jack and the car, however, were gone.

"Eggs or oatmeal?" she called from the kitchen.

"You must come out to speak to me," said the master. Maggie walked back into the main room. She noticed, however, that he seemed fairly pleased. *He probably likes being waited on.*

"What would you like to eat?"

"I shall prefer oatmeal." His tone was almost grandiose.

Maggie dipped her head slightly and returned to the kitchen.

Between the fire in the stove and the fire in the main room, the cottage was starting to feel comfortable. She boiled up oatmeal for two, spooned it out into two bowls, and brought them out with the bottle of milk. Or cream…she hadn't tasted it. She did notice that it had thick cream at the top of the bottle.

The two ate in silence after the master spent about five minutes in his prayer ritual. Maggie cleaned the table and went into the kitchen to wash the dishes. She had started the tea kettle boiling, so she had hot water to wash.

Living like this, I wouldn't be surprised if Jacobites themselves came a knocking. She was quickly becoming irritated.

When she went back out to the main room, the master was sitting at the table. He had a book in front of him. "Come, sit."

Maggie sat down on the opposite bench.

"It is time for your first lesson. I will instruct you on the Rule of Life for the Order of Brothers and Sisters of Penance. It is the Third Order of St. Francis, the first being the Order of Friars Minor and the second being the Order of St. Clare."

"Chapter One: daily life." The master turned a few pages and started to read. "Paragraph three applies to you. "The sisters shall wear an outer garment and tunic made of cloth of humble quality."

Clothes: check.

"Chapter Two: abstinence. We only eat meat Sundays, Tuesdays, and Thursdays, except for high feast days. We eat cheese and eggs Mondays, Wednesdays, Fridays, and Saturdays. We only eat two meals a day."

Maggie interrupted. "Can I write this down? I might have a difficult time remembering all of this."

"You will learn slowly, Margaret. Only one more lesson for today: before and after each meal, you must say the Lord's Prayer, or three Hail Marys, and also give thanks to God."

"So, oatmeal this morning… I assume bacon for dinner? It is Tuesday."

"Correct!" beamed the master as he closed the book. "It is prayer time. I have already said matins and prime. Now is terce." The master headed over to the fireplace and knelt. Maggie knew he meant her to follow, so she knelt next to him again.

Only two meals a day? I must remember to eat more in the morning, she thought as she knelt quietly.

~

And so it went. The master was highly regimented, and each day followed this exact routine. Jack came with provisions every other day, and Maggie cooked, stoked the fire, cleaned, knelt quietly, and took in her "lessons." One week into captivity, a clean set of clothes, nearly identical to the ones she had first been given, were set out for her. She washed her dirty clothes and those of the master in the farm sink. She wrung them out and set them in front of the fireplace, on the benches, to dry.

Maggie's prayer sessions were spent scheming.

How can I escape? I will have to get to either a ski lodge or town. I have no shoes, and it's winter. I have no coat. There is already snow on the ground.

There was a fairly decent snowfall about ten days into this ordeal, and Jack didn't show for two days. When he did appear, he had extra pantry food.

"Roads were closed for the snow," he said as he entered. "I brought extra food just in case. I need to talk to you, Clance. In private."

"Margaret, please go to your room and close the door," said the master.

Maggie got up and went down the hall.

"Clance. He has a name. Clance…maybe short for Clancy? Last name or first?"

Maggie closed the door after her, as instructed. She strained to hear the conversation but couldn't make out much. She heard some words: "phone," "town," "shoes." It made little sense to her. And when she heard approaching footsteps, she quickly knelt on the prayer bench and lowered her head.

Clance strode into her room without knocking and looked pleased to find her kneeling.

"I must go with Jack into town. You have your chores and prayers to keep you until I return." He then simply turned and walked out.

~

Jack drove Clance to Spittal of Glenshee, which was several miles south. Clance was speaking non-stop, which Jack found mildly irritating.

"Why do you think his eminence wants to speak to me? Do you suppose we will be summoned to Rome? And that Margaret, I can't understand her. She seems to be docile and respectful, and she learns her lessons well, but she has yet to release the artifact. I

152

wonder if his eminence wants to speak to her?" Clance droned on and on, and Jack simply tuned him out. He pulled in front of the local pub and parked the car. The two men got out and walked over to the public phone – Clance was somewhat of a techno-phobe and did not trust mobile phone technology.

Clance checked his phone and waited until 3 PM on the dot: that was the time he had been told to call. He dialed the number he used to contact the Vatican, and a familiar voice answered.

"Your Eminence," said Clance, "I am calling at your direction. How may I be of service?"

"Master of formation, have you made any progress on recovering the sacred artifact?" said the voice at the other end.

After an uncomfortable pause, Clance apologetically replied, "No, Your Eminence. Margaret insists she does not have it."

"Of course she doesn't have it. If she had it, it would be ours. She has not yet divulged the location? Then you must take additional measures, Master. We are displeased with the lack of progress. Do you understand?"

Clance stammered at the rebuke. "Yes, Your Eminence. I will see to it. We must go now, though, so I may obey your order. I will send you word when we have the location."

Clance hung up the phone and turned to Jack. "Before we return, let's grab a pint and something to eat. Margaret is not much of a cook."

At the Vatican, the deacon who had slipped into an empty cardinal's office quietly placed the phone handset back into its cradle and walked over to the closed door. He slowly opened it and peered out to make sure the hall was empty. It normally was at this hour, being that the pope had regular meetings with his cardinals. The deacon ducked out the door and down the hall.

~

Maggie had started thinking furiously. She would have some time alone, but she did not know how much. She didn't move off of the bench until she heard the oak door open and close. She carefully opened her bedroom door and listened. She could hear the car engine start and the faint crunch of the snow under the tires.

She quickly left her room and headed to one of the two other rooms she had never seen. The first door she tried was locked.

Of course.

She tried the second – it opened into a room nearly identical to hers.

This is of no help.

She then went back to her room, grabbed the blanket off of the bed, wrapped it around herself, and headed to the front door. She opened it but realized she couldn't step out wearing only sandals. She went back in, took the blanket off of the bed in the other open bedroom and carried it to the door. She spread the blanket over the snow and stepped out. She could only go six feet or so, but she saw the tire tracks heading to the right.

That's where the road must be.

She hoped that it was the A93. She couldn't remember many side roads through the mountains.

She looked around to the left: there was a very small stone out-building about fifty yards from the cottage. It looked to be boarded up. Beyond that, Maggie could see no signs of human activity. She stepped back into the cottage, picked up the blanket and shook it off, and closed the door.

Maggie searched every nook and cranny for anything that might help her identify her captor, but to no avail. There wasn't so much as a newspaper, book, or journal around. She sat on the bench, frustrated.

Think, Maggie!! What would Callum do?

Callum would start dissecting the problem. Problem One: clothing.

Even though Maggie had a good idea of where she was, generally, she would probably die of exposure in only sandals and a blanket. She walked through the cottage again.

Two blankets, two sheets… What can I do for shoes in the snow?

She stopped short.

Snowshoes!!

She went back into her room and picked up the rattan basket. The base was about thirty inches long and maybe eighteen to twenty inches wide. She stepped into it.

This will do if I cut off the sides.

She went into the other bedroom. Sure enough, there was another basket, same size.

Now, how am I going to attach them to my feet?

She inspected the weave of the rattan. It was tight, but not tight enough to preclude pushing something thin through. Maggie went over to her bed and looked at the sheet. It looked to be homespun. If she could cut strips, perhaps she could push them through to bind the rattan to her feet. She went into the kitchen, got a butter knife, brought it back, and successfully inserted it between two rattan sticks.

Next step: how to cut strips?

She went back into the kitchen, looking for the sharpest knife. There wasn't one, only the knife she used to cut the bread.

No sharp tip.

The only utensil with a tip was a fork. Maggie took it back to her room, stuck the handle between her knees, grabbed the edge of the sheet, and pushed it down as hard as she could against the fork tines. She managed to make four holes in the sheet.

"This is going to take a while," she muttered.

But if I make a string of holes, maybe I can weaken the fabric enough to tear it.

This would have to wait until her attempted escape.

Maggie returned the fork to the kitchen and looked out the window. The sun was setting – evening comes early so far north. It didn't take long before the hills were shrouded in night. The clouds had parted, and the stars were brilliant. She went back to the front door and opened it. She looked closely at the horizon to see whether there was any faint glow from a distant town. Nothing.

Maggie went back in the cottage, into her bedroom, and stood on the cot to look out the window. Unfortunately, there was a low mountain that blocked any view of a town. She then went across the hall, stood on that cot, and peered out that window.

Is that light?

She closed her eyes tightly for several seconds and then opened them and looked out again.

There's a glow on the horizon!

She could barely contain her excitement. She stepped off the cot, straightened out the blanket, and went back into her bedroom to remake the bed.

The master had said nothing about supper.

It must be suppertime.

She went into the kitchen and looked at the meager food on the prep table.

I actually have no idea what day of the week it is. Doesn't matter: there is no meat.

Maggie boiled up a few eggs and ate them with a couple of slices of bread. She drank a cup of hot water and went to her room.

Jack brought Clance back a little while later, and then he left. Clance, assuming Maggie had fallen asleep, did not disturb her. She heard them arrive and heard Jack leave. She lay in bed, motionless, her mind racing with the plan she was starting to hatch.

~

The next morning, after prayers and breakfast, Clance called Maggie over to the table.

"It is time for you to give us the relic."

"Relic? What relic?"

"Come now, Margaret. The iron crescent you had evaluated at the university."

So that's how he found me. Someone there must have said something.

"I don't have it."

"Not with you, we know. But you still have it."

"I'm sorry, but no, I don't. Whatever do you want with it, anyway?

"Young lady, that is no way to speak to the master." Clance's face was getting dark.

His tone did not deter Maggie. "Why don't you tell me about this relic, Master. Why is it so important to you? Perhaps if you help me understand, I may try and help you recover it." She hoped she sounded appropriately conciliatory.

"The relic belonged to St. Francis. That's why we require it." To him, that was a perfectly complete and acceptable reason. He then stopped suddenly and proceeded to drift into one of his internalized, muttering soliloquies, crossing himself frequently.

When he came out of his trance-like state, he continued. "His eminence is losing patience, Margaret. I have been ordered to recover the relic. As the master, I order you to divulge the location." His demeanor was of one of someone who totally expected to be obeyed.

I am sorry, sir, but you are totally mistaken." Maggie's voice had become surprisingly firm. She had never challenged Clance in this way before, but she was willing to take the risk. She needed more information to assess the situation.

Clance was obviously surprised by Maggie's behavior, and he let out one of his remarkably inappropriate chortles. "Well, young lady," he said after he composed himself, "I am surprised you are being so obstinate. You obviously have not taken your lessons to heart enough." He chortled again. Maggie found that deeply disturbing. "Therefore, you must increase your Our Fathers to six before and after meals." He paused and then added, "And you will have only one meal per day. You must learn obedience. Now, go to your room."

Maggie quickly left.

Starve me into submission. I need to get out of here sooner than later.

The next morning, Clance had eggs for breakfast, which Maggie prepared, but he had her kneel in front of the fireplace as he ate. Maggie cleaned up after Clance's meal, and while washing dishes, she hid a fork in her waistband. When she finally was alone in her room, behind the closed door, she started to perforate her sheet into one-inch strips, late into the night, until her fingers were numb with cold.

By the third day, Maggie was hungry and exhausted. While washing the morning dishes, she crammed a piece of bread into her mouth, hoping Clance would not notice. She noticed that she had to snug up her drawstring skirt more – she must have lost several pounds.

"Are you prepared to give us the relic?" asked Clance after morning prayers, just as he had done the last several days.

"I do not have it," Maggie replied, just as she had since the deprivation had begun.

Clance lost his temper and yelled, "You must submit to the order!" He strode to the door. "Go outside!"

"I haven't coat or shoes."

"Perhaps that will convince you to submit, then!" he shouted as he came towards her and grabbed her arm. He dragged her to the door, pushed her out, and slammed the door.

Maggie stood by the door and quickly started shivering. She loosened the neck of her tunic and drew it over her head to form a hood and huddled down, wrapping her arms around her knees to try and conserve her body heat.

I won't last very long out here. How far will this man go?

She was counting on Clance realizing she was the only one who knew the location of the amulet. She hoped she was playing her hand well – her very life hung in the balance.

After several minutes, Clance opened the door, grabbed her by the upper arm, and pulled her inside.

"You are trying my patience, Margaret." He was eerily calm. "Perhaps Jack will have better luck convincing you." He walked over to the fireplace and looked up at the cross. "Now go to your room."

Maggie quickly went to her room and climbed in under the covers. After several minutes, she got back up and started to do jumping jacks. When she had generated enough body heat, she got back under the covers and was finally warm. *The very next time he leaves, I need to make my move. I won't last long like this.*

Jack came with provisions the next day. Maggie was sent to her room, as she always was when Jack and Clance needed to talk. This time, though, she could hear that the conversation was becoming heated. Clance and Jack abruptly left together, slamming the door after them. She heard the car leave and ran to the kitchen with her sheet and blanket. She stopped, ran to the other bedroom, and grabbed that blanket, too. She had managed to perforate a good half of the sheet. Try as she might, though, she was having difficulty ripping the sheet. She grabbed a piece of kindling, lit it in the fireplace, and carefully burned through a few threads at the edge of the sheet. She stood on the sheet and yanked as hard as she could. It tore along the weakened line. Thrilled, she continued until she had yards and yards of strips.

Maggie then brought the two wicker baskets into the kitchen and broke off the sides by snapping them along the edge of the work table. She bound her feet in strips, leaving only enough strips to fasten the basket bottoms to her feet. Wrapping herself in the two blankets, she headed out the door.

Maggie headed towards the road, following the car tracks. It was snowing again, heavily, but there was no wind.

Good. Hopefully, the snow will cover my tracks. And maybe it will close the road, giving me more time.

When she got to the road, she saw that the car had turned right. She turned left. The road was not recently plowed, and there were no cars.

The road must be closed. Safer for me.

She headed north.

CHAPTER NINE

She didn't know how long it took her to reach the ski resort – maybe an hour? It was dusk as she walked up to a low building by a ski lift. The resort appeared closed, but she saw a man working on some equipment.

"Hallo!" Maggie called loudly.

The man turned around, startled by her voice. "We're closed, ma'am," he started to say, but he stopped when he could see her through the snow as she came closer. "What?" he said, startled as he saw she was wrapped in blankets, her feet wrapped in cloth. "Hell's bells, what is this?"

"Please help me," said Maggie through chattering teeth. "I was kidnapped and escaped. Is there a phone here?"

The man quickly walked over to the warming house door and opened it. "There's a phone in here, in the back." He stood back to let her enter, switched on the lights, and headed for a back room. "Do you need medical attention?"

"I am not sure, but I do need to call MI6."

The man was obviously startled at that.

That should keep me safe for the moment.

He opened the back-room door, turned on the lights, and pointed to a phone on the wall. Maggie stumbled clumsily up to it in her ramshackle snowshoes and punched in a number she knew by heart. "Hello, Callum? This is Maggie."

"Maggie!!! I am so glad you are alive!" His voice was filled with relief and excitement. "Where are you?"

"I'm at Glenshee, in a warming shed… I don't know which lift."

"Are you alone?"

"No, there's a workman here that let me in. The ski resort is closed."

"Can you put him on the phone?"

"Sure." She had been watching him while on the phone, cautious about keeping him in her view. She held out the receiver and said, "Sir? Callum Fraser would like to speak to you."

"Yes?"

"This is Callum Fraser of MI6. To whom am I speaking?"

"Andy Sharpe."

"Mr. Sharpe, Scotland Yard has been searching for the woman with you. She may be in danger. Is the resort closed for the evening?"

Andy Sharpe looked closely at Maggie as he spoke. "Closed for the evening and perhaps for tomorrow, too, Mr. Fraser. They closed the roads a couple of hours ago for the snow."

"Mr. Sharpe, I am about to give you orders that, if not followed, will land you in serious trouble," Callum said sternly, with great authority. "You are to secure her in that warming shed for the evening. You must remain totally silent about this encounter. You are to tell no one, is that clear?"

"Yes, sir."

"I will secure a helicopter and get there as soon as I can tomorrow. You are to release the woman to me, and to only me. I will ask for you by name at the registration desk. Do not be surprised if you are called due to an emergency. Look for a man in a business suit – that should not be difficult to spot. Walk up to me and shake my hand. I will say the following words: 'Mr. Sharpe, I am sorry to call you away with no prior warning. I am here concerning your Uncle Alistair.' Do you understand?"

"Yes, sir."

"And Mr. Sharpe, please understand that if anything happens to that woman, MI6 will find you. Now, please hand the phone back."

"Maggie, do not say much. Does Mr. Sharpe know your full name? Please answer in as few words as you can."

"No."

"Keep it that way. Shall I bring a medic?"

"No."

"Just listen, Maggie, and say yes if you understand. I will be there tomorrow by helicopter. I told Mr. Sharpe he is to tell no one of you. I instructed him to secure you in the warming shed for the evening. I also told him to release you to no one but me. Do you understand?"

"Yes"

"The warming shed locks from the outside. Is there a room that you know that locks from the inside?"

"I think so."

"You need to figure out how to lock yourself in a room from the inside for the night, or at least barricade yourself in. Clear?"

"Yes, sir."

"Fine. See you tomorrow, Mag. Now, please put Mr. Sharpe back on the phone."

Maggie handed the phone back to Andy. "He wants to speak to you again"

Andy took the phone.

"Now, Mr. Sharpe, please lock the warming shed up for the night. I shall see you tomorrow."

"Yes, sir." He turned to Maggie. "I'm to lock you in here for the night ma'am," he said apologetically. He looked at her quizzically, shaking his head at the strange situation that had so suddenly befallen him.

"I am aware, sir."

"Well then." And with that, he turned uncomfortably, walked out the door, and locked it.

Maggie removed her snowshoes and walked out to the main room to look around. She immediately turned out the lights.

Too many windows.

She went back into the office, examining the lock.

No deadbolt.

Anyone with a key could enter. *At least it swings in.*

She closed the door and looked around.

No windows — that's good.

It was a typical office: small, utilitarian, with an old metal desk, a couple of file cabinets, and an office chair. She turned out the light and went back out into the main room. She waited until her eyes became accustomed to the dark and looked around for something to sleep on. Most of the benches were simply wood, with no cushions. That wouldn't do. She looked around some more and noticed a first aid red cross on a metal cabinet, but when she tried to open it, she realized it was locked.

Guess it will have to be the floor. She headed back into the office, closing the door behind her.

The file cabinets were against the same wall as the door. She pushed and pulled and bumped against them one by one until they were in front of the door. She then pushed the desk up against them. Exhausted, she wrapped herself up tight in her two blankets and fell asleep.

~

Maggie had no idea how long she slept – the office was dark and quiet. She was startled by a noise in the main room.

"Ma'am?" said the voice. "Ma'am, are you all right? This is Andy Sharpe."

"You'll have to wait a moment, Mr. Sharpe. I have to move some furniture away from the door. Are you alone?"

"Yes, ma'am."

Maggie suddenly realized she had no idea whether Mr. Sharpe was alone or not.

"It took me a while to move the furniture in front of the door, Mr. Sharpe. I imagine it will take me a while to move it away. While I am working on it, do you suppose you could get me a cup of coffee and something to eat?" she called through the door.

"Yes, ma'am. I'll be back. I will lock the door."

"Thank you, Mr. Sharpe." She waited until she heard the door close, and then she quickly moved the desk and a file cabinet out if the way. She went to the window and looked out. Only one set of footprints in the snow. Andy had been alone. Now all she had to do was wait for Callum. Wait for Callum and hope that Clance and Jack had been held up by the snowstorm and were unaware that she had escaped.

Maggie watched out the window for Andy, in part to make sure he was still alone and in part because she was starving. It took Andy a good half-hour to return, but he brought a thermos of hot coffee and a bag of oat cakes. She offered some to him but was actually pleased when he declined. She couldn't remember being so hungry. She was halfway through her third oat cake before she slowed down and took a sip of coffee. All the while, Andy was eyeing her with curiosity.

"Are ye the lass that went a missin' a while ago back?" he finally asked. "The lass splashed in all the newspapers?"

"I'm not sure. I've been totally isolated for weeks. What did the papers say?"

"That a lass went a missin' doon in Fife and to be on the lookout."

"Do you remember a name?"

"Nae, I kinna remember."

"Might be, Mr. Sharpe. We'll have to wait for Mr. Fraser. I am sure he can clear up everything for you. Wish I could help more. I imagine he should be here soon."

"Aye, the storm's petered out. The copter can get through now."

An uneasy silence fell between the two.

"Am I keeping you from your work? I can stay here if you need to go."

At that moment, Andy's walkie-talkie chirped. "We're opening in one hour," squawked the voice on the other end.

"Aye, lass, I've got to get the lifts going. You'll be all right here?"

"I'm sure I will be. Perhaps it would be easier or you to simply bring Mr. Fraser here when he arrives. That will be less bother for you."

"All righty, then. Shouldn'a be much longer." He turned and left, locking the door behind him.

Maggie went back into the office, turned on the light, and shut the door. If the slopes opened before Callum arrived, she would need to stay in the office, as skiers would be using the warming room. She sat down in the chair, blankets wrapped around her, and waited. After about fifteen minutes, she suddenly realized that light would be visible under the door, so she took one of her blankets and pushed it against the bottom of the door. She then went back to the chair and sat.

She must have dozed off, because she was awakened by the opening of the outside door and the drone of several voices. She listened intently.

Skiers. The slope must be open.

She sat very quietly, glad she had thought about using the blanket to stop the light.

A few hours later, there was a knock on the office door, and Maggie heard Callum's familiar voice. "Maggie, it's me, Callum." She heard the key turning in the lock, and the door swung open to reveal Callum and Andy.

She bolted out of the chair and ran up to Callum, giving him a big hug. She then stood back and said, "Aren't you a sight for sore eyes!"

Andy stood rather uncomfortably off to the side, but Callum shortly turned to him and shook his hand. "Mr. Sharpe, on behalf of Her Majesty's service, I wish to thank you for what you have done here. This woman has been missing for weeks, and Scotland Yard had run out of leads. Thank you for keeping her safe."

Andy bowed his head a bit, face flushed red from the compliment, and muttered, "Och, it was nae much, Mr. Fraser."

Callum continued. "There will be some press about this recovery, Mr. Sharpe. At this stage in the investigation, we would like you to not offer any details to the press if they come a callin' here. We would very much like to catch the criminals that kidnapped this woman, and it would be unfortunate if we tipped our hand. Can you do that?"

"Aye, sir, that I can." He was awed at being part of a mystery.

Callum turned to Maggie. "Well then, let's get you out of here and into some proper clothes. Whatever do you have on your feet?"

"I'll tell you the entire story on the way back, Callum, but since you asked, I have sheets on my feet."

Callum looked at Maggie's bound feet, shook his head, and headed out the door. Maggie followed him out and hopped on the back of his snowmobile, wrapping her blankets tightly around her and tucking them between her torso and Callum's back, which she then leaned tightly against. It was going to be a cold ride back to the helicopter.

Callum had the helicopter land in Edinburgh, and he took Maggie straight away to the St. Leonard's police station, which caused Maggie a great deal of embarrassment.

I must look as if I just came from the poor house — two hundred years ago.

The many stares she received caused Callum to protectively grab her by the elbow and quickly shepherd her to a back office. He walked her in and shut the door.

"Stay here for a minute. I am going to fetch a detective."

Several minutes later, a pair of detectives returned with Callum, along with a young woman who might have been a cadet.

"Maggie, what size clothes and shoes do you wear?" asked Callum. "Constable Paton here will fetch you some appropriate clothing." He pointed to the young woman. "And these are Chief Inspector Purdie and Inspector Wilkie."

Maggie shook hands all around and then turned to the constable. "Size thirty-seven shoes, size six or eight for clothes. Thank you, Constable."

The Constable left as Callum said, "Maggie, please sit down." He pointed to a chair on the far side of the table. "We would like to take your statement."

Maggie sat down and let out a long sigh. "Do you suppose I could get something to eat during this? I am frightful hungry."

Inspector Wilkie nodded and left the room for several minutes. When he returned, he said, "We are having food brought in, Mrs. Tyler."

"Thank you." She then turned to Callum, words pouring out of her like an erupting Mt. Etna. "Callum, it's not an art collector after the amulet. It's some sort of religious cult. They are absolutely doo-lally!!! I mean, look at these clothes!! Right from the Middle Ages! And there I was, cooking over a fire stove and boiling water to wash dishes and tending the fire, which was the only heat, and—"

Callum interrupted her. "Maggie, please. Take a breath. We would like you to start from the beginning. Tell us what happened and when...and can you describe the person or people?"

Maggie sat back and took in a long breath. "Sure." She started recounting the kidnapping.

"What can you tell us about the woman?" asked Chief Inspector Wilkie.

"She was very plainly dressed. Maybe in her mid-forties. She could be younger, though – she wore no makeup, and that can make a body seem older. She had medium-brown hair and blue eyes. She was a bit on the slender side and maybe my height. Pretty nondescript. She told me her name was Martha, but I didn't get a last name. She said she worked in the Kingsgate Shopping Center. I doubt it now from the way she looked. She did have an odd scar on her right hand, though."

Maggie went on to describe the entire ordeal: how she had counted to figure out where she might have been taken, how she had fashioned snowshoes and bound them to her feet. She described both Clance and Jack as best she could between spoonsful of cock-a-leekie soup and a meat sandwich, trying to remember bits of conversation she had overheard. All the while, both Purdie and Wilkie took notes. They then brought in an artist to work with Maggie and sketch pictures of all three suspects. Halfway through, they were interrupted by Constable Paton, who brought with her a pair of winter boots, an overcoat, warm socks, a pair of slacks, and a thick sweater. Maggie excused herself to get dressed and returned to finish with the sketch artist.

It took several hours to complete the interview. When it was finished, Callum escorted Maggie to Dougal's house. It was well past dinner when they arrived, and the children were already in bed. Dougal, however, couldn't wait to ply Maggie with questions. And although Maggie was tired, she was very eager to tell Dougal what she had learned.

"Dougal, I don't think it was a collector. I think it was this crazy 'Third Order' group. They are pure mental! But they did say the amulet belonged to St. Francis. They found out I had it from someone in the lab, I think. No one else knew. I don't think they are going to stop trying to get their hands on it."

"We need to figure out who these people are," said Callum. "I'll get Scotland Yard trying to locate your kidnappers, Maggie. Perhaps you and Dougal can figure out just what this Third Order group is all about. And Maggie, we need to figure out how to keep you safe."

Dougal had gotten lost early on in the conversation. He finally interrupted. "Maggie, please tell me; what happened to you?

Third Order? What in the world is that? Where were you? You look thin... Are you sure you are all right?"

Maggie turned to Dougal. "I was kidnapped in the Kingsgate Shopping Center and taken up to the moors near Glenshee. I was held captive in an ancient stone cottage by a truly radge man that made me wear clothes from the Middle Ages and learn all of these bizarre rules about when to eat what foods, what to wear, and what to say when. But can I fill you in tomorrow? I have spent most of the day recounting my little adventure, and I am not wont to do it again. Maybe in the morning. I've had a very long day, and what I would really like is a long, hot shower and a warm, soft bed."

"Fair enough. Tomorrow, it is. Come with me to work tomorrow, Maggie. We can go over things in my office, and then I'll take you to Mum and Da's. They've been crazy with worry."

~

Maggie awoke and looked at her watch: 10:12. She stretched her arms upwards before sitting up and brushing her hair away from her face. She tossed the covers off and swung her feet off the edge of the bed, yawning and stretching again. It was a luxury sitting on the edge of a bed, warm. She looked down and wiggled her toes.

Even they are warm. It made her smile.

There was a robe that had been placed across the foot of the bed. She put it on and headed downstairs to the kitchen. Kate and Dougal were at the table nursing cups of coffee, both reading: him, test papers; her, the newspaper. They looked up as Maggie entered and smiled.

"Good morning, sunshine!" said Dougal as he rose. "Coffee?" He knew the answer as he headed to fetch a coffee cup.

"Ah, Dougal, you know me too well." She took a steaming cup of coffee from him.

"Here. Sit," he said as he sat back down. Kate moved over a bit to give Maggie more room.

"Good morning, Kate," said Maggie. "Thank you so much for allowing me to spend the night. I know it must be disruptive."

"Not at all. Getting the weans up and off to primary – now, that's disruptive." She laughed and got up to fetch some scones and jam. "Hungry?"

"I could stand a bite. Can I help?"

"Nae, no work to be done." Kate set a full plate down. "Eat up."

Dougal piled his papers in a neat stack and put them to the side. "Maggie, we are so glad to see you safe. You must have had some adventure."

"Nothing I'd care to repeat. I have a newfound respect for central heat, that's for sure." She got up to refill her coffee cup and returned to the table.

"What happened to you, Maggie?" asked Kate.

Maggie glanced at Dougal, who gave a nearly imperceptible nod, so she started recounting her kidnapping. She focused on the events, finessing around the parts of the story that she wanted to discuss with Dougal in his office privately. The parts that needed further investigation. Kate didn't need to know that there was more work to do or that there might be potential for additional incidents. Both Kate and Dougal were alternately captivated and horrified by the tale.

"You did well to leave when you did. Rattan baskets? Wherever did you learn to be so resourceful?"

"Let's just say that I was highly motivated," Maggie replied dryly. She arose and put her coffee cup and plate in the sink. "Let me get dressed, Dougal, and we can go to your office. I think we need to reconsider our prior assumptions." She turned to Kate before heading upstairs. "Kate, you are a saint. Thank you so much for everything."

Maggie waited until she and Dougal were in his office, behind a closed door, before she started telling him about the clues she had picked up while trapped in that ancient stone cottage.

"Dougal, there is definitely a religious angle. I did some research about the life of St. Francis, but I need to learn more about the Third Order he founded. Clance told me he was the master of formation of the Third Order. And whatever it is, it goes higher than him: there is someone else to whom Clance reports. 'His eminence,' he called him. At least, I assume it's a 'him.' He left the cottage a couple of times to speak with him.

"There is something else: Clance has a strange, square-ish scar on the back of his hand. That Martha woman had a very similar scar, also on her hand. I think that might have significance…maybe some sort of initiation-related mark. And there are more members of this cult… Clance knew about the amulet, and he knew my name.

There is someone at the testing lab that is connected, and I wouldn't be surprised if that someone sports a similar scar. Keep a keen eye, Dougal. Look out for a scar like that."

Dougal sat silent for several moments. "Thanks for the warning, Maggie." He picked up a pad of paper and a pen and, changing the subject, asked, "So you think the connection might be a Scottish crusader that crossed paths with St. Francis while he was on the way to, or coming back from, the Crusades?"

"That, or a Scottish crusader St. Francis met when he went through crusader lines to get to the court of the Sultan of Egypt."

"Well, that narrows it down quite a bit. The meeting could not have been before the Third Crusade or after the Fifth Crusade. So we are looking for a Scot crusader sometime between 1189 and 1221. That's only a thirty-two-year span." Dougal beamed. "That's progress! Now I really understand why you wanted that thesis."

"There is something else I found out. Apparently, no one knew exactly where the tomb of St. Francis was for centuries. It was finally located in the early 1800s by a team that broke through the floor of the basilica. Records indicate that along with the body, excavators found coins, a stone, beads, a ring, and a 'piece of iron.' That piece of iron has no further description. That makes sense because the Assisi locals that did the excavating would have never seen anything like it before. I think that's what we have."

Dougal looked sharply at Maggie. "Brilliant! That makes sense. It also ties in with your Third Order characters."

Maggie leaned forward. "And that's why, Dougal, I think I need to go back to Italy. I need to find out more about the Third Order. I would like to talk to Brother Ventimiglio. I know he's an ordained Franciscan, so he can't also belong to the Third Order. The Franciscans are kind of the First Order. I think I can trust him, and I certainly know he can fill in a lot of holes."

"Do me a favor, baby sister. Clear it with Callum first. Please? We don't want to lose you again."

"Fair enough. So, will you look into when this Scot crusader might have run into St. Francis between whatever years you figured out?"

"I most certainly will. Now we should see about getting you to Mum and Da's. You probably want to see your own clothes again. Come on – I'll drive you up."

Maggie grinned. "Amazing what one can take for granted."

CHAPTER TEN

Clance was furious when he and Jack returned to the cottage to find Maggie gone.

"It's your fault!" he screamed at Jack. "No shoes or coat, you said. She can't leave in a snowstorm, you said. And now look! You should have tied her up!" Clance was pacing, and he began rambling incoherently. "I might be replaced as master of formation for this! What shall I tell his eminence?" He turned and pointed his finger at Jack. "Go find her! Or find the relic!" Clance marched towards the oak door and forcefully flung it open. "Go!! Now!!" Just as suddenly, he stormed over to the fireplace, knelt down, and began to pray furiously as Jack walked out the door.

Jack was not concerned. He was never concerned.

If the money weren't so good, I'd give this job up in a minute. These religious fanatics are such a bore.

As he got into his car, he decided he needed to find out more about this relic that seemed so important to these nutcases.

Maybe it's worth something. I just might make some money off of this.

Jack headed to Edinburgh. He needed to talk to Oliver McQuiddy. For the entire hour and a half the journey took, Jack was formulating his cover story. He didn't want to alert anyone in the cult about his newfound interest in this sought-after bauble.

Jack was a classic con. He had an impressive criminal record that, long ago, had precluded him getting any honorable job. This gig had asked no questions and paid well, but it was wearing thin. Jack held no loyalties to anyone or anything beyond himself. He thought it perfectly reasonable to steal this relic and sell it if he could. He had an unshakable belief that he deserved whatever he desired. He was, after all, so brilliant, so handsome…the world owed him everything.

When Jack got to Edinburgh, he called McQuiddy's office and left a message that he would show up at ten the next day. He needed to control things, and that extended to phone calls and appointments. He didn't leave a return number.

Oliver got into the office at eight, and when he picked up the message, he was excited. He had gotten high praise from the Third Order for sounding the alarm when Dougal and Maggie had shown up. He knew that the piece they'd brought was authentic. What he didn't know was whether it was actually the "piece of iron" from the tomb of St. Francis. He thought that he was about to find out.

Jack arrived promptly and put on his most convivial face.

"Mr. McQuiddy! Good to meet you. I'm Jack. The master of formation sent me to ask you some additional questions."

Oliver eagerly offered Jack a chair across from his desk. After Jack sat down, Oliver walked around the desk and sat. "Of course! What can I do for you?"

"I am here to ask some additional questions about that piece of iron you dated. What can you tell me about it?"

"It is an ancient Pictish relic. Pictish. It is amazing in that most of the relics we have from that tribe are stone carvings. It's quite rare."

"And how did you come to call the master? What led you to think it was a holy relic?"

"The woman that brought it told me it was found in Assisi during the earthquake that toppled the roof of the basilica." He then stopped, pondering. "I guess I assumed. I have no real evidence it was from the tomb of our most sacred saint. If it really is from the tomb, I have no idea how or why it might have gotten there. It's Scottish, through and through. I was told it was found in the basilica, but proving it is a sacred relic? I am not sure how we might do that."

"It's rare, though? And verified Scottish? Perhaps it isn't from the tomb at all." Jack paused and bowed his head. "We had such high hopes, but this does present a wrinkle. I will inform the master that we have no evidence that this is truly a sacred relic." Jack raised his head and looked directly at Oliver. "But let's assume it is. If that is true, we would like to protect it. Tell me, are there private collectors that might try to acquire it? Someone well versed that would care to acquire it even if it is not sacred? People we would need to guard against?"

Oliver looked directly at Jack while he thought. "Well, besides the government, there are two renowned collectors here in the U.K. One is Lord Anthony Whittall – the other is Lady Cecily Barminster. They both have fairly extensive collections, and they are both sought after to speak at conferences and universities on ancient artifacts from these isles."

Oliver stood up and walked over to his bookcase. He pulled out a book and turned, opening it while he walked back. "Here's a book on Lord Whittall's collection," he said. Thumbing to a photo near the middle of the book, he showed Jack a picture of a Pictish carving in a very similar form as the iron piece. "See? See how similar this carving is?"

Jack took the book and studied it intently. Through all of this, he'd had no idea what the relic looked like. "It's like this, but in iron." Jack was only half-questioning. He wanted to verify what he was seeking without letting on that he had neither ever seen it or had it in his possession.

"So, I know it is Pictish," continued Oliver. He then took a deep breath. "I saw in all of the papers that the woman that was here with the iron piece was missing for several weeks. I assume it was the Third Order? And I assume you retrieved the piece from her? I heard she was found unharmed."

"Mr. McQuiddy, there are things that the master wishes not to share." Jack's tone was sharp. "As a true follower, you are bound to honor his wishes. Until we verify that this is from the tomb of our most sacred saint, please ask no more questions and do not speak with anyone about this. The master believes that the safety of the piece hangs in the balance." Jack stood up, shook Oliver's hand, and turned to leave. "Thank you for your time, Mr. McQuiddy."

As he was opening the door, Oliver said to his back, "I didn't catch your last name."

Jack didn't answer, but simply walked out and closed the door behind him.

CHAPTER ELEVEN

Maggie stepped out of the gangway in Perugia and headed to baggage claim. She grabbed her bags and made her way to the rental car she had reserved. She pulled out the Italian-English dictionary she had purchased and, using it, was able to complete the car rental transaction. She felt elated. Her solution to not speaking Italian had passed its first test.

Next challenge: get to the hotel.

She pulled out a map, studied it, and started the engine.

Destination: Hotel Ideale.

She smiled to herself. Success was sweet.

It didn't take her very long to pull into Assisi and find the hotel. She parked the car, grabbed her luggage, and walked into the lobby. Dictionary in hand, she walked up to the desk, opened the dictionary, and looked up "reservation." The desk clerk was clearly amused but very impressed that Maggie was putting forth the effort to communicate in Italian.

"Signora, I speak English," he said with a kind smile. "Thank you for speaking Italian to me. I truly appreciate the effort."

Maggie checked into her room, opened up her suitcase, and started putting things where they would be needed: toiletries in the bathroom, nightgown by the bed. She set the alarm clock on the nightstand for 7 AM, took her notebook and pen over to the work table, and sat down. She had written down a list of things she wanted to learn while she was in Assisi, and she was going to need Brother Ventimiglio's help with most, if not all, of her to-do list. She looked at her watch: it was 3 PM. She grabbed her purse and headed over to the basilica.

She had no idea where to find Brother Ventimiglio. She walked down the steps into the lower church and saw several Franciscan brothers. She walked up to one and made the mistake of speaking. She was quickly whisked out and walked upstairs by one of the brothers.

"Non parlare nella chiare inferiore, signora," he said. Maggie pulled out her dictionary and tried to translate what she had heard. The brother, seeing what she was doing, put his hand on the book and looked at her, raising his eyebrows and asking permission to take it. Maggie gave it to him, and after a few moments, the brother said, "No talk lower church."

"Scusa," said Maggie. She indicated she wanted the dictionary back. Armed with a few Italian words, she asked if the brother knew where Brother Ventimiglio might be. The friar nodded, held up his finger to indicate Maggie should wait, and left. Several minutes later, he returned with Brother Ventimiglio.

In anticipation of this meeting, Maggie had written a note in fractured Italian, and she gave it to Ventimiglio. He read it, smiled, and nodded enthusiastically. Maggie had asked if they could meet tomorrow – did he have several hours? She smiled at him and shook his hand.

"Grazie." She turned and left.

Maggie went back to the hotel, had a lovely dinner, and went back up to her room. She spent the evening writing another note in Italian: the questions she wanted answered.

(1)   *Can you tell me about the Third Order?*

(2)   *How is the friar organization related to the Third Order?*

(3)   *I read that St. Francis was a soldier. Can you tell me about that time in his life?*

(4)   *Can you tell me about the tomb of St. Francis? Was he buried with any artifacts?*

(5)   *Have you ever seen anything like this?*

Maggie drew a sketch of the amulet at the bottom of the piece of paper. She again set the alarm clock for 7 AM, took a shower, and went to bed.

~

Maggie arose before the alarm went off. She went to the window, opened both sets of shutters, and watched as the sun rose over the valley below. There was a bit of foggy mist lying in the low areas.

This looks like an Impressionist painting.

It was quiet and absolutely lovely, and so peaceful that Maggie found herself falling into a state of relaxation just gazing upon it.

She snapped back, remembering her reason for returning to Assisi. She quickly dressed and headed to the café for coffee and a roll before heading over to the basilica. Morning Mass was just letting out when she arrived. She waited for the parishioners to leave, and then she entered the main church. There were several brothers rearranging hymnals and tending to the other responsibilities of the post-Mass routine. She spotted Brother Ventimiglio and walked over to him, touching his elbow. He turned and smiled.

"Buongiorno, signora. Bella giornata, no?"

Maggie pulled out her dictionary and spent a few minutes deciphering what Brother Ventimiglio had said. She finally replied, "Buongiorno, Fratello Ventimiglio. Si, e bello."

Ventimiglio motioned for the two of them to head over to a small garden, where they sat on a bench. Maggie gave Ventimiglio the note, which made him laugh out loud. He quickly turned to her, his body language asking for the dictionary. After a moment, he said, "No laugh you, signora. Grazie try speak e write Italiano." He spent several minutes in the dictionary and then said, "I write answers. Give you tomorrow?"

Maggie grinned. "Si. Buona. Grazie." She picked up the dictionary and, looking for the words, told Ventimiglio to write it in Italian… She would translate it later. They stood up, shook hands, and parted.

Maggie found herself with several free hours on her hands. She walked around town for several hours, admiring the beauty of the city, before heading back to her hotel. To her surprise, she ran into Agent Leone in the piazza.

"Agent Leone!! What a surprise to see you here!" Maggie rushed up and gave the agent a hug.

"You too, signora!" replied Leone. "What are you doing here?"

"I came back to speak to Brother Ventimiglio again. And you?"

"Part of my territory. Have you eaten lunch? I'm hungry. Want to catch a bite to eat?"

"Sure!"

The two headed to an outdoor café Leone knew, sat down at a table, and studied the menus. After ordering, Leone looked at Maggie intently. "How have you been? I have been wondering."

"As well as can be expected, I guess. I am not quite sure of my direction yet, but I am not wallowing in despair. I haven't settled down yet, but I know I have no desire to return to New York. I'm still looking. We'll see."

Maggie and Leone chit-chatted about nothing in particular over lunch. When it was over, Leone asked if Maggie would help her get something out of her trunk. Maggie said "Sure!" and bent down to pick up her purse, which was under her chair. As she was leaning over, she noticed that the heel of Leone's shoe had slipped off of her heel and was dangling off her toes on her crossed leg. Then Maggie saw it: a rectangular scar just above Leone's toes, mid-center. It startled Maggie so much that she hit her head sitting up. Quickly gaining her composure, she rubbed her head vigorously and muttered, "I am so clumsy!" She made a concerted show of pawing through her purse.

"Darn! I must have left my dictionary in the basilica. Sorry to back out on you, Agent Leone, but I am totally lost without that dictionary. Please excuse me, but I have to go find it."

With that, Maggie quickly got up and rushed back towards the basilica. When she turned a corner some distance away, she stopped and peered around the corner to see whether she was being followed. Agent Leone was nowhere to be seen. Maggie looked around, trying to figure out how to become inconspicuous. Her hair did not help. She walked up to one of the street vendors selling memorabilia and bought a souvenir hat. She twisted her hair into a bun and tucked it into her hat. Looking around again, she noticed a tour group coming out of the basilica. She waited until it was close and quietly slipped into the group, near the back, on the side away from the piazza. She walked with them until they got to their tour bus, and then she split off and headed to her hotel.

Maggie ran up to her room and locked and bolted the door behind her. She pulled out her mobile phone and dialed Callum. Luckily, he answered.

"Callum, this is Maggie. Remember I told you about the scars I saw on the woman accomplice and Clance? I saw another one, but this time, it was on a foot. The foot of Agent Leone. Are these people everywhere?"

"How did you run into Agent Leone? Did you tell her you were returning?"

"No. I ran into her in Assisi. I didn't tell her I had come back to Italy. I think she knew I was here, and I think she came to Assisi specifically to kidnap me. She asked me to help her get something out of her trunk. After I saw her foot, I made up an excuse and got away."

"Do you think she bought your story?"

"No idea. But it wouldn't surprise me if she didn't."

Callum thought for several minutes. "She knows you as Maggie Tyler?"

"Yes."

"Your passport – did you ever get a new one with your married name?"

"No. By the time I got back to the U.K., Ben had died. I've been traveling under my British passport, under the name Margaret Fraser."

"Let's gamble that she is looking for Maggie Tyler, not Maggie Fraser. She might even assume you are a U.S. citizen. That should buy you some time, maybe. You need to get out of there, Maggie."

"I'll try and get a flight day after tomorrow, or maybe tomorrow night. I've come all this way, and I already met with Ventimiglio and asked him to answer several questions I gave him. I need just one more meeting."

"Don't be by yourself, Maggie. And I'll see you soon."

Maggie ordered up room service and ate in her room that night. The next morning, she ate in the dining room early, looking out to see whether there might be a tour group staying in the hotel. She noticed a couple wearing lanyards with some sort of tour identification, and she timed her departure to coordinate with theirs. She arrived at the basilica after morning mass and sought out Brother Ventimiglio. They walked over to the same garden and sat on the same bench. In fractured, dictionary-assisted Italian, Maggie told Ventimiglio everything. The amulet. Where it originated. The ransacking of her parents' house. Her kidnapping. The master of formation. The scars. Even Agent Leone. It took most of the morning. Brother Ventimiglio was dumbfounded. Maggie hoped she was not making a big mistake.

As Maggie was wrapping up her missive, her mobile phone rang. It was Callum.

"Scusa," she said to Brother Ventimiglio. "Mio fratello." She took the call.

"Maggie, what's going on?" asked a very concerned Callum.

"What do you mean? I've spent the entire morning at the basilica with Brother Ventimiglio."

"There's an arrest warrant out for you, issued by the Italian police."

"An arrest warrant? For what? I haven't done anything! I ate dinner in my hotel room last night and left this morning with a tour group, got here, found Brother Ventimiglio, and we have been chatting here in the garden ever since. I have done nothing!"

Maggie thought for a moment. "Damn. Do you suppose it is the work of Agent Leone?"

"Could be, but there's very little I can do from here. Do you want me to get the embassy involved?"

"I don't think so. At least, not right now. What you can do is find out my 'crime.' Let me work on getting out of Italy."

Ventimiglio could see the concern in Maggie's eyes. She grabbed the dictionary and got him to understand the situation, hoping that he would not report her whereabouts. She was shocked at his immediate response. He lowered his head and silently prayed. Very quietly, very peacefully, he simply prayed.

"Ho un idea," he finally said. "Aspettare qui." Maggie grabbed her dictionary while Ventimiglio left.

*Idea…wait…here…*Maggie understood.

Ventimiglio soon returned with a nun. She was quite diminutive, perhaps in her late fifties, with a very kind face. She motioned for Maggie to follow her. Ventimiglio nodded, encouraging Maggie. The three of them headed to the back of the basilica, through a nondescript door, and into a small, sparse room. There, the sister brought out a nun's habit and motioned for Maggie to put it on.

Maggie had no issue with the tunic, but she had a problem with the coif – her long hair. She looked at the sister, grabbing her hair with one hand and making a scissors movement with the fingers of the other. The nun left, returning with a pair of scissors. Maggie unceremoniously cut off her hair and donned the coif and wimple. The nun adjusted Maggie's habit, stood back, and nodded approvingly.

Maggie held up her index finger, indicating for Ventimiglio and the nun to wait. She pulled out her mobile phone and called Callum.

"Can you get me a box of black hair dye and a pair of brown contacts? Have them delivered to Brother Ventimiglio – and please, make everything very nondescript."

"I'll have it there tomorrow morning."

Maggie pulled out her dictionary, studying frantically. "Pacchetto…domani…per me…da…mio fratello." *Package tomorrow for me from my brother.* Ventimiglio nodded his understanding.

The sister motioned for Maggie to follow her and led her to one of the rooms for cloistered sisters.

The silence of the order is a very good thing.

Maggie entered the room. "Grazie, Sorella," she said to the nun. The nun bowed slightly, turned, and left. Maggie saw the wisdom of staying sheltered in the basilica for the evening. Having no desire to leave, she took off her habit and pulled out the notes Brother Ventimiglio had given her. She started translating and stopped only when daylight faded. Then she crawled into bed and fell asleep.

It was still dark when she heard quiet murmurs outside her door – the sisters heading towards matins, she supposed. She lay silently until she heard no more rustling, and then she got up. She put on her habit, hoping that without a mirror or the ministrations of the helpful sister, she had it right. She knew she couldn't leave the room until after matins, so she waited until she heard sisters returning. She quietly opened her door and waited, head bent, until the last sister had passed and followed the others into the dining room for breakfast.

Silence is wonderful.

Maggie unobtrusively but carefully studied the movements of the sisters and followed suit. Breakfast over, she was wondering what was next when the kindly sister summoned by Brother Ventimiglio motioned for her to follow.

The sister took Maggie into the vegetable garden, where several sisters were tending to the plants. The sister motioned Maggie to join in and pointed to the green beans. Maggie knelt and began weeding around the beans. Head bent, she didn't even notice the two policemen who were looking around. Apparently, the two were convinced that these studiously weeding sisters were not suspicious, and they turned and left without further incident. Maggie never even realized they were there.

The sisters broke for prayer before lunch. The elder sister sought Maggie out and motioned for her to follow. The two went to the quiet garden, where Brother Ventimiglio was waiting with a small, brown-wrapped package. He handed it to Maggie.

"Grazie," she said.

He also handed her a note, handwritten in Italian. "Traduci."

Maggie took the package and the note and nodded in understanding – *translate*. She turned to the silent sister and gestured that she was going to go back to her room. She then stopped and, using her hands to pretend to wash her hair, she looked questioningly at the sister. The sister nodded and led Maggie to a washroom with a large utility sink. Maggie locked the door, took off her entire habit, and proceeded to dye her hair and eyebrows. Without a mirror, she had to rely solely on touch. She worked that dye thoroughly, hoping she covered everything, hoping the skin around her hairline wasn't telltale black…hoping that her eyebrows did not look grotesque.

Her hair was still wet when she put her habit back on and returned to her room. She quickly removed it and was extremely pleased that she had rinsed the dye out so well that her wimple was still white. Wet but white. She finger-combed her hair, scrubbed her face over her eyes vigorously, and let everything air dry as she sat down to translate the new note.

Signora Tyler, if you were taken by individuals claiming to be from the Third Order, please know that is not an officially recognized order by the Vatican. I have a concern that you told me that the men that held you left to speak to someone in a higher position, someone you referred to as "his eminence," which causes me some concern. I will try and learn more, but I must tread lightly, especially if the "eminence" refers to someone within the Vatican hierarchy.

I was interested in the scars you mentioned. St. Francis was the first person recorded as having stigmata. I assume that the scars you have noticed are in reference to that. Perhaps this Third Order has a practice of inflicting stigmata-referencing scars? That may help identify those that wish you harm.

The note went on, and as Maggie slowly translated the words, she became more and more excited – Brother Ventimiglio was going to get her out of Italy, him and the silent sister with no name. Maggie needed to call Callum. There were two problems, though: first, she had no signal; second, she couldn't risk speaking.

~

The next day, the sister with no name slipped Maggie a note after breakfast. Maggie needed to return to her room to translate it. She slipped out after matins and went directly to her room, sitting on the edge of her bed, translating. The note said Maggie was to meet Brother Ventimiglio in the quiet garden at 2 PM. Maggie tucked the note into the dictionary and checked her watch. She had over four hours to wait. She put in the brown contact lens and quietly opened the door and checked the hall – it was empty. She slipped out and headed for the vegetable garden, unobtrusively picking the closest corner to start working. She doubted anyone even realized she had come late, being that the sisters were very diligently working with heads down, concentrating on their tasks.

After a couple of hours, everyone headed to the dining room for lunch and then devotionals. Maggie sat in the back, surreptitiously checking her watch for the time. Devotionals ended at 1:55, giving her five minutes to get to the quiet garden. She was met by Brother Ventimiglio and the silent sister.

Maggie wanted to address the sister by her name, so she had memorized a phrase: "Qual è il suo nome?" which she asked Ventimiglio.

He smiled and replied, "Sorella Cecilia." Maggie turned to Sister Cecilia and grabbed her hand in both of hers. "Grazie, Sorella, mille grazie."

Sister Cecilia smiled at Maggie and, lowering her head a bit, shrugged in self-consciousness.

Brother Ventimiglio motioned for Maggie and Sister Cecilia to follow him. He headed out the back of the basilica grounds to a black Alfa Romeo with clergy signage that was parked not far away. The three got in, and Ventimiglio started driving west, to the coast. Three hours later, they pulled into the beautiful little Tuscan town of San Vincenzo. Ventimiglio drove to the marina and parked the car. The three got out and, Ventimiglio in the lead, headed into the marina and down a quay to a waiting boat. The captain smiled at the three and, with arms extended, said "Benvenuto!" Maggie and Sister Cecilia climbed on board first, followed by Brother Ventimiglio and the captain. Maggie, unable to translate without causing suspicion, decided to simply follow and hope for the best in silence. A short time later, they landed in Arcipelago Tuscano and disembarked. The national park was a well-known destination, and apparently, it was very easy to visit without suspicion.

Once the three were alone, Maggie checked her mobile. Still no signal. She then pulled out her dictionary and, after consulting it, said in Italian, "Where go now?"

Ventimiglio simply answered, "Corsica." It was getting late, and the three headed to the church of San Gaetano in Marina de Campo, where the local priest put the three up in the rectory for the night.

In the quiet of her room, Maggie again tried to contact Callum.

Now or never.

She hoped that being in the middle of town would help. She was overjoyed when she saw three bars. It was not the best, but at least she could try. She dialed Callum's number and hoped that the call not only went through, but that Callum would answer.

"Callum? It's Maggie. The signal is not terribly strong here – hopefully, you can hear me."

"Maggie!" Where are you?"

"I am on an island in the Mediterranean, spending the night in a rectory. We are on our way to Corsica. Brother Ventimiglio and Sister Cecilia are getting me out of Italy by boat. We stopped here under the pretense of taking in the national park. Brother Ventimiglio has planned this entire trip, but it's nearly impossible to communicate with him because I need a dictionary, and that would obviously raise suspicion. I am dressed as a nun, I've cut my hair and dyed it black, and I am wearing brown contact lenses. If I can disembark in Corsica, can you get me out of France?"

"You don't know where in Corsica?"

"No, I don't. When I get there, I might be able to call you and tell you. I would imagine Brother Ventimiglio will have us take refuge in a church. I obviously don't have any papers I can use. I am going to need some help."

"Let me see what I can do. Keep your phone charged."

Maggie plugged in her phone, took off her habit, and fell asleep.

Brother Ventimiglio knocked on Maggie's door at daybreak. She quickly dressed and walked out, following Ventimiglio and Sister Cecilia to morning prayers. Afterward, the three headed to the marina, where, once again, a captain of a small commercial fishing boat was waiting.

"Bonjour, monsieur!" said Brother Ventimiglio. "Merci de nous avoir ramènes à Bastia!"

Maggie tried very hard to hide her surprise: Brother Ventimiglio spoke beautiful French. She'd never known. Maggie had watched Sister Cecilia in her silence and followed suit. The two nodded to the captain and boarded the boat. Her biggest concern now was disembarking without papers. That and how to tell Callum she was headed to Bastia.

The drone of the engine hid the fact that Maggie could not speak to anyone and be heard, and she was grateful. When they pulled into Bastia, the fishing boat moored at a buoy, amidst other commercial fishing boats. The four took a dinghy to a marina quay landing, where the captain dropped them off. "La douane est là-bas," said the captain as he turned to leave, indicating that the three should head over to the customs building on shore.

"Merci beaucoup," said Ventimiglio as he paid the man. The captain waved them off, and the three headed down the quay towards shore.

What now?"

Maggie had no idea how they were going to finesse customs, and she was nervous. She had no idea whether Italy had contacted Interpol to alert them, and she wasn't sure at all how she could pull off getting into France. Then she saw them…a dozen or so clerics heading towards the docks, each with a thurible to bless the ships. They walked in concert, half blessing ships on the right and half on the left. Everybody stopped to watch the spectacle. When they got to Maggie, Ventimiglio, and Cecilia, they parted enough to form a circle around Maggie and Cecilia and gave Brother Ventimiglio a thurible. The group thus blessed the remaining fleet and left the marina en masse, Maggie and Cecilia protected within a circle of priests.

The group piled into a waiting van and headed across the island to St. Dominic Convent of Corbana, hidden high on a hill overlooking idyllic countryside.

Excellent place to hide. But how can I tell Callum where I am?

Maggie settled in her room and pulled out her dictionary. She painstakingly wrote a note to Brother Ventimiglio, hoping he could get a message to Callum on her behalf: *Ti prego, di' a mio fratello dove sono – Please tell my brother where I am.* She wrote down Callum's phone number and waited to see Brother Ventimiglio again. That happened sooner than expected, as the call to vespers happened almost immediately.

After the service, Maggie slipped Ventimiglio her note and was surprised that he had one for her. She went back to her room to translate.

My sister Signora Tyler, Sister Cecelia and I will be leaving to return to Assisi in the morning. We pray that you will remain safely here and sincerely desire that you find your way back home. Please know that I will attempt to alert the Holy See of the organization that took you, and know that the church, and definitely the friars, condemn such behavior. Please ask for Sister Marie-Claude Pasqua if you require assistance, as she is my contact here. I pray that you and I might meet again in the future, and I pray that you and I together can return the amulet of St. Francis to its intended resting place. May God bless you and keep you. In Christ, Brother Ventimiglio.

Maggie folded the note, placed it into her dictionary, and went to bed. She needed to find Sister Marie-Claude.

~

Maggie didn't have to find Sister Marie-Claude. Sister Marie-Claude found her at matins the next morning. The sister sat next to Maggie and slipped her a note before prayers started. Maggie quietly slipped the note under her cincture, waiting until she returned to her room to translate. Upon opening it, however, she was dismayed to find the note written in French, and she did not have a French-English dictionary.

I hope this is just an introduction. I wonder whether the sister speaks Italian.

Maggie wrote a short note back: *Parli Italiano?* She folded the note, placed it next to her bed, and pulled out her dictionary and Brother Ventimiglio's long missive that answered the questions Maggie had first given him. While it had only been a few days since that day in the garden, it seemed like an eternity ago.

It took several days for Maggie to fully translate Ventimiglio's answers.

Signora, the Third Order is a lay order founded by St. Francis in 1221. It is no longer called the Third Order: the name was changed by the Pope in 1978 to the Secular Franciscan Order, when the Pope also changed and made the order's Rule of Life less austere.

St. Francis founded three orders, the Friars Minor, the Sisters of St. Clare, and the Third Order. The Friars Minor are not organizationally related to either the Sisters of St. Clare or the Secular Franciscan Order.

Yes, before his awakening, Francesco Bernardone was a soldier…and before that, a vain, fashion-conscious man about town, reveling in drinking and gambling with his friends. When he became a soldier, he was promptly captured by the Germans during strife with Perugia. He was held captive for over a year before his father managed to raise the required ransom to free him. However, the ransom was not happily paid, and St. Francis and his father had a great falling out, especially when St. Francis later gave a pauper his vestments in sympathy. St. Francis left his home, donned rags, and begged, preaching and beseeching followers to forego worldly pleasures and wealth, and preaching peace. He even traveled to Egypt and was given permission to preach at the sultan's court.

The tomb of St. Francis was lost for centuries. People believed it was in the basilica, but they didn't know where. It wasn't until the 1800s that it was found underneath the floor of the main sanctuary. Yes, St. Francis was buried with artifacts, and to this day, the meaning of those artifacts remains a mystery. St. Francis was buried with 12 silver coins, 29 beads, a ring, a stone, and a piece of iron. When the tomb was discovered, it was restored, made into a place of worship, and the artifacts were re-buried with the Saint's remains. There are no pictures or detailed descriptions of those artifacts beyond what I have told you.

Finally, I have never seen anything like the picture you drew. You said it was found among your late husband's belongings. It is an odd piece of iron... I wonder whether it is the piece of iron that was buried with the Saint. Your late husband did fall through the floor after the roof caved in, and perhaps the area that held those buried artifacts was disturbed. I will attempt to research the writings of St. Francis held in the Vatican's catacombs to see if I can learn anything more. Peace be with you.

After finishing, Maggie pulled out the last written note from Ventimiglio.

I found out something else. The amulet belonged to St. Francis!

Maggie wished that the timing had been different: that she would have had time to translate earlier; that plans had not been so terribly disrupted by the unfortunate meeting with Agent Leone; that she was somewhere else than sitting in a remote contemplative convent in the hills of Corsica with no contact with the outside world except through Sister Marie-Claude, who didn't speak or understand English and with whom she could only, and maybe, communicate via clandestine notes. She most fervently hoped that Brother Ventimiglio had contacted Callum.

~

Maggie was tiring of the monastic routine: only being able to use her voice in prayers, again toiling in the garden. She had been unable to communicate with Sister Marie-Claude due to an insurmountable language barrier. A good week had passed with no word from the outside world, and she was starting to think she might have to risk arrest by leaving the convent and venturing out on her own. The hair dye would not last forever. Just as she was developing an escape plan, though, one morning at dawn, she was directed to join the other nuns and pile into the convent van. The sisters had baskets and bags – it looked to Maggie that they were going shopping.

Probably for foods they don't grow here.

Sister Marie-Claude sat next to Maggie and gave her a covered basket.

The van headed to the coast and stopped in Algajola, near the open-air market. The nuns clambered out of the van and made their way to the vendor stalls. Sister Marie-Claude, however, held Maggie back and motioned for her to inconspicuously look into the basket. Inside were street clothes and a note with an address, a name, and a time. Sister Marie-Claude gave Maggie a blessing and shooed her away from the market, towards a quiet residential street. The sister then quickly turned to join the other shopping sisters. Maggie quickly headed away from the market and ducked into a perpendicular street.

How am I going to change? In the middle of the street?

It seemed ridiculous. Looking around, it seemed that the only place that might have a quiet nook was in the ancient fortress overlooking the coast. The tower was quite visible over the rooftops, and she headed towards it. It was still quite early, and the fortress was empty. Maggie found a darkened, arched nook sunken into the stone wall overlooking the beach, ducked in, and changed into khakis, sneakers, a cotton shirt, sunglasses, and a floppy hat. It felt wonderful. She wondered whether she should keep the habit: she might need to change back into it, but conversely, if discovered, it might not only create suspicion but link the convent to her escape. She walked back to the market – Sister Marie-Claude needed to take the habit back with her. Maggie left the basket by the empty convent van, hoping that Sister Marie-Claude would recognize it and take it back with her.

Maggie re-read the note that was enclosed: *"U Castellu, Chemin de Ronde, 2 PM, Alex Caldwell."* She glanced at her watch: she had four hours to find "U Castellu," whatever that was. She was more intrigued by "Alex Caldwell."

Wasn't that the man from the embassy in Milano? Common name, but will it be him? If it is, at least I will be able to recognize him.

She stuffed the note into her pocket.

She wandered the market. It was getting to be late morning, and she noticed tourists heading towards the beach.

This must be a resort town. Good for me.

She walked up to a vendor selling beach towels and sunglasses and, pulling out the note, pointed to the address written on it. The woman manning the stall pointed west. Maggie said, "Grazie," and headed away from the rising sun. She had to ask several other people along the way, but finally, she found the sign: "U Castellu." It was a restaurant. Maggie had no money, so she walked slowly around, playing tourist, until just before two. As she was heading back to the restaurant, she saw Alex Caldwell waiting at the entrance.

"Mr. Caldwell! So good to see you again." Maggie shook his hand.

"Good to see you, too, Mrs. Tyler." He extended his arm towards the door, palm up. "After you!"

After the two were seated, Alex asked, "Are you hungry? I am. I haven't yet eaten lunch."

Maggie grinned – the first time she had grinned in a long time. "Starving." She lowered her voice. "I am glad you recognized me."

"To tell you the truth, I wouldn't have. Good thing I had a description of your clothes. And the hat – that was the tell. Thanks for remembering to wear it."

Maggie had so many questions for Alex, but he shushed her. "Not here, Mrs. Tyler. Too many potential ears." The questions gnawed at Maggie, but she tamed her impatience and ate lunch. Soon after they finished, the two left and headed towards Alex's waiting car. In the privacy of the car, Alex handed Maggie a somewhat worn U.S. passport, already with several travel stamps and in the name of Margaret Stuart, a wallet with a matching New York driver's license, several credit cards, and both French and U.S. currency. He also handed her a return ticket to New York. "If they ask, the record shows you came to France on holiday two weeks ago. You landed in Marseilles on the fifteenth." Maggie looked at the documents and marveled at the picture of her – with black hair and brown eyes.

"I don't even want to ask how you did all of this, but thank you. I am just so grateful."

"My pleasure, Mrs. Tyler. I will take you to the airport. Your baggage is already checked." He gave Maggie two luggage claim tickets. "Your flight leaves in three hours." With that, Alex started the car and headed to the Calvi airport.

When Alex pulled up to departures, he reached into the back seat and gave Maggie a shopping bag. "Here are the souvenirs you bought. You need to declare the necklace. You bought it in Nice. The receipt is enclosed." He gave it to her and smiled. "I hope you like it." She climbed out of the car and reached back in to squeeze his hand. "I am deeply in your debt, Mr. Caldwell."

"Don't thank me, Maggie. Thank Callum."

Maggie shut the car door, and Alex drove off, leaving her to wonder in amazement about the intricate web Callum had obviously developed and maintained and kept silent about, only to use when required…an intricate web that lay silently under normal life, known to only a few.

Just like the Third Order.

She wondered how many other such networks existed.

Probably thousands. What else don't I know?

CHAPTER TWELVE

Maggie landed in JFK and cleared customs with no issues. She picked up her bags and hailed a cab back to her apartment. It was easier walking through the apartment door this time, easier taking a shower, easier falling asleep in the bed she and Ben had once shared. Easier but not easy. Maggie felt the melancholy she had felt the last time she was in New York, but it wasn't quite as suffocating. She fell into a long and deep sleep, feeling safe for the first time in weeks.

It was past ten when she awoke. She looked around, momentarily confused, before she remembered where she was. She threw off the covers, sat up, and threw her legs over the side of the bed and stretched. She rather groggily stumbled into the bathroom and looked in the mirror. She was startled at the reflection staring back: she hadn't seen herself with short, ragged-cut black hair, and it took her quite aback.

First stop – hairdresser.

She climbed into the shower. However, after taking a hair blower and brush to her hair and putting on makeup, she thought she didn't look half bad.

Gray eyes and black hair. She analyzed herself in the mirror again.

Rather startling.

She rummaged through her closet, a sense of comforting familiarity settling over her. She grabbed one of her favorite weekend outfits – loafers, khakis, a white T, and a jean jacket – and headed out to her favorite coffee shop. She grabbed a table near the window and, sipping her grande latte, picked up a copy of the New York Times someone had left. Coffee finished and paper read, she glanced at her watch: it was nearly noon. She headed back to her apartment, locked the door behind her, kicked her shoes under the entry table as she always did, and headed to the phone. She called Callum but got his answering machine instead.

"Callum? This is Maggie. I made it back to New York – but something tells me you already knew that. I'm in the apartment – you probably already know that, too. Anyway, call me when you get a minute. I need to touch base so you can catch me up on events. I'd like to come back to Scotland and go to the Isle of Bute, but I would like to know the coast is clear. Love you, Callum."

She placed the phone back into its cradle and turned on the TV. She flipped through the channels and, finding nothing of interest, turned it back off. She went to the living room window and looked out. It had turned out to be a lovely afternoon. Maggie went to her closet, pulled out some running clothes, and took off to Central Park. As she ran, she cataloged what she needed and wanted to do: she needed to get out of the Third Order's line of fire; she wanted to understand how St. Francis was in possession of a Scottish artifact; she needed to figure out what to do with the amulet. And here, she was torn. The relic had such important Scottish historical and Italian religious meaning – both Scotland and the church had legitimate claims to it. She wanted to honor both but had no answer as to exactly how to pull that off.

These thoughts carried her through her entire run, and as she was headed back to the apartment, she ducked into a deli for a Reuben to go. She took it back to the apartment, and as she was sitting at the counter eating it, the phone rang. It was Callum.

"So, lass, you are safely in New York." It wasn't a question; it was a statement. "I take it you are well?"

"Aye, well rested and full. I want to thank you for getting me out of Corsica. I must admit I was terribly impressed. Remind me never to get on your bad side."

Callum laughed. "Mind ye, lass," he said with a chuckle. "It took all of this to get ye ta finally mind me."

"Callum, do you know whatever happened to that Italian arrest warrant? One of these days, I need to go back and thank Brother Ventimiglio and Sister Cecilia."

"The arrest warrant has been rescinded, and if you do ever return, I would not worry about Agent Leone. Apparently, she was caught in a compromising position and has been forced out of the police force. It was quite the scandal, and she has left Umbria."

"And I am sure you had nothing to do with that." Maggie's sarcasm was palpable.

"Of course not." Callum matched her sarcastic tone perfectly.

"Do you suppose I can return home? Have you made any progress on those people that kidnapped me?"

"We believe we know who they are. However, there was not enough evidence at the cottage to properly charge them. We have them under surveillance, but they are not in custody. If you don't mind being bait, you might help us apprehend them."

Callum's suggestion caught Maggie off guard. "Are you trying to get back at me for something?" she said teasingly as she bought some time to think through the suggestion. "No – don't answer that." They both chuckled. Maggie thought things through. "I trust you, Callum. If you think that is a good idea, I am game. Just make sure I don't end up in a trunk again."

"May I ask you to fly into Heathrow? We would like to go over the plan with you before you go up to Scotland."

"Sure. Let me get a ticket. I'll let you know when."

"Let me handle that. And Maggie, you will be traveling under the name Stuart. I will call you with the travel arrangements." And as an afterthought, Callum added, "And please leave your hair black for now. And your eyes brown."

Maggie ended the call and hung up the phone, wondering exactly what Callum had in mind. She then picked up the phone and dialed Dougal. Kate answered.

"Hello, Kate!" said Maggie. "Good to hear your voice! How are you?"

"Hello, Maggie! You have been quite the gypsy lately! Are you ready to come home?"

Maggie wondered whether Callum had said anything about her adventures. Assuming not, Maggie answered, "Well, Italy is gorgeous, and I decided to spend more time there. I will be coming back home maybe in the next week or two. I will definitely let you know. I came back to New York for a bit to make sure nothing has gone amiss. How are the weans?"

"They are braw. Rascals, the lot." Kate and Maggie both laughed at that.

"Say, is Dougal around?" asked Maggie.

"I'll put him on. Good talking to you, Maggie. Hope to see you soon."

"You, too, and thanks."

After a few moments, Dougal took the line.

"So, lass, what have ye been up to?"

"Just the usual. But I have some news: Brother Ventimiglio confirmed that the amulet was buried with St. Francis."

"Really? That is fantastic! Did he have any idea how it came to be in St. Francis's possession?"

"Unfortunately, no. At least, by the time I left, he didn't have a chance to tell me. One of these days, I need to go back and both thank him for his help and ask him more questions. Have you found out anything more?"

"Not much. But then, I haven't gone myself to Bute. And the research papers my students did have not been much help. I have been very schooled in the rise and fall of the Picts, but nothing has surfaced to link them to the Crusades."

"I trust you haven't had any issues?" Maggie was half afraid of the answer.

"No. Nothing. Nothing at all."

"That's a relief. Have you spoken to Callum? Have they made any progress on tracking down who tore apart Mum and Da's house?"

"No, I haven't. But I don't think they've caught anyone yet. Mum and Da would have said something, I'm sure. When are you coming back?"

"Probably in a week or two. There are some things I need to take care of here in New York first. I will let you know, though, when I fly into Edinburgh. Maybe you and I can go to Bute together."

"All right, then. I look forward to it. Keep ye safe, lass. See you soon!"

Maggie pushed the button on the phone, waited for a dial tone, and dialed a third number. "Hello? I would like to make an appointment for a haircut."

~

Callum had Maggie fly into Heathrow three days later, and after meeting her by the luggage carousel, he drove her to his office. She had never been there before, and she was both curious and a bit apprehensive.

"Callum, I've been very good about not asking you about your job, but why am I here? What is going on?"

"Come on in, Maggie." He ushered her into his office and closed the door. "I brought you here for this." He pointed to a bit of pliable, flesh-colored plastic attached to a clear piece of hard plastic. "I want you to wear this on your hand." He reached over and picked it up. He picked up a small vial next to it as he spoke. "This, my dear, is your scar. Let me glue it on. Hold out your left hand."

Callum took Maggie's hand and swabbed the back of it with alcohol. He then opened the vial, pulled the pliable plastic off of its backing, and applied some adhesive to its back, pressing it firmly onto the back of Maggie's hand, between and about a half-inch above her index finger and middle finger knuckles. "This should give you some protection from any Third Order people you might run into and also might allow you to glean some information. This adhesive will last for two weeks before it sloughs off. Between the black hair –

nice cut, by the way – and the scar, I doubt anyone will mistake you for Maggie Fraser Tyler."

"What do you want me to do? I thought you said I was bait."

"You just go about your business. Let Scotland Yard lead the kidnappers into temptation."

"Dougal and I are considering going to Bute. What say you?"

"That should be fine. Just let me know where you are."

Maggie looked intently at Callum and hesitated. "Callum, I must admit I was impressed with what you arranged in Corsica. Impressed and intimidated. There is a lot I don't know, isn't there?"

"Probably more than you would want to know." Callum turned somber. "It's a different world for me, Maggie. You just got a little glimpse. Now you know why I will never marry. Too much of my world is dark. Dark and more dangerous than my family should ever experience."

Maggie walked over and gave Callum a hug. "You have sacrificed a lot for your job, Callum. I am both proud of and sad for you."

Callum began to look extremely uncomfortable. He was not used to feeling vulnerable, and what Maggie had said had put him squarely there. He turned to put the adhesive back on his desk and headed over to the door.

"I've arranged a room for you at the Rembrandt, and you have a ticket to Edinburgh day after tomorrow. I thought you might want to spend tomorrow in Harrods."

"You think of everything." Maggie smiled broadly.

"I try." Callum smiled and ushered her to his car.

~

Maggie went shopping. She hadn't been shopping for clothes since before the wedding, and it lightened her spirits. She bought several lovely things and treated herself to a proper afternoon tea in the food hall. It just felt so very normal. Lovely and normal. Normal, that is, until her waitress came over with the bill and made a subtle but unmistakable nod while using her left, scarred hand to place the bill on the table. Maggie gave a very slight nod back and quickly moved her left hand to her lap. Her reverie shattered, she quickly left and returned to her hotel.

She caught her late-morning flight to Edinburgh the next day and caught a cab to the university. She walked over to Dougal's office and knocked on the door, but there was no answer.

He must be lecturing.

She left and went to the library for a few hours. When she returned to Dougal's office, the door was open. She knocked on the jamb. "May I come in?"

"Maggie? Is that you? What in the world have you done with your hair? And your eyes! Why are they brown?" Dougal rushed from behind his desk. "I thought you said you would call and tell me your flight plans!" He paused, gave her a big hug, held her back by her shoulders, and said, "So good to see you!"

Maggie laughed. "Good to see you too, Dougal." She closed the door behind her. "Is it safe to speak freely in here?"

"Of course." He peered at her with great curiosity before saying, "I sense a tale coming on."

Maggie spent the next hour telling Dougal what happened in Italy. He listened in near disbelief, occasionally interrupting her tale with an expletive or exclamation. At the end, she pulled out her passport and, handing it to him, said, "And that's why I am, for now, Maggie Stuart, U.S. citizen."

"Unbelievable," he said finally as he read her passport. "What now?"

"Well, I thought you and I should head on over to Bute."

~

"Maggie, I just can't get used to your brown eyes." Dougal put Maggie's bags in the cab taking them to the train station.

She grinned. "Have to match my driver license now, don't I? All part of getting out of Italy – looking somewhat Italian. Tell you the truth, I want my red hair and gray eyes back again. But Callum told me I should stay Maggie Stuart until Scotland Yard apprehends the dobbers that snatched me, so black-haired, brown-eyed Maggie Stuart, it is."

Dougal and Maggie boarded the train for Bute and took the ferry to the island. Dougal brought his research notes; Maggie brought her translations of the letters from Brother Ventimiglio and a sketch of the amulet. The two headed straight for the Bute Museum.

The museum was devoid of visitors at opening. The two headed over to the welcome desk, behind which sat a kindly, plump woman with egret-white hair.

"Welcome to the museum," she said as she smiled. "Tickets are four pounds sterling."

Dougal pulled out his wallet and bought two, and tickets in hand, he asked, "We are interested in early Rothesay history; is there perhaps a historian available with whom we can speak?"

"Aye, certainly. You'd be wantin' to speak wi' Bruce MacAlister. I'll ring him up."

Several minutes later, an elderly but spry man came up to the desk. He was immaculately dressed in dark tartan slacks, a pressed shirt, and a green Harris tweed jacket. He extended his hand with a warm smile as he announced, "Hello. I'm Bruce MacAlister. How can I help you?"

Dougal shook his hand. "Mr. MacAlister, I am Dr. Fraser, history professor at the University of Edinburgh. And this is—"

At this point, Maggie suddenly interrupted, not wanting Dougal to innocently blow her cover. "Maggie Stuart. I am here from New York, and I asked Dr. Fraser to assist me in some research. How do you do?" She extended her hand to shake MacAlister's, glancing at his hands before looking directly into his eyes. She noticed no scars.

Bruce MacAlister's eyes lit up. "You are looking for your roots, are you? Couldn'a be too far gone, I hear a strong brogue, lass."

Maggie smiled. "I moved across the pond about three years ago, so no, not too far gone."

Dougal interrupted, "Mr. MacAlister, is there an office room with a table? I would like to show you my research."

"Follow me." MacAlister headed to a staircase to the left of the front desk and up the stairs to a cozy room with a table and six chairs. "I am keenly interested in what you have!"

The three settled around the table, and Dougal started the conversation. "We are interested in the very early history of St. Blane's and any involvement of local residents in the Crusades – the early Crusades."

Maggie added, "Anyone that might have been involved prior to 1226."

MacAlister looked at the two quizzically. "I thought you were here for Stuart genealogy and the building of Rothesay."

Maggie glanced at Dougal. "I was in Italy and spoke to a priest that said something like this is buried with St. Francis." She pulled out the sketch and laid it on the table. "And it looks Scottish to me, so I came to Dr. Fraser, and he told me it looked very Pictish. He suggested we come here."

Dougal interjected, "My research indicates that the most likely link to this artifact and the timing – St. Francis died in 1226 – would be a Scot that participated in the Third, Fourth, or Fifth Crusade. Someone that either traveled through Italy to get to the Holy Land or someone St. Francis met when he went to Egypt to meet with the sultan during the Fifth Crusade. That or a cleric that traveled between Bute and Assisi. I am leaning towards the Crusades connection, though."

Bruce looked at Dougal quietly, obviously running facts through his head. "Wait a minute." He got up and left the room, returning shortly with a couple of well-worn books.

MacAlister looked directly at Maggie. "There is one of your ancestors that did participate in the Third Crusade with Richard the Lionheart. Alan Fitz Walter. This was even before the family assumed the surname Stuart. He returned safely from the Holy Land and was a staunch patron of the Knights Templar." Bruce stopped and read for several minutes. "He returned to Scotland in 1191. He seems to be the only person from Bute that fits what you mentioned – at least, the only one for whom we have a record. Now, the only question would be, if it was Fitz Walter, how did he come by a Pictish carving?" Bruce stopped and, picking up the second book, started reading again.

Maggie looked quickly at Dougal, and his return glance told her that neither of them should correct Bruce's assumption that the sketch was of a stone carving.

After several minutes of reading, Bruce continued. "The only connection I can find would be involving Kingarth. Kingarth was founded by St. Blane, and St. Blane was a missionary and confessor to the Picts." Bruce stopped again and switched tomes.

"Fitz Walter was well acquainted with Kingarth, as records show he attempted to have it placed under the authority of Paisley Abbey."

Bruce stopped, closed the book, and looked up at Dougal and Maggie. He smiled. "History is a big puzzle. A big puzzle with missing pieces. It is very possible that somewhere along the way, Fitz Walter came into possession of that carving, and it is possible that somewhere along the way, he ran into St. Francis. Or someone who knew St. Francis. Unfortunately, I have no further information."

He stood up, picked up the books, and started to turn around. He stopped halfway and turned back to Maggie and Dougal. "You know what… You might want to go over to the Royal Stuart Society and ask whether they have any more information. What we have here mostly relates to the castle… The sennachie at the society might have more information on the man himself."

Bruce smiled at Maggie. "You come from a long and distinguished line, my dear. Even though they originally were imported from Breton."

Dougal reached across to shake Bruce's hand. "You have been most helpful, Mr. MacAlister." He pulled a business card out of his pocket. "Please feel free to contact me any time at the university's history department. It has been a pleasure."

Maggie smiled and bowed her head just a bit. "Thank you, Mr. MacAlister, for taking the time to help us out. This has been most interesting."

"Any time. And good luck to ye!"

Dougal and Maggie headed back to catch the last ferry of the day. "Alan Fitz Walter," she said. "So, really, we're not even Stuarts? We are Fitz Walters?"

Dougal laughed. "Apparently, on that side, we're not even Scottish."

"And what in the world is a sennachie?"

"I think we're going to be finding out."

The two clambered aboard the ferry.

The Royal Stuart Society had headquarters in Norfolk. Dougal and Maggie decided to drive, as there is no easy way to get to Walsingham from Edinburgh using public transportation. That gave them over six hours together, which they filled alternately with small talk and silence. Maggie stared at the glued-on silicone scar on her hand, wondering just how long it would last. She pulled down the visor and checked to see whether her red roots were starting to show.

Maybe I'll channel Sinead O'Connor and just shave it all off when the time comes.

Finished inspecting herself, she flipped the visor back up rather sharply, growing impatient with being Maggie Stuart. The last thing she wanted to do was have to dye her hair black again.

Dougal, noticing Maggie's impatience, guessed at her frustration. "It's not that bad, lass. It quite shows off your lovely complexion."

Maggie harrumphed. "I just want to be me again. No word from Callum or Scotland Yard. Seems like forever."

I'm sure it won't be long now. They are top drawer, you know." The two lapsed back into silence.

Maggie and Dougal spent the night in a bed and breakfast and headed over to the Royal Stuart Society right after a hearty breakfast. They were greeted by a lovely elderly woman dressed in Stuart tartan.

Well, of course.

Maggie smiled and shook her hand.

"Hello. We are looking to speak with the sennachie? Is he, or she, here today?"

"Oh, I'm afraid the clan sennachie works from his home. May I inquire as to your reason?"

"My name is Maggie Stuart. I was speaking to a docent at Rothesay, and he thought that the society sennachie would be able to answer questions about an ancient ancestor. Alan Fitz Walter."

The woman smiled warmly. "We are always pleased to assist our clan members. Are you a member of the society?"

Maggie's mind raced for an acceptable answer. "To tell you the truth, I am not. I moved to New York right after graduating university, and I never thought to even look for a local chapter."

"Well, we would love to have you. We love to have younger members to sustain the society." She opened a drawer and brought out a business card. "Here is the contact information of our sennachie." She then reached over to the side of the counter and pulled out a brochure. "And here is information on how to join." She looked at Dougal expectantly.

"Oh, ma'am, I am Dr. Dougal Fraser from the University of Edinburgh. Not a Stuart, I'm afraid."

The receptionist, ever polite, smiled. "Well, at least you are Scottish." The three laughed.

"Thank you so much for your help," said Maggie. At that, she and Dougal turned and left.

Back in the car, Maggie called the number on the card. "Mr. Stuart? My name is Maggie Stuart, and I was wondering if I could arrange an appointment with you." She paused as she listened. "We are in Norfolk at the moment, so it would be helpful if we could meet later today. We are in from Edinburgh." She paused and listened again. "Three o'clock? That would be perfect. At the address on the card? Perfect. See you then." She disconnected and turned to Dougal. "Between now and three, we need to find this place," she said as she read from the card. "This just says 'High Street, Walsingham NR22.' How are we going to find a home without a street number?"

"Let's go into town, Maggie. We have a few hours to kill, and there are several ancient monasteries here we can tour. We can ask someone."

"I'd rather drive out to Holkham Hall. I hear it's quite magnificent. I could spend a few minutes staring out to sea."

"Holkham Hall it is, then." Dougal headed to the coast.

Holkham Hall is a massive manor house, like many scattered across the island country. However, the hall overlooks the North Sea. Maggie and Dougal walked out to the beach, and she let the wind blow through her hair as she surveyed the empty beach and lapping waves. The sea air, cool and crisp, calmed her as she took deep breaths. She shoved her hands into her pockets, tilted her head back, and closed her eyes.

"Lovely, isn't it? There's something about the sea that makes our lives seem so little." She and Dougal stood there in silence for several minutes, and then she turned to Dougal. "We really should undertake finding High Street." They walked back to the car.

"Thanks for bringing me here, Dougal. It was a good break."

"I agree, lass." They headed back to town and went into a small pub for lunch.

"Fish and chips and a pint," said Dougal to the waitress who came up to their table.

"Same for me, please," added Maggie. "Say, would you happen to know this address?" Maggie showed the business card to the waitress.

"Oh, yes," the waitress answered. "That would be the old chapel. Converted into a home several years ago. Take this street down to the light and turn right. You'll be able to see it from there. Just look for a tiny chapel." She left to fill the order.

Dougal and Maggie finished lunch, and Dougal glanced at his watch. "Nearly perfect timing. It's 2:30. Let's head out, shall we?"

The two left the pub and Dougal looked down the street. The light was maybe only a quarter-mile away. "Want to walk?" he asked Maggie.

"Great idea."

They headed down the street, Maggie window shopping as they walked. It turned out to be a lovely day, and she was enjoying the sunshine and the exercise.

At three on the dot, Dougal knocked on the door of the converted chapel. A rather wizened man answered the door. "Would this be Ms. Stuart?" he asked Maggie, looking questioningly at Dougal. "Yes, Mr. Stuart," Maggie replied, "and this is Dr. Dougal Fraser from the University of Edinburgh. He has been assisting me in my research."

"Robert MacIntosh Stuart," announced the man, extending his hand to Dougal and then to Maggie. "You can call me R.M. Please come in."

R.M. led Maggie and Dougal to a cozy study to the left of the door. The room had apparently been a small nave, and the conversion had kept its vaulted ceiling. While the square footage was modest, the dramatic arched ceiling gave the room an impressive feel.

"How can I help you?" asked R.M.

Maggie started. "We are looking for information on Alan Fitz Walter." She pulled out her sketch of the amulet. "We spoke to the historian at Rothesay, and he suggested we contact you. This," she said as she handed the sketch to R.M., "was found in the Basilica in Assisi after the earthquake brought down the roof. We believe that it might have been Fitz Walter that gave it to St. Francis, and we thought you might have some proof or additional information to confirm that."

R.M. studied the sketch. "Very interesting," he said finally. "It is possible. Fitz Walter did return from the Third Crusade, and most likely, the route he took back home was through Italy. May I ask, why are you pursuing this line of research?"

Damn. I didn't look at his hands.

She glanced at Dougal and then looked calmly back at R.M. "I was vacationing in Italy when the earthquake struck. I was in the basilica when the roof collapsed and was stuck in the debris until paramedics freed me. They found this and asked me if it was mine. I said no, but it looked Scottish to me. So, when I got back, I went to Dr. Fraser – he is a professor of history – and asked him whether this piece would have any historical significance. We are trying to determine how something like this would end up in Assisi."

R.M. peered intently as Maggie relayed this tale. "Interesting," he finally responded. He studied the sketch, and as he did, Maggie checked the back of his right hand.

No scar there.

She flicked her eyes at Dougal and then quickly down to R.M.'s hands twice. Dougal's face lit up in understanding, and he checked R.M.'s left hand. He made a nearly imperceptible shake of his head. Maggie was at least partially relieved.

"We have an archive of personal papers from many generations of Stuarts," said R.M. finally. "I haven't gone back this far in time, but let me see whether any pertinent journals or diaries are in our archives. We have slowly been scanning documents to preserve them from the ravages of time. Perhaps I can find something."

Dougal reached into his pocket and brought out a business card. "If you find out anything, please contact me at this number. Your assistance might help us understand an event that would have quite the historical significance. We appreciate any assistance you might lend."

"Glad to be of service. Thank you for coming! We are always interested in more fully understanding the contributions made by the esteemed House of Stuart."

Maggie and Dougal shook hands with R.M. and left.

Safely out the door and halfway back up the street to the car, Maggie commented, "I really need to be more careful."

CHAPTER THIRTEEN

As Jack walked into the library, he went over the several tasks he had at hand. He needed to determine the most lucrative target: Whittall or Barminster. He needed the Third Order network to keep an eye out for Maggie while keeping Clance at bay – that needed some finesse.

That Maggie is feistier than I gave her credit for. I won't make that mistake again.

He started researching peerage records. Whittall had the more extensive collection, but Barminster was quite wealthy. Adding the amulet to her collection would give her an immense boost in all the right circles. Besides, she was a "she." Jack could turn on his charm. Barminster, it was.

Jack had contacted the Third Order network requesting a BOLO on Maggie through Martha. He also called Oliver McQuiddy, advising him that the orders from the master to locate Maggie were in reference to other possible missing artifacts. No need to disabuse him of the notion that the Third Order was in possession of the iron piece. He had heard that Agent Leone had managed to lose Maggie, which led him to believe that Maggie could be pretty much anywhere. He decided he needed to pump Martha for more information, so he headed to Dunfermline.

Jack called Martha from the coffee shop. "Martha, I'm at the coffee shop. Can you meet me here? In fifteen minutes? I have some questions for you." He ordered a large coffee, black, and a scone and sat by the front window, nursing his coffee and watching for Martha. She arrived in ten minutes, not fifteen, and sat down across from him.

"Martha, what can you tell me about Maggie?"

"Not very much. Her parents live in Dunfermline, in Ayton Lodge. She didn't tell me where she lives – she just told me she was visiting for only a few weeks."

"Can you ask around and find out if anyone knows more about her? Where she lives? Where she works?"

Martha's face lit up. "I did see her walk out of the dance studio down the way from here. I can go in there and ask if you like."

"That will not be necessary, Martha. The master is pleased with your diligence in serving the order. I will inform him of your continued obedience and assistance."

Martha blushed and bowed her head. "I live to serve the order."

Jack stood up, took the last gulp of coffee, and tossed it in the trash.

"Thank you, Martha." He left the coffee shop, immediately located the dance studio, and walked in.

"May I help you?" said Fiona.

"Yes. My family has recently moved into the area, and my young daughter has shown an interest in ballet. I heard you have lessons for children. She's six."

"We do. However, our current classes are full. We had to cancel an entire class, unfortunately, due to the unexpected absence of one of our instructors. I am trying to find another instructor to take her place."

"I heard from one of my neighbors that there was a really good instructor here. One with red hair? I think her name is Maggie."

"Oh, that's the teacher we lost. Would you like to leave your name and number? I can call you if a slot in an existing class opens up or when I hire a replacement."

"Do you know if Maggie intends to return? "My daughter also has red hair, and I think she would do so well with another ginger."

"I'm not sure Maggie is still in the country. She left Scotland when she got her degree. I was surprised when she returned, frankly. I don't know what happened to her, but it was something big. She was different. I think she's gone back – I haven't seen her in quite a while. New York, I think, is where she got a job. Or London, maybe. Give me your name and number, though, and I'll call you when I have an opening."

"That's all right. I am not sure my daughter will be as eager to dance a month from now. She's got a very short attention span. It was either dance or horses. I might go investigate horses. I might be back in a couple of months. Thanks for your time." Jack turned and left.

Fiona watched Jack until he was out of sight. Then she headed to the phone and, pulling out a scrap of paper from her drawer, called a number scribbled on it. When a voice answered, she said, "You asked me to call you if anyone came in asking for Maggie? Someone did, and he just left."

Jack wasn't pleased that Maggie might be in New York. London was doable, but with his criminal record, he knew he wouldn't be able to easily get into the US.

That has to wait for a bit.

He considered his next move.

Hopefully, she's in London.

He switched gears suddenly.

I could really use a picture of the amulet.

He checked his watch: it was nearly 5 PM. He hailed a cabbie and headed over to McQuiddy's lab. He had decided to let himself in and look around – he was sure that Oliver had a photo somewhere. He sat outside and watched the activity around the building. Shortly after five, staff started streaming out, and a half-hour later, security came to lock the main doors. There were still lights on in some offices, so Jack surmised that there was a back or side entrance for those still working. He started walking around – slowly, like he was pondering a great idea as scholarly-like as he could muster. He noted doors on both sides and two in the back, facing a parking lot. He walked to the back of the lot and, leaning up against a car and lighting a cigarette, waited. Sure enough, after ten minutes or so, someone walked out of the east door. Jack snuffed out the cigarette and left to find some dinner.

An hour later, he walked back to the lab building. There were few cars left in the lot, and nearly all of the office lights were out.

Lost my window of opportunity. Well, there's always tomorrow.

Jack arose early the next day and went back to the lab, getting there at 6:30 AM to watch the foot traffic into the building. Tech workers started dribbling in at 7:15, and by 8:30, there was a large influx – some in business clothes, some in lab coats. By nine, the parking lot was full of cars and bereft of people. Jack went to the far corner of the lot and started to casually look into car windows. The third car in had a wrinkled lab coat in the back seat. Jack looked around cautiously and, seeing no one, broke into the car and took the coat. He rolled it up tightly, like a satchel, and headed home to wash and iron it. He was meticulous about his looks and used them wisely to further his own ends. At six foot two and 185 pounds, he had an enviably proportioned and athletic body. He had wavy black hair with distinguished-looking graying temples, a very square jaw, and piercing blue-green eyes. He was arrestingly handsome. His looks gave him incredible advantage, which he exploited frequently.

The lab coat had the university crest embroidered on its chest pocket, with "Carbon Testing Lab" embroidered under it. There was a crimp in the pocket edge that he assumed had been made by a name badge. He washed and pressed the lab coat and hung it up on the back of a door.

The next day, just before lunch, he went to a fish and chips place and bought three orders to go. He drove over to the lab building and parked in the back, watching for McQuiddy to head to his car. Luckily, Oliver obliged – Jack thought he might, given his rather ample girth. Jack then parked right in front and ran in with the food. He went up to the reception desk, watching people walking in and out. He was checking on the badges they wore. Workers were swiping their badges to open doors.

"I have a lunch order here for…" He stopped and looked at the receipt that was stapling the bag shut. "Oliver McQuiddy?"

The receptionist picked up her phone and dialed a number. She waited for several seconds and then hung up. "Mr. McQuiddy is not answering," she said to Jack. "You can leave the food here, and I'll see it gets to him. As long as he has already paid."

"He charged it." Jack reached over the counter and handed over the bag. "Thanks."

He left and went to a stationery store. He bought some substantial card stock, some laminating sheets, and a badge clip. He then went and got a couple of passport photos made. His plan was to mock up a lab identification badge, which took him the rest of the day.

Bright and early the next morning, he arose and drove to the lab, parking in the back lot. He waited until about 8:30, when most of the workers were flowing into the building. Donning his coat and badge, he walked in with a throng of technicians, gallantly holding the door open for others after a woman in front of him swiped her badge. Trailing after, he entered.

Jack was quite adept at blending in... He spent time in various bathrooms and visiting various break rooms, taking his time making coffee, and walking halls purposely towards imaginary meetings when required. He parked himself with a view to Oliver's office just before lunch and waited for him to leave for lunch. When McQuiddy obliged, Jack slipped into his office. He had about an hour to search. He started with the file cabinet. Finding nothing, he carefully rifled through Oliver's desk. In the lower-left-hand drawer, in an unlabeled manila file, Jack found the photos. He took one, slipped it into his coat pocket, and making sure the office was as he left it, headed towards the door. He opened the door very slightly and, noticing an empty hall, slipped out and headed to the exit.

He went back home and started researching. His next task was to find an event where he might run into Lady Barminster. He started combing the social pages in the newspaper and looking into conferences and charity events she might attend. He quickly discovered that Lady Barminster was not deep into the royal social scene, but he did find mention that she had pieces from her collection on loan to the British Museum and that the Friends of the British Museum were hosting a lecture on ancient Scotland within the week. Jack decided that was his most likely opportunity. He called and got tickets.

He drove down to London several days prior to the museum event. He familiarized himself with the area surrounding the museum: the car parks, the nearby shops, the neighborhood. After spending a day making a mental map of the area, he entered the museum and walked up to the information desk.

"Pardon me," he said politely to the young man behind the desk. "I have tickets for the ancient Scotland lecture in a few days, and I have never attended a lecture here before. Can you tell me where it will be held?"

"Yes, sir," replied the young man. "Let me check that for you." He looked down at a calendar of events, running his index finger lightly over the page. "Ah – here it is," he said with a smile. "The lecture will be held in the Hugh and Catherine Stevenson Theatre, which is in the new Clore Education Centre. It is located below the Great Court. You can take the stairs or the lift down." He pointed towards the center of the building.

"Thank you very much," replied Jack. "Would you happen to have a building map? I would hate to get lost."

The young man lifted a museum brochure off of the counter and handed it to Jack. "The facility map is in the centerfold," he said, still smiling.

Jack raised the brochure in a salute to the pleasant young man, smiled, and walked past the desk, opening the brochure to the map. He walked downstairs and located the Stevenson Theatre, but the door was locked. All of the lecture hall doors were locked. He went back upstairs and left.

~

Jack took great care in dressing for the lecture. He pulled out his best gray flannel slacks, his Grenson Albert brogues, a bespoke Davies and Son shirt, and classic navy blazer. He splashed on some cologne and applied a bit of bronzer to his face. He looked at himself admiringly in the mirror, straightening his collar with an arrogant grin, and then he noticed his hands. He pulled out a nail file and shaped his nails and then buffed them to a respectable shine. Checking himself one last time in the mirror, he left for the museum.

Jack didn't enter the lecture hall right away. Instead, he found an unobtrusive spot to watch people file in. He knew who he was looking for: a very well-manicured, tall, and trim woman in her fifties, her chin-length blond hair flawlessly styled. That was Lady Barminster. She arrived fifteen minutes before the start of the lecture, walking in with several scholarly-looking gentlemen, deep in conversation. Once they entered the lecture hall, Jack quickly followed.

The hall was arranged as a classic auditorium, with audience seats descending towards the stage, placed in a gentle arc around the equally curved stage front. There was a lectern mid-stage and a curtain across the back. It could have just as easily been on a college campus. Jack stood back and watched as Lady Barminster headed down the center aisle, taking a seat on the aisle about halfway down. There were several young men and women on stage, moving tables and encased artifacts to either side of the lectern. Jack didn't give them much thought until, out of the corner of his eye, he saw a flash of long, wavy red hair disappear stage right.

Is that Maggie?

His mind raced. It certainly looked like her: same height, same build, same hair.

Could she be announcing the amulet at the lecture?

Working Lady Barminster would have to wait a bit. Jack hurried down the far aisle, towards the door that led backstage. As he rushed, he noticed that he hadn't seen any press. If the amulet were being announced, there would have been plenty of media present.

That might not mean anything. She might not have wanted to make herself an obvious target.

What he did know was that he needed to stop her – and he wanted the amulet.

This might just be my lucky day!

Maggie or the amulet – or both.

Jack slipped backstage and stood in the shadows, against the wall. When his eyes had gotten accustomed to the dark, he studied the people moving back and forth… The redhead was not moving items to the tables. He watched for several minutes and was about to turn and go back and concentrate on Lady Barminster when he once again caught a glimpse of wavy red hair – this time leaving out a door on the far side of the stage. He quickly moved across the stage, behind the curtain, and followed the redhead out the door.

He found himself in a well-lit corridor with walls on both sides dotted with doors. Offices, storerooms…the business end of the lecture halls. He started down the corridor, trying doorknobs as he went. Locked. Locked. The corridor took a ninety-degree turn to the right, and as he made the turn, he saw the flash of long, swinging red hair leaving through the exit door at the end. He took off running and burst through the door – and stopped dead in his tracks. He had run into a semicircle of police. In back of them, the redhead slowly turned around, smiling. It wasn't Maggie.

"Hello, Mr. Walker," said the sergeant in the center. "May we ask you why you have burst out here in such a rush?"

Jack swore under his breath. "You must be mistaken. I am not Mr. Walker."

"Oh, come now," said the sergeant, smiling as he pulled a police photo from his pocket. "Can we please dispense with the charade?" He held up Jack's picture to his face. "We are placing you under arrest for breaking and entering and kidnapping. And based upon your most recent act, we just might add attempted kidnapping.

Constable, will you please take Mr. Walker into custody?" The sergeant then pulled out his cell phone and made a call. "Mr. Fraser, can you please bring in Mrs. Tyler for a positive identification?"

Mrs. Tyler? Who the hell is Mrs. Tyler?

Jack was trundled into a waiting police van, wondering where his plan had gone wrong.

CHAPTER FOURTEEN

Maggie stood behind the one-way mirror and stared at the six men standing against the far wall. It took her only a second to confidently say, "Number three. That's the man named Jack that kidnapped me."

"Are you positive, Mrs. Tyler?" asked the chief detective.

"Absolutely."

"Thank you, Mrs. Tyler. You may go."

Maggie turned and left to join Callum, who was standing outside the door. "Callum, you must tell me. How did you catch him?"

"It wasn't me. I told you: let Scotland Yard led him into temptation."

"Oh, come on, Callum. Give me a hint!"

Callum laughed. "If you must know, Scotland Yard lured him into trying to nab you again. With a ginger decoy."

"Amazing. So, can I become a ginger again?"

"We still have the other character to deal with, Maggie, but I promise it won't take long. Maybe another week at most. Be patient just a little bit longer."

"Well, I guess I'll just have to wear hats until the coast is clear. I am getting red roots, and I am not keen on dying my hair again."

"Speaking of things that don't last, how's the 'scar' holding up?"

Maggie held out her left hand. The silicone on her hand was still firmly attached.

"Just a little longer, Mag. This should be over soon."

"Callum, is it okay for me to go back to Assisi? I have more research to conduct."

"Absolutely, Ms. Stuart. Just stay Maggie Stuart. For now."

"I will. One down, one to go. And hopefully, that will put an end to this." She paused again. "A decoy. Hmmmm. Pretty clever."

Maggie gave Callum a little kiss on the cheek. "Thanks, big brother. Now I think I need to talk to Dougal – see whether he's found out anything new." She turned and left the police station.

Maggie returned to her hotel room and checked her watch.

Dougal should be in his office now.

She called, and Dougal answered.

"Dougal! Thought I would tell you that I just came back from the police station. They captured the man that kidnapped me and told me he was also responsible for the break-in at Mum and Da's."

"That's wonderful news, Maggie! So, we can all get back to normal?"

"Not quite yet. Callum tells me we still have to be concerned about Clance. But one down – that's good news. Not to change the subject, but have you heard from R.M.?"

"Yes, but not the best news. He said that the clan had no documents that would tie Alan Fitz Walter to the artifact."

"Darn. That's unfortunate. But Callum said I am free to return to Assisi. I am dying to find out exactly what Brother Ventimiglio discovered."

"Are you sure you want to go back?" There was unmistakable concern in his voice. "After what happened to you last time?"

"Yes, I really need to go back. Thinking I need a chaperone?" She chuckled.

There was a brief silence on the end of the line. "Maggie, that's not such a bad idea. Not that I am Callum, but you would definitely be less of a target if you weren't traveling alone. Let me talk to Kate and get back to you. When do you suppose you would want to go, and how long do you suppose we would stay?"

It was Maggie's turn to go silent, thinking through Dougal's offer.

"Well, I didn't expect that. But there is merit to your offer. We actually wouldn't need more than a long weekend, I think. I already know that Brother Ventimiglio has confirmed the artifact was buried with St. Francis. All we would need is to ask him how he knows that. I must warn you, though – he speaks no English. We do everything via an English-Italian dictionary."

"Let me talk to Kate and get back to you. Within a day, I promise."

"Okay, then! I'll wait for your call."

Maggie hung up the phone and looked at herself in the mirror, studying her hairline closely. She sighed, grabbed a jacket, and headed to the nearest pharmacy for a box of temporary hair color.

I certainly hope this is the last time.

She returned to her room and opened the box.

~

Maggie and Dougal got off the plane in Perugia and headed to the rental cars.

"You have this down pat, I suppose," commented Dougal as he loaded the overnights into the trunk.

Maggie laughed. "This is starting to feel like a second home," she replied as she slipped behind the wheel. "You have your own personal tour guide, brother." She drove the relatively short distance to Assisi and pulled up to the Hotel Ideale. The concierge smiled as they walked in. "Buona sera, signora, signore. Posso aiutarla?"

"We are not Italian. Do you speak English?"

"Yes, I do," replied the concierge. He looked intently at Maggie. "Have you been here before, signora? You look somewhat familiar."

Maggie had to finesse the question – her previous stay had been under a different name and passport. "No, signore, this is our first time in Assisi. My brother and I are here on a short holiday. We plan on spending the weekend here before we head to Fiorenza."

"Well, Benvenuto," said the concierge with a smile. "Signore, do you have reservations?" he asked, turning to Dougal. As he turned his attention, Maggie furtively inspected the back of his hands. Upon seeing a familiar scar, she coughed to get Dougal's attention, and as she bent over with her fist covering her mouth, she pointedly caught Dougal's eye and glanced down at the concierge's hand. Dougal picked up on the signal.

"We do," answered Dougal smoothly. "A room under the name Maggie Stuart and a room under the name Dr. Dougal Fraser."

The concierge rummaged through his files and pulled out the two reservations." Ah, here they are," he said as he laid out the paperwork in front of the two. "Please sign where indicated and leave your passports." He studied Maggie again intently. "Excuse me, signora, but I can't help but think we have met somewhere before."

"Highly unlikely," interjected Dougal. "My sister lives in New York. I had to almost drag her away from Wall Street, with its ridiculous hours, to take a small holiday. She's quite the workaholic."

Maggie put her passport on the desk. "I did get to France earlier this year, but Dougal tells me that ninety-hour workweeks require a lot more respite. He suggested Assisi for its calm and Fiorenza for its art and beauty. Do you agree?"

"Lovely choices," the concierge demurred. He registered the two, gave them their keys, and wished them a pleasant stay. After Maggie and Dougal had left the lobby, he thumbed through Maggie's passport. The only clearance through Italian customs had been earlier that day. He shook his head, thinking he must have made a mistake.

I rarely forget a face. But this passport doesn't lie.

He placed the two passports in the safe and got back to work.

Dougal and Maggie walked out to dine at an intimate restaurant a few blocks away, and after dinner, they took a stroll about town. It was an absolutely glorious evening, and they admired the narrow, winding residential streets with their abundance of heavily blooming window boxes. They ended up in front of the basilica just as vespers were beginning.

"Let's go in," said Maggie impulsively. "The music bouncing off the walls must be incredible." The two walked in and sat in a rear pew off the center aisle. The Gregorian chants sung by the chorus of monks was indeed breathtaking. Maggie leaned back and closed her eyes, drinking in the sonorous and mesmerizing sounds surrounding her. A deep sense of calm took residence in her, and she was captivated by the experience. When it ended, she and Dougal got up to leave. Maggie spotted Brother Ventimiglio but failed to catch his eye.

He probably doesn't recognize me, she thought. *He would be looking for long red hair.*

"Dougal, let's linger outside for a while. If Brother Ventimiglio comes out this way, we can speak to him."

"Do you have your dictionary?"

"Won't need it. All I have to say is 'Domani' and 'Giardino' and hold up a few fingers. He will totally understand."

"That black hair and those brown eyes are rubbing off on you, Mag. Next thing you know, you'll be making your own pasta."

"Oh, stop! As soon as this is over, it will be back to ginger. Never knew I would miss it so much."

Dougal and Maggie waited outside, watching the long golden streaks the setting sun made across the stone piazza. After ten minutes or so, Maggie turned to Dougal. "Looks like we missed him. There's always tomorrow, though." The two turned to go just as a couple of monks walked out the front doors to shut them. One was Brother Ventimiglio. Doors shut, the brothers started to walk away. Maggie quickly walked up to Ventimiglio and said, "Scusate, Fratello," touching his arm. Ventimiglio was startled as he turned… He recognized the voice. The voice, but not the hair or eyes. He took a second to stare at Maggie, and then his expression turned to one of joy. "Signora! Stai bene!"

"Yes, I am well," Maggie replied. "Fratello, this is my brother. Mio fratello Dougal. Parlare domani? Giardino?" She held up all ten fingers.

"Si! A dieci!" he replied as he gave her a hug. Slightly embarrassed, he quickly turned to Dougal and shook his hand. "Felice di conoscerti, signore."

"I am sorry I don't speak Italian," replied Dougal sheepishly. "But I am happy to meet you."

"A dieci," repeated Maggie, taking Ventimiglio's hand and squeezing it. "Grazie. Molte grazie." They parted, and Dougal and Maggie headed back to the hotel.

"We have to be careful around that concierge," said Maggie. "He was trying so hard to place me."

"I agree. We need to get in and out before he figures out who you are. Very good idea to have a U.S. passport in a different name. And brilliant to dye your hair." Dougal self-consciously ran his hand over his head. "I should have thought of that… Here I am, your brother, with reddish hair and blue eyes. He might wonder how our coloring is so different."

"We can always plant a seed in his head that you and I are on a secret tryst," Maggie teased. "The married man and the wanton woman."

Dougal guffawed. "That we could," he finally said, still laughing. "That would take the cake, now."

And when they reached the hotel, Dougal grabbed the door handle with one hand and wrapped his other arm around Maggie, holding her close as they entered. The two couldn't help but laugh. The concierge noticed. He noticed most everything.

~

Dougal and Maggie had a leisurely breakfast at the hotel before leaving to meet with Brother Ventimiglio. Maggie had her dictionary, a note she spent most of the evening writing in Italian, and the sketch of the amulet. Dougal had notes on Alan Fitz Walter. They got to the garden ten minutes early, so they sat and waited. At ten sharp, Brother Ventimiglio walked up. Maggie and Dougal stood up as he entered. Ventimiglio gave Maggie a big hug; his happiness at seeing her safe was undeniable. Maggie motioned for Ventimiglio to sit, and she gave him her note and the sketch of the amulet. Ventimiglio became very animated after reading the first question: *Have you ever heard of Alan Fitz Walter?*

"Si! Si!" Ventimiglio replied excitedly. "Questo è l'uomo!"

Maggie turned to Dougal and grinned widely. "Bingo!! That's the man!" She then pulled out her dictionary.

"Ha…dato…amulet…per San Francesco?"

"Si!! Si!!", said Ventimiglio. He grabbed the dictionary and thumbed through it.

"He…gave…I…find…writing…San Francesco…Vaticano…catacombe." He was so excited he kept slipping into Italian. "When…boy…Cavaliere Templare." It was enough. The three were elated.

Maggie then became somber. Looking into her dictionary, she translated, "I still have the amulet."

Brother Ventimiglio grew very silent. He took the dictionary. "Bad…people…want?"

Maggie nodded and tipped her head towards her brother. She took the dictionary and translated, "Protection."

Brother Ventimiglio nodded and took Dougal's hand. "Grazie, fratello."

Maggie held up her finger and took back the dictionary. In Italian, she said, "I…write…more…bring…tonight…vespers." Ventimiglio nodded in understanding. She then turned to Dougal. "Between now and then, you and I need to figure out what we are going to do now." Dougal simply nodded.

The three parted ways, and Maggie took Dougal outside the city walls to a private, wooded area.

"Dougal," she started to say, but he interrupted her.

"Maggie, what are we going to do? The artifact has incredible historical significance, but it also has incredible religious significance."

"I know. Part of me knows it belongs back here, but what about your paper? What about the Scottish Museum? The Clan Stuart? All of that?"

"We shouldn't ignore our heritage, Maggie. It's just as important."

"I know. That's what I am struggling with."

The two sat down, leaning against trees. The small forest was quiet except for a chorus of songbirds that occasionally sang antiphonally. They sat in singular silence, each lost in their own thoughts.

Finally, Maggie looked at Dougal. "Dougal, what if we had a replica made for display?"

Dougal sat up. "Tell me more."

"Well, you could publish your paper. We could perhaps have a joint announcement with the Vatican. The amulet and the journal

Brother Ventimiglio found should be ample proof of authenticity. Then we could return the original to the basilica, telling the world that it is back with St. Francis. You and I wouldn't be chased anymore, the church would be happy, and the story would be out. The replica could go on tour to whatever museums would be interested."

Dougal considered Maggie's proposal. "This would entail some pretty complex logistics. We will have to assure the amulet's safety in transit. I'm not comfortable with it seeing the light of day, frankly."

"We would still need a replica made."

"We have pictures, so we can get dimensions. Where is it, anyway?"

Maggie looked around cautiously before replying under her breath, "It's in the States. In a safe."

Dougal stared at Maggie for several seconds. "Okay. You tell Brother Ventimiglio that you intend to return the relic to its resting place. Ask him if the plan to make a replica has the Vatican's blessing. Also ask him if the Church has any issues with a scholarly paper on the amulet and its provenance and ask whether a joint announcement would be acceptable. If he says there are issues, I think we need to call upon some diplomats to pave the way. Callum can help with that, I bet. I think that the amulet should travel across the pond only once – to go home. If everything works out, do you suppose you can find an artisan stateside that can make a replica for us? I can start writing up my paper in the meantime. Can you ask

Brother Ventimiglio for the citation referencing the journal he found in the Vatican catacombs and ask him about a joint announcement?"

"I'll work on it. Let's get back to the hotel. I've got a lot of translating to do for a letter I need to give to Brother Ventimiglio before we leave."

CHAPTER FIFTEEN

Clance was getting worried – he hadn't heard from Jack in several days.

Very unlike him. He said he knew where the relic was.

Clance paced back and forth. He stopped as a statue of the Virgin Mary caught his eye.

"Hail Mary, Full of grace, the Lord is with thee," he started in a monotone voice as he stared at the statue. He finished the prayer mechanically, by rote, and immediately continued with his prior line of thought.

"I need to find the amulet," he said out loud to the room. "His eminence is not pleased. I will be replaced. What will I do if I lose master of formation? I have been so faithful! This is not fair! Jack needs to bring me the relic soon!"

Clance went to the phone and called Jack's line, which went straight to voicemail. Again. Just like the six times Clance had already called. He became even more agitated.

"What if he is hurt?" Clance again spoke to the empty room. "What if he's been caught? What if… What if he has given up? What if he has the relic and wants to become master of formation? What if he's already called his eminence?" Clance had worked himself into a near frenzy, and he began pacing furiously, back and forth. He suddenly bolted to the door, flung it open, and headed to a kneeling bench in front of a statue of the crucified Christ. He threw himself down on the bench, crossed himself very quickly and started furiously praying. He kept at it for a good half hour, and then just as quickly got up and went to the phone. He dialed the number he had been given for his eminence. It was not an appointed call, there was no call scheduled: Clance decided that this was just too important.

"Dio sia con te," said an unfamiliar voice at the other end. "Questo è il Cardinale Santiago."

"Your Eminence, this is Clance, the master of formation of the Third Order. I am sorry to bother you unannounced, but I have a concern of the highest order," said Clance, as humbly as he could muster.

There was a long silence on the end of the line. In broken English, the cardinal said, "I am confused. I know of no 'Third Order', or any 'master of formation'… how did you get this number?"

Clance fell silent for a moment. "Yo...Your Eminence, I am calling about the relic. You know, the relic of St. Francis? We spoke of it not two weeks ago."

Again, there was a long silence. "Sir, you called this number and discussed a holy relic?"

"Yes, Your Eminence. We usually speak at 3 PM Greenwich time, but I felt that we needed to speak about my concern. Do you not remember?"

Again, a long silence. Finally, the cardinal said, "I am sorry, but you caught me at a bad time. I am heading to a meeting, and I do not have my calendar with me. Do we have another call scheduled?"

"Yes, Your Eminence. Next Tuesday, at three, as usual. Every other Tuesday at three. Correct?"

"Call me then, sir. I will assure you that you will have my full attention. We will speak of your concerns then."

"Yes, Your Eminence. We will speak then." Clance hung up the phone, went back to his prayer bench, knelt, and prayed.

~

The deacon looked at his watch – nearly three. He gathered some papers and headed down the hall to the cardinal's offices. He nodded as he passed a few other staffers heading past him. It was not unusual for deacons to deliver papers to cardinals' desks, so he caused no suspicion.

When he reached Cardinal Santiago's office, he glanced up and down the hall and slipped in. He headed to the desk and, glancing at his watch, checked the time again. He had three minutes.

He put the papers down and headed over to the window to gaze out, hands clasped behind his back, waiting for the phone to ring.

Lovely day.

The ringing phone roused him from his reverie, and he went back over to the desk to answer.

"Hello, Your Eminence? This is the master of formation."

"Yes, Master. Have you news of the relic?"

At that moment, the door opened, and in strode Cardinal Santiago and two gendarmes. The deacon's jaw dropped open, and he quickly put the phone back in its cradle.

"What are you doing in my office?" the cardinal asked almost gently.

"I… I…" stammered the deacon.

"Deacon, I took a call last week from the master of formation," said the cardinal quietly. He didn't need to say more.

The deacon hung his head. "Forgive me, Father," was all he could manage to get out.

"Now, you and I are going to have a little chat," continued the cardinal. "Then, afterwards, these gendarmes will escort you to their offices. Come over here and have a seat." The cardinal motioned to a couple of armchairs near the window. Right then, the phone rang again. The cardinal walked over to the phone and picked it up.

"Your Eminence? We must have been cut off," said Clance.

"Sir, you have reached the office of Cardinal Santiago. I regret to inform you that the person to whom you have been speaking is no longer associated with this office." At this, the deacon slumped into the chair. The cardinal took a deep breath. "I think the best thing would be for you to come to the Vatican. We can discuss this in person. Would you be able to do that?"

"Oh, yes, Your Eminence! I am humbled that I have been summoned. I can be there as soon as I secure a flight." Clance's presence had never been requested, and he took that as a vote of confidence.

Perhaps I will be promoted!

The cardinal glanced at the calendar open on his desk. "I can see you next Wednesday at 11 AM. Will that be possible?"

"Absolutely, Your Eminence. I shall see you then. If you would give me your leave, I need to start making arrangements."

"Go then, my son. I will leave word at the gate to allow you to be escorted to my office." The cardinal hung up the phone and turned to the deacon.

"Now, where were we?" He strode over to the facing armchair and sat down. "What have you been up to, my child?"

~

Clance spent two days obsessing over what to wear for his all-important meeting. He had no monk's robe, so it would have to be street clothes. Should he dress humbly, as a follower of the order? That was what the Rule of Life would have him sport.

They might not let me in if I appear a beggar. No, something more impressive.

He could not appear overly vain, though. That was not in keeping with the order. He visited his closet at least a dozen times, rummaging through the hangers. Nothing seemed appropriate. He wanted to appear humble but important. He finally decided that he owned nothing that fit the bill, so he headed out to Saville Row, where he spent four months of his pensioner income on a quietly tailored blue-black suit of fine quality. Between the suit, the remainder of the humble-but-important outfit, and his airfare, he had gone through the majority of his meager savings.

Clance arrived at the Vatican an hour early and announced himself to a Swiss guard and asked for directions to the administrative offices. The guard asked Clance his name and the party he was to see. He indicated that Clance should stay where he was and walked over to another guard, who then walked into a nearby building. Several minutes later, the guard came out of the building and motioned for Clance to approach. He was escorted by both guards to a large buff-colored building that sat directly behind St. Peter's Cathedral. The guards stayed with him until a clerk approached and shepherded Clance up to the cardinal's office. The clerk knocked.

"Si prega di entrare," said a voice from behind the door. The clerk opened the door, stepped to one side, and motioned for Clance to enter. He then quietly shut the door and left Clance alone with the cardinal.

All of Clance's planning and rehearsing what he would say vanished in the presence of the cardinal – Clance was simply awestruck at the magnificence of being in the presence of such an important man.

"Please, come and sit," said the cardinal, motioning to the armchairs near the window. He had a disarming way about him that only somewhat broke through Clance's wonderment. Clance hurried over to one of the chairs and sat.

"You are the master of formation?"

"Yes, Your Eminence."

"And can you tell me about your responsibilities?"

"Your Eminence, I do your bidding. I recruit members, I teach the Rule of Life, and I follow the Rule myself. I say all the correct prayers before and after meals, I only eat meat Sundays, Tuesdays, and Thursdays. I say matins and terce and vespers–"

The cardinal interrupted. "Which Rule of Life?"

Clance was startled by the question. "Why, St. Francis's Rule of Life, as originally written for the brothers and sisters of the Order of Penance of St. Francis. The true Third Order!"

The cardinal rested his elbows on the arms of the chair and brought his hands together so that all five fingers were touching their mates.

"Ah, I see. And how did you come to join this order?"

Clance hesitated. "Your Eminence, I have been a follower since I was a young man, in my thirties. I was dismayed when the pope relaxed the Rule and changed the name of the order in 1978. I wrote the Vatican at the time but received no answer. In the beginning, the small group of people that felt as I did kept the old ways. However, after about a year, I was contacted by a cardinal that agreed with the true and original Rule. Under his protection and guidance, the Third Order flourished, and after about a decade of faithful service, I was given the honor of being named the Master of Formation. That cardinal passed – you know, the cardinal you, I assume, replaced? And then I started being instructed by your offices. I thought I had been speaking to you personally, but I certainly understand that Your Eminence is extremely busy and apparently delegated the communication to another cleric."

"So, tell me, what specific directives have you accomplished, and what directives remain?"

Clance involuntarily puffed out his chest a bit.

Now's my chance to shine!"

"Your Eminence, I have grown the Third Order by two dozen people in the past year alone. I have a network that spans all of Europe, and I can call on the faithful at any time to do your bidding."

"What directives remain?"

Clance squirmed a bit. "Your Eminence, we have yet to secure the holy relic. We searched the home where we believed it was, and when we realized it was elsewhere, we detained the woman who has it. I was teaching her the Rule of Life and fully expected her to relinquish the relic as she came to understand the wisdom of the Rule, but she escaped before I completed the lessons."

"She escaped? You were holding her against her will?"

"We brought her against her will, Your Eminence, but only to teach her the way and to recover the relic. She would have seen the wisdom of our ways, had I only had more time."

"Hmmm. And this relic? How did this woman come to have it?"

"I am not entirely sure. It ended up with her after the basilica roof collapsed after the earthquake in Assisi. It is authentic, though: the technician that dated it is a true believer and contacted us when it was brought to him for authentication."

The cardinal took this all in and then leaned forward in his chair. "Sir, there has been a great misunderstanding. I am an obedient servant of the pope and respect his infallibility. I do not support your Third Order; I support the pope, the Secular Franciscan Order, and the new Rule of Life as decreed by Pope Paul VI. I believe anything else is heresy."

Clance's face went white, and his mouth fell open. He couldn't bring himself to utter a word, but his expression spoke volumes.

The cardinal sat back. "Apparently, there was a heretic on our staff who inappropriately used this office to further his own agenda. He has been discovered, and he is being dealt with. As for you, sir, I am directing you to disband your rogue 'order' immediately. If you want to truly be in the service of the Church and the pope, I direct you to steer your followers to the Secular Franciscan Order and the only and true Rule of Life for the penitent."

Clance started stammering and became more and more agitated. His stammers turned into rapid muttering, and he started to pace back and forth. Seemingly forgetting where he was, he suddenly crossed himself several times, fell to his knees, and started praying. The cardinal watched in disbelief and then got up and walked to his desk, picking up the phone. Clance seemed unaware the cardinal was even in the room. The cardinal called for the gendarmes, who came to escort Clance out.

"Your Eminence, shall we take this man into custody?" said one of the gendarmes.

"No," replied the cardinal. "He needs to be taken to the hospital and be evaluated psychologically. Please see to it."

The gendarmes approached Clance, who was still lost in his rapid-fire incantations, picked him up by his arms, and walked him out.

After they left, the cardinal placed a call. "Giordano? Santiago. We have a potentially embarrassing situation for the church. Are you in your office? Good. We need to talk. I will be right there." The cardinal immediately left and walked down the hall.

~

"Giordano, I don't think I convinced him," said Santiago after had explained what had just happened. "He had a woman kidnapped! He has definitely crossed the line, and I'm not sure we can reel him in. If this gets out…"

Giordano interrupted. "Friend, let me take care of this. I have some experience handling minor crises. Go about your business. I will manage this situation. You say this man is in the hospital?"

"Yes – I had him taken for psychological evaluation."

"I will follow up on the evaluation. You have nothing to worry about. All will be well."

Santiago looked intently at Giordano, searching his face, wondering what he intended to do to make sure the problem never surfaced. His desire for remedy overcame his lingering trepidation of what Giordano might do, though, and he clasped Giordano's hand between his own. "Grazie, Giordano. God be with you."

"And with you," replied Giordano with a smile. With that, Santiago left.

Two days later, Santiago learned that while in the hospital, Clance had suffered a major cardiac infarction and had unfortunately passed away. When Santiago asked about the circumstance, Giordano simply replied, "It's God's will." Santiago asked no more questions.

CHAPTER SIXTEEN

Dougal and Maggie flew back to Edinburgh after meeting with Brother Ventimiglio one last time to share their proposal. Ventimiglio took Dougal's office address and said he would have someone in the Vatican weigh in on the proposal. In the meantime, Dougal and Maggie decided that having a replica made would be a great idea, even if it ended up being used differently than originally anticipated.

"Maggie, when are you going back to the States?" said Dougal as they left the concourse and headed to find a taxi.

"Soon, I would imagine. I need to call Sarah and see if she is still willing to have a house guest. I have a lot of explaining to do. And I need to talk to Callum to see whether I am still Maggie Stuart or if I can revert to Maggie Fraser." Maggie paused, and a wave of sadness swept over her face. "I never did get a new passport or driver license as Maggie Tyler, you know. I never had the chance. I am starting to feel that I never really became Maggie Tyler at all."

Dougal stopped and turned to face Maggie directly. "Mag, I am in no position to suggest what to do. Lord knows I have no idea. Just know that a name is only that – a name. You and Ben loved each other deeply: that was very evident. And that's what is important…the love you hold in your heart. He will always be there – he will always have a very special spot in your heart regardless of your name or the path you end up taking in your life. Cherish the love you felt for one another. Allow that love to radiate warmth and comfort throughout your body. It will never leave – it will never die. Decades from now, you will be able to feel that warmth, and it will make you smile."

Maggie's eyes started to well up, but then suddenly, her face turned resolute, and she abruptly changed the subject.

"Are we going to your house or to the office?"

"Let's head to the office. We can call Callum from there, and you can call Sarah if you like."

"Great idea." Maggie climbed into the back of a cab waiting at the airport curb. "Office, it is."

When they got to Dougal's office, Maggie immediately called Callum. "Hello, Callum. We're back. We solved the puzzle of how the amulet ended up in the basilica! Our trip was blessedly uneventful, you'll be happy to hear."

"I was a bit worried for you. The UK Border Agency told us that Clance traveled to Rome. We lost track of him and are trying to locate his whereabouts. But since he hasn't returned and you have, I am much less worried."

"Callum, I need to travel back to the States. Should I travel as Fraser or Stuart?"

"Are you going to retrieve the amulet?"

"You always were one step ahead. That was my intent."

Callum was silent for a moment. "Is there any chance you could enlist someone else to transport it? We have identified many people associated with this Third Order of Clance's, and we don't want to risk putting you in the crosshairs if someone finds out you have it on you."

"Are you telling me not to travel?".

"No, not at all. Go to the States. But when you come back here, it will be better for the amulet to not be on your person."

"Well, let me see what I can do. I think I would rather send it. That's how it made it to the States to begin with. And Callum, there will be two. Dougal and I are going to have a replica made."

"Brilliant! That should add a lovely layer of complexity. Just let me know your travel plans."

"Yes, sir!" Maggie replied with exaggerated inflection. Dougal laughed at that.

"I have been waiting my whole life for that response from you, little sister. It's about time. I'm glad you're home, Mag. Talk to you later."

Maggie pressed the disconnect button and waited for a dial tone. "Now for the hard part," she said under her breath. She dialed an international number, and when it connected, she said, "Hi, Sarah! This is Maggie. I hope you are still talking to me."

"I have been so worried about you! Are you okay?"

"I have quite the adventure to tell you. I thought I would do it in person if you wouldn't mind. I am coming to Ann Arbor very shortly, but I have a question for you: if I gave you and Jake tickets, would you consider returning to Scotland with me for a little vacation?"

"Wow, Maggie – that is very generous of you. I would love to come, but I need to check with Jake. And I have news myself I have been dying to tell you: I'm pregnant."

"Oh, Sarah, that's wonderful! I am so happy for you and Jake! Are you sure you are up for travel?"

"Definitely. I'm only in my second trimester. Let me call Jake and see what he says. When were you thinking?"

"Whatever is convenient for you two. Tell me when I get there. But if you can't find a time within the next month or two, let me know. I might need to go to Plan B."

Sarah paused. "Maggie, can you give me a little hint about your adventures? Just a little one?"

Maggie laughed. "Okay, then – just a little hint. I had to get smuggled out of Italy. As a nun. My hair is now short and black, and I have brown contacts. You will need to know this to find me at the airport."

"Are you kidding me! Really?? I can't wait to hear the rest."

"Let me know as soon as you can, will you, Sarah? I am so looking forward to seeing you again. Bye now." Maggie hung up the phone.

~

Maggie boarded British Airways direct to Detroit Metropolitan Airport within the week. Sarah was waiting for her at the luggage carousel – Maggie spotted Sarah first and ran up to her to give her a hug.

"Sarah! So good to see you again! I've missed you," gushed Maggie sincerely. "You look fabulous!"

Sarah smiled as she looked down at her abdomen, and then she hugged Maggie and stood back, analyzing her new look.

"Thank you for giving me the lowdown. I am not sure I would have recognized you. Not bad, but I think I like the red better."

"You and me both." Maggie headed to the carousel and grabbed her bag as it went by. "I can't wait to get back to being me." She then turned to Sarah. "You do look wonderful. Pregnancy suits you."

"Thanks! I feel much better than I did a few weeks ago. Doctor says I am doing well. I'm halfway there!"

The two found the car in the short-term parking garage, loaded the suitcase in the trunk, and headed west on I-94. Once on the expressway, Sarah couldn't contain her curiosity.

"Getting smuggled out of a country as a nun? You must tell me the entire story!"

"It's all because of the amulet, Sarah. It's a very good thing I stashed it here in the States. I was kidnapped because of it."

"Kidnapped??? Really??"

"Oh, yes." Maggie then relayed the entire story: about how she had been taken and how she escaped. She told of visiting Brother Ventimiglio and nearly getting kidnapped in Italy, too. She told of the arrest warrant, the escape to Corsica, and hiding out in a monastery, and how her brother got her a new identity, so she could return to New York. She also told Sarah what she had learned about the amulet.

"That's quite some tale. What's next?"

"We want to get a replica of the relic made so it can go on tour while the original goes back where it belongs – with St. Francis in the basilica. Do you suppose you know of anyone that could make one from pictures and dimensions? Maybe your dad knows someone?"

"I think you need an artist, not an engineer. We have a really robust artistic community here. I am sure we can find someone. I'll ask around."

"That would be great. But after what happened to me, it's probably wise to not let on the nature of what we need replicated. I don't think I am being too paranoid: these people seem to be everywhere. Watch for an odd, rectangular scar on the backs of hands. It's telltale – they belong to the cult."

Sarah and Maggie pulled into Sarah's driveway. Maggie popped the trunk and pulled out her suitcase as Sarah unlocked the front door. Jake came out of the kitchen as he heard the front door unlock, and he gave Sarah a hug and a kiss. As Maggie brought her suitcase in, she said, "Dinner, everyone? My treat." Jake came up, gave Maggie a hug, and grabbed the suitcase from her and placed it on the first step going upstairs.

"I thought you'd never ask," joked Jake. "Are you up for some Thai?"

Over dinner, Sarah and Maggie took turns relaying Maggie's adventures. Jake frequently stopped eating and interjected exclamations of wonderment. And then Maggie got to the replica part.

"So, Jake – do you know of anyone that could make a very good replica of the amulet?"

"I will look into it, certainly."

Maggie then said rather timidly, "We need a way to get both the original and the replica back to the UK without endangering anyone. I was thinking we could send one to Dougal and one to Callum. Do you think that would work?" She then paused. "You can come for vacation, can't you?"

"Sarah and I talked about it, Maggie," said Jake. "When the baby is born, our lives will change forever. We thought that one last trip, just the two of us, would be delightful. We would love to come!"

Maggie lit up. "I am so glad! I will be your personal tour guide. I promise I will make your visit unforgettable!" Her face then darkened a bit. "Do you think sending the pieces back by post is a good idea? Or should we carry them in our bags?"

Jake looked at Sarah before he replied. "With the story you have told, I think mailing them is a better idea. No telling whether a baggage handler might rifle through the bags. Or someone could switch bags on the carousel. I would be very displeased if anything got taken."

Maggie changed the subject. "Now all we need is an honest and discreet…jeweler? Metalworking artist? One without a scarred hand."

Sarah piped up. "I think we should go to Cranbrook. They have a marvelous art school there, and their artists work in all media."

"Cranbrook? I have never heard of it. Where is it?" asked Maggie.

"It's in Bloomfield Hills – about forty-five minutes from here. I think that would be our best bet. You and I can call tomorrow if you like and then take a drive out there."

"Let's give it a try." Maggie turned to Jake. "And your choice of a restaurant was spot on, Jake. This food is delicious!"

The next morning, Sarah called Cranbrook. "Maggie, we can go this afternoon. Let's leave at about 11:30. We can get lunch at the Fox and Hounds and then travel over. I think you'll love it. It's a huge complex, and besides the art school, there's a gorgeous Tudor mansion, a natural science museum, several prep schools, and gorgeous gardens. It's quite something."

"Sounds beautiful. Say, can we pull out the amulet so I can get dimensions?" She pulled out her sketch while Sarah unlocked the safe and retrieved the amulet. Maggie picked it up and placed it in the palm of her hand. It was cool and surprisingly heavy, and she could see rust on her fingers.

"I probably should get some gloves. Do you have any around? And perhaps a ruler?" Sarah left and came back with some rubber kitchen gloves and a rigid desk ruler.

"Will these work?"

"Perfect." Maggie rubbed her fingers on her jeans and put the gloves on.

Maggie and Sarah carefully started measuring the piece.

"Okay. It measures three and three-eighths of an inch from the tip of the crescent to the other." Sarah drew two parallel lines on the sketch, crescent tip to tip, and wrote down the dimension.

Maggie continued. "Interesting. It's also three and three-eighths of an inch from the furthest point on the left, on the do-jiggy that extends from the V, to the furthest point on the right. But they are offset…" She hesitated while she measured again. "Offset by an eighth of an inch to the left." She stopped again. "The crescent, at its deepest point, is thirteen-sixteenths of an inch, and the V below it extends three-eighths of an inch. Now, about the depth…"

Maggie turned the amulet. "It's not perfectly even, Sarah. The crescent is…a quarter-inch deep in the middle. The rust may have degraded the piece. I think the best we can do is take several pictures and pinpoint measurements. The artist will have to fill in the rest."

She placed it in the palm of her hand again. "Do you have a kitchen scale? It would be nice to weigh this."

"We have to go into the kitchen for that," said Sarah, getting up and heading to the door. Maggie followed. "Where's your camera?"

"Twenty-nine point two ounces," announced Sarah as she removed the amulet from the scale. "And now for some pictures." She retrieved the camera from the den, and she and Maggie took several pictures, placing the amulet on a piece of white baking parchment paper. After all was said and done, Maggie and Sarah locked the amulet back in the safe.

Maggie glanced at her watch. "We probably should leave within the hour. I think I'll run up and take a quick shower. Before I do that, though, I'd like to go through Ben's box again. I want to feel close to him once again."

Sarah fetched Ben's box from a closet and gave it to Maggie. "Want me to sit with you?" she asked gently.

"No. I just want to feel close to him again. My way of sharing what I have been through."

Maggie took the box with her and went upstairs. Once there, she took out Ben's wedding ring. She took her wedding band off her finger and slipped it inside of Ben's. There was room to spare. She kissed both rings as tears welled up in her eyes. She pawed around the inside of her purse and found a paperclip, which she wrapped around both rings. She hung them on the chain around her neck and went into the shower.

Sarah waited until she heard the water running and then called Jake. "How much money did that man offer you for the amulet?" she asked in a muted voice.

"Twenty thousand dollars. We could fund the baby's entire college education with that, Sarah. All we would have to do is have a second replica made. No one would ever know."

Sarah bit her lip. "I don't know, Jake. That's a lot of money, but it just doesn't feel right. After all that Maggie has been through, we shouldn't. We will be fine without the money."

"Sarah, forget I ever said anything, okay? I don't want you to worry. You and Maggie are taking the pictures and dimensions to Cranbrook?"

"Yes – we're leaving in about an hour."

Drive safely, then. Love you."

"Love you, too." Sarah hung up the phone.

Sarah heard the water stop, so she quickly went over to a chair and picked up a book. Maggie came downstairs, drying her hair with a towel. "This is one good thing about cropped hair. Drying it is a breeze. Ready to go?"

"That, I am." The two locked up and headed to Bloomfield Hills.

Half an hour after they left, Jake came home. He opened the safe, took pictures and measurements of the amulet, put it back in the safe, and left again.

~

Maggie and Sarah had no problem finding a metal-working artist at Cranbrook who was willing to replicate the amulet – one Peter Brenner.

"Mr. Brenner, you will be making a replica of an ancient Pictish piece that will be used by a university to go on loan to museums and the like to spare the original," said Maggie. "Here are photographs and dimensions. Dr. Fraser of the University of Edinburgh will unveil the piece when he holds a press conference on the paper he is writing about it. As you would imagine, we would like you to age the metal to match as closely as possible. Are you interested?"

"I've not made a practice of making replicas, but this is intriguing. The metal aging part, in particular. With whom should I negotiate a commission, and will the replica be attributed to me?"

"I am sure that the university's solicitor would be pleased to draw up an agreement. Have you a card? I will arrange for the proper person to call you to make all of the appropriate arrangements. There is one thing that you should know, though: the sketches and photos must be returned, and you must pledge to not make another. May I please have the photos and sketch back until we have a signed agreement?"

"Certainly." Although the piece would not be original, Peter was excited about the challenge of aging the metal appropriately – if he figured out the appropriate technique, he thought he would be able to apply that new skill to his original art. "If we can work out the details, this will be fun. I think it will take me about a month."

"Very nice to meet you, Mr. Brenner" Maggie shook his hand. "We will be in touch."

Satisfied with their accomplishment, Sarah and Maggie traveled back to Ann Arbor.

"Sarah, I think we should put the pictures and drawings in the safe with the relic. Just in case."

"Not a bad idea." She and Maggie headed into the living room to pull up the rug and open the safe.

"Wait, Sarah," said Maggie, staring at the rug. "That chair has been moved." She was pointing to an armchair whose feet were slightly off the depressions it had previously made in the rug. "You moved it back exactly, right?"

Sarah looked nervous. "Yes, I believe I did. At least, I think I did."

Maggie's eyes narrowed as she looked at Sarah. "Sarah, I don't think the amulet is safe here anymore. If it is still in the box." Sarah leaned over and unlocked the safe, pulling out the relic. She sighed with relief. "Here it is, Maggie. I must have not moved the chair back perfectly."

Maggie went over and took the relic from Sarah.

"I don't want to put you in danger, Sarah. Something just doesn't feel right. I am going to take these down to a bank and put them in a safe deposit box. Right now." She put the relic in her pocket with the pictures and sketches and headed towards the door.

"Lock up tight, Sarah. I'll be back when this is safely out of your house."

Maggie didn't wait for a response from Sarah – she simply left. She walked the mile into town and right into the Bank of Ann Arbor. She was back at Jake and Sarah's within a couple of hours. The key to the box hung from her necklace chain under her blouse. She didn't say another word about it to Sarah except that the relic was locked up. She took care not to mention the name of the bank.

The next day, without mentioning it to anyone, she retrieved the contents of the lockbox, boxed and taped them up after a quick trip to OfficeMax, and took the box to the post office to send to Callum. She slipped in a note: *This is the original and my documentation. Something's up here. Keep these safe. Dougal might need the photos and sketches. Love, Mag.* She then went to the arboretum and found a quiet place to call Dougal but got his answering machine.

"Dougal? I found an artist willing to make a replica. Peter Brenner, out of the Cranbrook Art Institute. Can you get the university's solicitor to draw up an agreement? I already told him he must return all photos and sketches and agree not make more. His commission and artist attribution need to be negotiated. He said the work would take about a month. I sent the original, photos, and sketches to Callum. Something is not right here. I think someone got into Sarah and Jake's safe. They didn't take the relic, but I am not taking any chances. I think you should have your paper ready to go when the replica arrives. I am going to get to Assisi as soon as I can to see whether Brother Ventimiglio has made any headway in getting approval from the Vatican. I think we need to get this out in the open sooner rather than later." She hung up the phone and called the airline for reservations.

~

"Jake, did you open the safe?" Sarah was visibly upset.

"Sarah, I said you shouldn't worry about it." He tried to give her a hug.

"You did, didn't you! The chair was moved! Well, the joke is on you. Maggie noticed and took everything to a safe deposit box. She's leaving in the morning. How could you do that?"

Jake just stood and stared at her. "The original is gone? Do you know where?"

"That's all you can say?" By now, she was screaming. "Who are you, anyway? How could you do this to family?" Tears were streaming down her face, and she was shaking with anger. Jake had never seen her so angry.

"It was for the baby, honey. I wanted the money for the baby."

Sarah suddenly composed herself and became very quiet. I think you should go now, Jake. Leave." She turned away from him. "Now."

"Sweetheart…" he began, approaching her turned back. He tried to hug her.

"Leave, Jake. Right now." She was stiff, and her voice was flat. "Right. Now."

Jake left the front door open as he left, and Sarah slowly closed it after him.

CHAPTER SEVENTEEN

Maggie looked at her hands as the plane landed in Perugia.

No more silicone scar. Hope I don't need it anymore.

She grabbed her overnight bag from the overhead bin and headed to the gangway. She had the drill down pat. She procured a rental car – easily this time – and drove with sure foot to Assisi. Right to the Hotel Ideale. The concierge recognized her.

"Buon pomeriggio, Signora Stuart," he said, recognizing her.

"Buon pomeriggio," she replied, smiling.

"You are alone this trip?" he asked, looking over her shoulder to see whether Dougal – or some other man – was walking in the door.

"Si. "Short trip back."

She checked in, left her bags in her room, and promptly headed to the basilica. She glanced at her watch: vespers would begin in about an hour. She hoped she could find Ventimiglio before then. She walked up to the first priest she saw and asked for her friend. Several minutes later, Brother Ventimiglio appeared. He was smiling.

I hope that's a good sign, Maggie thought.

Pulling out her trusty dictionary, she asked if there had been any progress on her request for a joint announcement.

Brother Ventimiglio smiled broadly. "Si, signora. La Chiesa sarebbe felice."

Felice… Maggie knew that word. Happy. She grinned broadly. "Excellent!"

That needed no translation. Brother Ventimiglio grinned broadly, too, and nodded.

"E una replica?"

"Si, una replica."

Maggie clapped her hands in excitement. "Oh, that is wonderful!" She didn't even bother to translate.

Brother Ventimiglio laughed at her obvious elation. He held up a finger and ran into the church, returning moments later with paper and a pen. He motioned for Maggie to turn around, and he used her back as a writing board.

Cardinale Giordano. Vaticano. Farà l'annuncio.

When Maggie felt the pressure off her back, she turned around. Ventimiglio gave her the note. She hesitated just a bit and then decided she would hug Ventimiglio anyway. He was a bit taken aback but laughed after. He pointed to his watch and left for vespers, waving goodbye as he turned and headed into the Basilica.

Back in her room, Maggie called Dougal. "It's a go. The Vatican's representative will be Cardinal Giordano. Get that paper ready, brother."

Maggie was only in Assisi one night – she left for London the next day.

~

Maggie called Callum on her cellphone. "Callum, has the package I sent you arrived?"

"Yes – it came yesterday. Your note sounded a bit ominous… What happened?"

"I think someone knew about the amulet. I had to get it away as soon as I could. What I would like to do is get it back to Assisi right away. No pomp – no circumstance. I think it needs to be quietly put back by St. Francis's side before any announcement. Before anyone knows. I think that's the only way it will be safe."

Callum was silent for a moment. "Come to my office, Maggie. Right now, if you would. If that's what you want to do, I am going with you. I will carry the relic. Let me make a few calls… I think we should take a military transport. I think you have gotten too much exposure as Maggie Stuart."

When Maggie walked into Callum's office, the first thing he said was, "We are in luck, Mag. What about" – he paused as he looked at his watch – "in two hours?"

Maggie laughed. "I've only been in London for three hours, and now I'm headed back to Assisi? Amazing." She checked her watch. "We will be getting there in the dead of night. Any idea where we might stay?"

"We can stay on base until daylight. It will take a couple of hours to drive to Assisi. Do you have a plan?"

"I am going to go right to Brother Ventimiglio. I think he will approve of quietly making things right. The grand announcement can use the replica and the journal that was found in the catacombs."

"Grab your overnight, then."

"It's right here." She pointed to the floor by her feet. "I guess I can go another day."

The two headed to the base to catch their transport.

~

Brother Ventimiglio was very surprised to see Maggie again so soon. She had spent the flight writing a note in Italian explaining her intent. He became very silent as he read it and then quietly nodded, looking at her. He held up ten fingers and then pointed at his watch. He then said, "Notte."

"Diece, notte," repeated Maggie, nodding. She turned, bringing Callum up by his forearm. "Un altro fratello. Callum."

Callum extended his hand and shook Ventimiglio's. "Piacere di conoscerti, Fratello Ventimiglio."

Maggie looked at him in disbelief. "Since when do you speak Italian?"

"Oh, I just know the social niceties, like 'pleasure to meet you.' That's about it. Let's grab a bite to eat. I'm starved."

Maggie turned to Ventimiglio. "Ciao, Fratello Ventimiglio. Diece."

"Diece," repeated Ventimiglio. He turned to go into the Basilica, and Callum and Maggie went to the nearest restaurant.

They spent the day enjoying Assisi, waiting for night to fall.

"Assisi is magical at night," Maggie said as she and Callum strolled from the wall where they were looking over the valley below. "When it's dusk and the cobblestones darken – when the last vestiges of sun drop behind the hills on the far side of the valley and a hush blankets the streets – you can't help but feel peace."

Callum walked silently next to his sister, hand in his pocket over the relic. He was glad that the object of all of the intrigue was soon going to be put back into its original resting place. The two arrived at the Basilica at ten minutes to ten – Brother Ventimiglio was by the front doors. He motioned for Callum and Maggie to enter, and he locked the door behind them. The three walked downstairs to the tomb of St. Francis. Ventimiglio had removed one of the blocks of stone from the side of the tomb – a secret niche where the relic would be safe. Callum reached into his pocket and gave the relic to him. Ventimiglio examined and then kissed it. He knelt in front of the niche, placed the relic inside, closed his eyes, and started to pray. Callum stood back and bowed his head.

Maggie had taken off her necklace and placed it in her pocket. She slowly took it out... The two weddings bands hung together, linked by a paper clip. She silently kissed the two rings, tears running down her face, and placed the necklace into the niche. She hoped that neither Callum nor Brother Ventimiglio noticed. She mouthed, "I will always love you, Ben," and blew a kiss. "Together for eternity." She then knelt down next to Ventimiglio and bowed her head.

Ventimiglio finally stood up and slid the stone back into place. If he noticed the necklace and rings, he said nothing. He crossed himself and took several steps backward before he turned. The three left.

Outside, Father Ventimiglio hugged Maggie and shook Callum's hand. "Dio sia con te," he said to them both. God be with you.

Grazie, Fratello, mille grazie." Ventimiglio smiled sadly and wiped a tear from Maggie's cheek. "La pace sia con voi," he said gratefully to her. "Peace be with you." She was shocked to hear him speak English. "I learn," he said haltingly.

She squeezed his hand and then turned to Callum. "Let's go, Callum." The two walked back to the wall overlooking the valley. A full moon had risen, and a silver sheen covered the valley below. And out from the shadows of the forest came a graceful doe. She briefly grazed on some grass and then looked up, seemingly right at Maggie. An intense calm came over Maggie at that moment, and she suddenly knew what she wanted to do. She turned to Callum.

"I've decided to make my home in London."

I can go on. I can do this. I think I just felt the peace of St. Francis.

ABOUT THE AUTHOR

Wendy Sura Thomson holds both undergraduate and graduate degrees in business. She is a first generation American, her father being born in Scotland. She has visited Italy more than once, and fell in love with Assisi after performing in a classical vocal concert there.

Wendy is semi-retired and keeps herself busy keeping the back office for her older son's business, painting, gardening, writing, and tending to her two beloved Irish Setters.

She is also the author of *Summon the Tiger*.

www.ingramcontent.com/pod-product-compliance
Lightning Source LLC
Chambersburg PA
CBHW050701290626
47170CB00016B/2560